A GOVERNESS SHOULD NEVER... TEMPT A PRIZEFIGHTER

THE GOVERNESS CHRONICLES - BOOK ONE

EMILY WINDSOR

SENARA PRESS

This is a work of fiction. All names, characters, places and incidents are products of the author's imagination. All characters are fictitious and any resemblance to real persons, living or dead, is purely coincidental.

ASIN: B08MB7C1J6

ISBN: 978-1-9161139-5-4

This book is written using British English spelling.

DEDICATION

To all my 'Wednesday's Waistcoat' voters – thank you!
I hope I did your fine choices justice.
Love Emily x

CONTENTS

NOTE TO THE PROSPECTIVE GOVERNESS...

"...to you, do I presume to offer a few scattered remarks, founded upon experience, on the particular station of life in which the Almighty has, of his divine will, been pleased to place you."

ELIZABETH APPLETON. 1815.

CHAPTER ONE

"...the profession of a private governess is an honourable and genteel one."

PRIVATE EDUCATION: A PRACTICAL PLAN FOR THE STUDIES OF YOUNG LADIES.

ELIZABETH APPLETON. 1815.

Hawkins Boxing Academy. Outskirts of Piccadilly. May 1816.

"So tell me, Miss Griffin, why should I employ you as governess?"

Oh botheration.

And Matilda fidgeted in the unyielding chair.

The interview had been progressing quite satisfactorily until now. They'd greeted one another in a cordial manner, lamented the bitter spring weather and Mr Hawkins, her prospective employer and owner of this famed Boxing Academy, had shown her to his somewhat masculine study.

Chestnut panelling smothered the walls from floor to ceiling, a few drawings of sturdy ruffians in pugilistic stance embellishing its manliness. A battered chaise of dun leather sat in the corner whilst the desk gleamed with fresh wax.

Matilda's lips parted to answer, but for once words failed her, so instead she contemplated a bird fluffing its wings upon the windowsill outside and ardently wished she could swap places.

Although perhaps not with a scrawny sparrow but rather a brightly coloured Bird of Paradise. To be far away on the tropical Molucca Islands and not shivering in this rugged study, being interviewed by a man who'd once been a prizefighter.

Males of the species could be so savage.

His cough prompted for attention and she returned her gaze to Mr Hawkins.

"It appears," he said, flicking her application letter and hoisting an eyebrow, "that you have no previous experience."

Matilda crossed her arms.

How hard could it be? Although Mr Hawkins may be factually correct, she had thrice read *Private Education: A Practical Plan for the Studies of Young Ladies*.

The somewhat crisp author, a Miss Elizabeth Appleton, had been hired by the 9th Earl of Leven no less, so she must have known what she was writing about.

Mr Hawkins set to scrutinising her application letter once more...and Matilda set to scrutinising Mr Hawkins.

Dark hair the colour of chocolate, ruthlessly trimmed and without curl; a light linear scar to his right eyebrow; a firm chin which could never hide its burgeoning stubble; sultry olive-toned skin; and a classical nose that looked to have been forcibly inclined to the left.

A decidedly handsome man, the crooked appendage adding a certain *je ne sais quoi*.

Then there were those...muscles.

Even clothed, they were noticeable – which was curious because as a rule, Matilda would not notice at all. Muscle and brawn, in her humble opinion, were uninspiring, belonging to men of paltry intellect.

Yet these *were* inspiring. Never had she studied real ones before, and she longed to prod and measure. Purely for anatomical endeavour, of course. How would they feel when–

"Ahem."

Double botheration...

She'd been caught inspecting that broad chest encased by a pale-gold waistcoat with pleasing feather motifs, its oval collar and glimpse of brass buttons drawing one's eye. Whatever his former vocation and current profession, Mr Hawkins dressed with exquisite distinction: a midnight-blue coat stretched along extensive shoulders, and tight pantaloons sculpted a callipygian figure.

A widower, she'd read as a part of her preparations for this interview, with some three decades to his name, Mr Seth Hawkins had apparently set the prizefighting world alight before opening his Academy.

He thrust the letter aside, clasped his substantial hands and sighed deeply. "Do you have any experience whatsoever?"

Well, no. Hence her rare silence.

In that now shunned application letter, she'd penned with keen verbosity her knowledge of geography, history, astronomy and so forth, hoping to bamboozle the man with protracted explanation and incomprehensible words – she was good at that.

Perchance she ought to fib about her past experience: state she'd educated a younger brother who'd gone on to discover a cure for boils, or imply her references had gone astray on her return voyage from India, having educated a Maharaja's daughter.

Matilda sighed and slid her spectacles up the bridge of her nose.

A close confidante, Miss Evelyn Pearce, had told some blistering fibs recently in order to escape dire circumstance, which had resulted in her being abducted by the richest duke of all England.

So perhaps being circumspect with the truth did have its benefits.

Sparkling hazel eyes gazed at her in query across the desk, his fingers shifting to splay upon the leather inlay.

Robust knuckles and calloused skin.

Matilda shivered.

However, those broad knuckles did not belong to a rich duke.

They belonged to a muscled beast of a man whose wits had most likely been knocked out in some prizefighting field in Somerset.

SETH BRIEFLY SHUTTERED his gaze and concluded that this fifth candidate for interview had been at the gin, her wits most likely washed out into some rank gutter of a London alley.

Shame, as she had appeared promising upon arrival. Flower meadows had teased his nostrils as she'd marched to his study, a striped yellow dress with a pelisse of velvet, also yellow, encasing a most comely figure.

Neat of demeanour, Miss Griffin had sat with grace, neck straight, spine not daring to brush the back of the chair. Black tendrils of hair curled from a hat more suited to promenading in Mayfair, and behind gold-rimmed glasses, eyes the colour of his favoured brandy had dissected him.

Yet a simple question had rendered her mute except for strange mutterings and a scrunched brow. She fidgeted, foot tamping and fingers tapping, obviously agitated by her breakfast tipple of blue ruin.

How difficult could it be to find a governess?

Bloody difficult, as it so happened. More onerous than brawling with Jumpin' Jack Scroggins, whose trotters had never remained in one place.

"I repeat, Miss Griffin…" Because he felt he had to try one last time. "Why should I employ you?"

The previous four applicants had reduced him to this desperation.

A Miss Rippleton had cursed better than he, Miss Broadhurst had divulged her conviction that the world was flat in response to his geography question, and Miss Frost had…issues with his daughter's upbringing. The last, a Miss Murphy, who'd seen him beat Rugged Rick in 1811, had offered additional services.

"I-I…"

His eyes flicked up at the stutter, caught on her sumptuous bosom, upped to exquisite ripe lips that parted, pursed, and then fell silent.

Damnation.

Wearily, Seth rose to his feet. "Perhaps we should conclude this interview, Miss Griffin, as I do not believe–"

"I need to hide, you see, Mr Hawkins."

Seth reclaimed his seat. That was the most intriguing answer he'd heard thus far, but for now, he merely cocked a brow.

That ripe lip was bitten once more. "Only until my birthday in August."

He folded his arms but kept the brow aloft, thoughts sifting – her absurd answer, those eyes which shimmered as though lit from behind by candlelight, her heaving chest and that impeccable accent proclaiming her a lady of the *haut monde*.

"Please continue to enlighten me, Miss Griffin."

"I suppose there is little point in untruthful perfidy…" And she peered to the left, then to the right.

Seth did the same – window overlooking Green Park to one side, empty shelves to the other.

What a curious female.

The gentry were a rum lot and he ought to be used to their idiosyncrasies by now, but every so often one still flummoxed him.

"Until I attain twenty-one years in August," she confessed, leaning near, "my guardian cousin dictates my life, but lately his behaviour has become most…unreasonable."

Perchance this guardian had threatened to cut her clothing allowance or curtail her coiffure appointments? "I suppose you wish me to deal with him?"

Most visitors to his door wanted no more than the prowess of the famous pugilist. The last woman he'd courted had, it turned out, only wished him to threaten her brother, who'd cut her pin money to five guineas a week. She had believed Seth would be quite content to pummel the fellow and hence exhibit his valour.

"Goodness, no." Miss Griffin's small nose creased in repugnance. "I do not require your brawn or any such uncouthness. I believe the mind to be mightier."

All well and good, but she'd never been thumped by Gaslight Gary, whose fists had certainly been mightier than his mind.

Yet he had to acknowledge that a prizefighter sans brains did tend to meet St Peter somewhat prematurely.

Gaslight Gary had in fact accidentally shot himself while demonstrating how his friend had accidentally shot himself.

Irish Tom had expired after volunteering for the Astley's Amphitheatre knife thrower.

And Big Bill had been found dead in his bed with three doxies and four empty gin bottles – cause of death unknown.

Hence Seth had retired and opened a boxing academy.

"Pray continue then."

With a rustle, Miss Griffin straightened her pelisse. "Whilst...snooping in my cousin's study, I discovered he had contracts for me to marry a debauched libertine of advanced years, all without my knowledge or consent." Her shoulders hunched. "I am...fearful of what action my guardian may take in order to seek my compliance."

Her gaze dipped, spectacles sliding, and now he noted the cobweb of shadows beneath her fine eyes, the tremble to her fingers which she swiftly suppressed.

But even so...

"Miss Griffin, I cannot appoint you as governess for my daughter simply because you wish to hide–"

"I merely seek employment until August when I am no longer beneath his control, and then I can access the money my parents left me and forge ahead as a proper governess. I agree my lack of experience is...contestable, but I am well versed in all subjects." A slender hand reached across the desk in entreaty. "In addition, I can teach the full breadth of a lady's accomplishments – fork placements, quilling tea caddies and how to back from a room without tripping over one's train."

Clenching his fists, Seth faltered, yet this indecision had naught to do with misplaced cutlery and all to do with the yellow colouration upon her delicate wrist, revealed as the sleeve had pulled up. A couple of weeks old, to be sure, but he knew a bruise from a harsh grip when he saw one.

A damsel in distress.

Damn.

In silence, he rose from his seat to pace in front of the smouldering fire – always thinking better on his feet. Never had he been one for rushed decisions, and this petite female had trouble written all over her charming cheekbones.

If he hired her and this possessive guardian emerged, a wealth of upset could descend upon the club he'd spent so long building up.

Nevertheless, he could not deny that a lady such as Miss Griffin would be the perfect influence to give his daughter choices in life. Feminine company, exquisite manners and a wide scope of knowledge were required, and from this application letter and her obvious *haute monde* upbringing, Miss Griffin encompassed all.

And besides, there was no one else.

Wide eyes beseeched, and his thoughts turned to what might happen if he refused. Seth could not bear to imagine this dainty lady cowed into submission by some callous guardian and thus married to a degenerate with more diseases than a London rat.

Surely any strife this runaway bride might bring to his club could be dismissed with an innocent shrug or a cod of blunt. The fact he'd a swathe of influential patrons also detracted any nuisances.

"You pledge you are able to teach a wide range of subjects?"

She nodded frantically, spectacles sliding once more. "My parents were both bibliophiles so I had a wealth of matter to read as a child." She peered around his bookless study and returned a benevolent smile. "I could bring some with me."

Clearly Miss Griffin thought him a witless dolt, but he was in no hurry to change that opinion. She would take pity on his daughter, having to live with such a brutish ignoramus, and impart all the accumulated education in that noggin of hers.

"I will employ you as governess for a one-month trial."

Liquid cinnamon eyes gleamed up at him and he cursed his own soft heart.

If honesty was to be their byword, then he'd not merely employed her for those reasons alone, but for her sensitive wrists, gaze of purity and the wildflower scent which bloomed around her.

"When could you begin?"

"Would Thursday be too soon?"

"Of next week?"

"No, the morrow." She fiddled with her pelisse cuff. "My guardian is in the country, you see, so I've only the servants to evade."

Devil take him – evading servants? Whatever next? "Please tell me your name is not false and that you're not the daughter of some duke."

"How dare you, Mr Hawkins." She gracefully sniffed. "My name is my own. And the Duke of Aberdare is a mere half-cousin thrice removed. I've never even met him. He resides in Wales."

Bloody hell. "And your guardian, this cousin... A nobleman also?"

"Merely a viscount."

It could be worse; he was sure it could be worse.

"The salary is seven guineas a month with chambers next to the schoolroom included. As you are obviously a gentlewoman, I have both a housekeeper-cum-cook and a maid who could chaperone should the need arise."

"Oh." She removed her glasses and polished them on her striped dress. He'd been mistaken – her eyes flashed the colour of tawny sherry, tantalising and sharp all at once. "That will not be necessary, for if I am to embark upon the career of governess, I will have to learn to do without such chaperone shenanigans. I believe a working life has much freedom."

Poor innocent.

"Indeed," he murmured instead. "My daughter Chloe has been previously tutored, but only by myself and the vicar's wife. Do you require any additional books?"

She replaced her glasses and smiled, causing a dimple to wink enticingly.

Heaven help him.

"For a girl of three and ten, I daresay the first abridgement of Mrs Trimmer's *Ancient History* would be useful. Molineux's *Introduction to the Globes,* of course, Mr Goldsmith's *Grammar of Geography* is a must, and Salzmann's *Elements of Morality*...without the translator's preface."

Heaven help his daughter.

"'Knowledge is the wing wherewith we fly to heaven'," he muttered, holding out a hand to aid her rise.

Incredulous lips pursed. Suspicious eyes narrowed.

Seth grinned as he drew the study door wide. "Must have read that on some discarded theatre print, Miss Griffin, as I have little time for literature. On the morrow, I shall introduce you to my daughter. Good day."

With a regal nod more suited to a duke's half-cousin thrice removed than a lowly governess, she marched ahead of him and twisted left for the hallway.

Some years past, he'd gutted this old-fashioned, three-storey townhouse to create both a boxing academy and home for himself and daughter, hence the old back door to the garden now functioned as the family's main entrance – the colonnaded façade at the front of the house on Arlington Street serving as the Academy's impressive threshold.

She paused at the door, presumably awaiting his non-existent butler, which told him much of her current abode and circumstance, so he opened it himself.

A blush lit her cheeks, eyes flitting and fingers fluttering.

"You must think me naive, Mr Hawkins, a privileged lady seeking a new life with little knowledge or experience, but I have to take my future into my own hands, you see, before it is wrested from me." She tightened the ribbons on her bonnet to continue her soliloquy. "Thus far, I have been shielded from life. Sheltered by the love of my parents or guarded by Cousin Astwood for my marriageability value. Curbed by my birth and gender. Now I shall endeavour to make my own choices, with all its forthcoming perils and blessings."

Miss Griffin appeared like a fledgling bird, so eager for freedom that she'd dare a boxing academy for her refuge.

"On the contrary, Miss Griffin, I think you brave," he murmured, sketching a bow.

The blush heightened and she scurried down the three steps which led to the garden.

An awaiting maid rose from the bench beneath his willow tree and together the females bustled down the path. As a cloud shifted and one single ray of sunlight beamed forth, the maid swiftly opened a pink parasol and hoisted it aloft to protect her mistress's delicate skin.

Seth pinched his forehead.

What had he done?

CHAPTER TWO

"One's dress is more handsome than fine; more neat than showy; one's clothes are made genteelly, but within extremes."

Private Education: A Practical Plan for the Studies of Young Ladies.

Elizabeth Appleton. 1815.

Could a governess wear buttercup yellow for her first day?

Clad in chemise and stockings, Matilda studied her wardrobe, praying that a monotonous brown or overcast grey might spring from the froth of colour.

All the sorrowful mourning gowns worn after her parents' tragic deaths had been replaced with startling shades of yellow silk by her guardian cousin a year past. Some young ladies might have been only too pleased – but he'd informed Matilda that with her petite stature, obscuring spectacles and dull conversation, she required all the help she could muster.

Charming.

Presently, Cousin Astwood was at some dissolute house party in the countryside, but before his butler and minions could awaken this morning, she was stuffing all she could into a small carpet bag. Most had already been filled with life's essentials:

- Three packets of filched tea leaves as, after all, she had no idea of a governess's allowance – if any.
- Miss Appleton's wholesome tome on education – she sensed she would need it.
- One bar of her favoured soap.
- The solicitor's address for when she reached one and twenty.
- Undergarments and two gowns of a darker shade – a saffron and nankeen, which could almost be described as brownish...yellow, but crucially both could be buttoned up without the assistance of a maid.

The gilt cherub mantel clock chimed the approaching dawn so she swiftly donned the buttercup gown, hoping a shawl might smother its vivacity. Then without further ado, a last frock was shoved into the bag, its silk billowing in puffs of golden beige.

Besides that, she thought dismally, heaving the bag shut, she owned little to her name.

Matilda peered around her beloved bedchamber at the well-thumbed books, elegant paintings and dainty writing desk.

Yet none of these items were hers. Even the books, she now realised. They all belonged to Cousin Astwood, a crawly toad as a child who'd shattered her spectacles and ripped her diaries, but now as viscount and her guardian, strutted like a mangy peacock.

Still, she'd considered him a harmless creature till of late, when he'd packed her great-aunt off to Wales and commenced introducing her to potential husbands – raddled old aristocrats who pinched her cheeks, leered at her bosom and requested to view her teeth. At first, she'd refused and acted the termagant, but in recent weeks…

Her cousin was becoming impatient: his grip pinched and bruised, marriage demands spat in hate, plum face contorting with anger.

She was…scared. Fearful of his rising temper.

Tales of abduction, ravishment and forced marriage by pistol abounded, and she could not tell truth from fiction.

Only that Cousin Astwood frightened her.

That before he'd left for the countryside, he'd shaken her hard and yelled she was chattel, to be used at his will, to be sold at his will. Auctioned off like a goat for sacrifice in that marriage contract she'd discovered to the Earl of Sidlow, a *gentleman* who'd cornered her in a closed room and outlined her marital duties, pinching her with skeletal fingers and attempting to kiss her using his…

She could scarcely bring herself to think upon it.

But now she would do all within her power to avoid a sentence of marriage to such a revolting roué.

Of course, a boxing academy was not her ideal choice of sanctuary, it being likely to contain pugilists, but after eight posted employment applications, Mr Hawkins had been the sole replier, and surely a governess remained secreted away in the schoolroom all day, teaching things, and should not have to stumble upon…muscles.

A bird groggily cheeped the first signs of dawn, so she shrouded her slight frame in her father's ancient cloak and snatched up the carpet bag along with a cloth smothered in pig fat.

Opening the bedchamber door, she peered out – silence, yet a bated one.

Astwood had replaced all her parents' staff with his own and they'd clearly been told to keep an eye on her. Purely her lady's maid had remained in her service, but at Matilda's behest yesterday, and with one of her gold bangles to sell and a promise to write, her maid had taken the stagecoach to family in Wiltshire, far away from questions as to her mistress's forthcoming disappearance.

Now, with a lone candle to light the stairs in one hand and the carpet bag gripped firmly in the other, Matilda crept as though a stealthy thief. Nevertheless, her starched petticoats dragged on the wooden treads like leaves rustling beneath a broom, her light steps as those of a hulking gollumpus in the attentive dark.

Each night, Matilda had watched from the landing outside her chambers as the butler had locked up, and now, standing before the solemn front door, she rubbed the foul-smelling cloth upon the shrill second bolt.

Tossing the cloth aside, she gripped the barrel.

The mechanism slid, a scant whisper of metal as it glided back.

Even the silence sighed.

She gathered her bag, clasped the handle and pulled open the hefty door. The wood groaned and she stilled.

Naught roused but for a brush of warm air which caressed her cheek, strange and vivid.

Matilda knew not its cause, only that it felt as though her childhood home was declaring its farewell, that it wished her Godspeed for an unknown future.

A solitary thick tear streaked her cheek, but after thrusting the door wide, she sped into the sombre dawn.

And did not look back.

SITTING beneath a sprouting willow tree with the faint glow of daybreak shimmering above the rooftops of Piccadilly ought to be quite the romantic scene.

But Matilda's buttocks had numbed, and she was quite sure her feet had succumbed to frostbite.

At least she was safe though.

She had scurried along the deserted streets, head down and pace frantic. Never before had she been out of the house alone, especially at dawn, and her heart had knocked in her chest like a nest-building cuckoo in spring.

A few jug-bitten bucks had staggered along the way and a keen night watchman had watched – which she supposed was his job – but he'd eyed her with a lascivious gleam and licked his lips.

The door to Mr Hawkins' home was located upon the rear of the property at the end of this tidy garden, with a spectral Green Park opposite, a nebulous fog drifting. Once a swampy burial ground for lepers, an air of sad expectancy gloated from within the park's lush green lawns, and eerie tales of the ill-famed haunted tree at its heart, avoided by birds and people alike, had compelled her to hum to herself as she'd passed by.

As a rule, she was perfectly clear-minded in relation to such matters – ghosts and whatnot – yet she'd sworn a sinister figure in scarlet had stridden through the mist this dawn and so she'd darted through the gates of No. 25 as though the devil himself had been tugging at her skirts.

The high-up chimneys had eventually spluttered a pitch smoke, and a dim glow had flickered at the rim of the closed shutters; yet surely to hammer upon the door at such an hour would have been the height of rudeness.

Cousin Astwood's butler refused to admit callers between the hours of midnight and nine, unless they were scantily dressed.

Needless to say, Matilda did not fit into that category, hence she remained in the cold upon this incommodious garden bench.

At what hour could a governess call upon her employer?

Matilda knew the exact hour for a lady to call upon friends in London, had read of when the Batok tribe took supper in East Africa and at what hour the Russians considered early enough for vodka. Yet conduct for this vocation was all so unknown.

What she did realise was that if she waited out here in the cold much longer, Mr Hawkins would not have a governess to house but a body to bury.

Surely he arose early to open his Boxing Academy? Or did he have staff for that?

With no small amount of prejudice before the interview, Matilda had thought he'd be an unpleasant character with hammy fists and lumbering steps, barely able to understand the King's English – if indeed anyone could, since their liege had gone mad.

For research purposes only of course, she'd scrutinised drawings of prizefighters and mulled over match reports, barely grasping the detail – fancy coves, mufflers, plumpers and whiffles...

Incomprehensible.

Mr Hawkins, however, had been most well-spoken and mannerly. And last night, for no apparent reason that she could fathom, she had dreamed of those sizeable calloused knuckles…

She rubbed arms that had lost all feeling and contemplated what her first-ever student might be like.

The pithy Miss Appleton, she of the governess tome, had compared her charges to opening blossoms of morality, to be shielded from the scorch of error until they burst into maturity.

Matilda wondered whether she herself had yet to burst forth.

A faint glow slanted through the May greyness, the downstairs shutters parting to reveal a buxom female with apron and lantern, hazy light spilling upon the plants still struggling to leaf.

Thank the heavens, and Matilda stiffly rose from the stone bench, gathered her carpet bag, strode for the steps and confronted the door, praying the housekeeper would allow her entry. Frequently such women guarded the household with hostile contempt for both employer and fellow employees alike.

After a timid knock…then a strident blow, it opened a sliver.

The buxom female scowled with suspicious brow and thinned lips, a rolling pin held aloft.

"What yer want?"

"Er… I am the new governess. I realise the hour is a little discourteous but…"

Matilda trailed off as she was gathered into that buxom bosom perfumed with flour and sugar.

"Yer poor child. Look at yer, as cold as Milling Mike after ten rounds with Big Bill."

Matilda floundered.

Her parents had never been ones for embracing. They'd

been loving without doubt but undemonstrative – a pat on the head for a book well read had been positively melodramatic. Her friend Evelyn oft placed a comforting arm, but Matilda had forever felt peculiar, not knowing where to put her hands, her body stiffening with the close contact.

Such warmth from a stranger should have caused an upset, a taut stiffening of spine and sinew, but after the frigid weather, the fright of Green Park and her cousin's callous dictates, she wished to bury deep into this motherly bosom and plead for hot tea.

Which doubtless Miss Appleton would tartly decry as unbefitting of a proper governess on her first day.

"I am fine, thank you," she muttered into white cotton. "Just rather...chilled."

The woman drew back, and if ever a countenance epitomised homely, it was this one. But not in a plain way. No, she radiated joy and welcome, eyes blue as bilberries.

"Mr H suspected yer might be early. Alert as a bull in Maytime, that boy."

Matilda opened her mouth, then closed it.

With a tongue chatting nineteen to the dozen, the housekeeper-cum-cook, a *Mrs Havistock but call me Betty,* bustled her to a kitchen and placed her before the open fire, causing those icy toes to twist and tingle.

"Mr H said he wanted to see yer the moment yer arrived, but them at Billingsgate could hear that belly rumbling so he'll have to wait." And *Mrs Havistock but call me Betty* opened the oven to produce a plate of hot crumpets, followed by a ladle full of chocolate from a pot upon the range.

Never had Matilda been allowed to partake of breakfast in a *kitchen* before, and although the chair was without a velvet cushion and the table of bare wood, it was perhaps the cosiest location she'd ever had the pleasure to sit in.

Nattering as though they were bosom friends, *Mrs Havistock but call me Betty* commenced making bread – bemoaning the bitter weather, the coal smoke that stained the washing and how Parliament didn't give tuppence for common folk like them.

"Now," she pronounced, pounding dough as though she ought to be in the Boxing Academy instead, "Mr H is sparring upstairs in the practice room but I'll get flour on the rugs, so it's one flight up and turn left." A speculative gaze perused. "Take yer hat off, dearie, and yer pelisse. I've had the fires lit since dawn."

"Oh, but…" Beneath the pelisse was that brash buttercup-yellow day dress – although 'twas true she was toastier than Betty's buns. "I am awaiting collection of my governess attire," she fibbed, peeling off her coat to reveal the vividness.

"Dunno why, yer could charm them bees from their hive in that dress."

"I suppose this colour does rather resemble a pollen-filled flower of spring."

Betty stared. "Girlie, where have yer been all yer life?"

"12 George Street."

A shake of head and Matilda was shooed from the kitchen by cumulus clouds of flour.

In the hallway, she dallied, taking stock of the curious layout, as in any normal abode the kitchens were hidden in the basement. A door to the right lured – which as a rule would lead to the drawing room and parlours – but the odd grunt of pain could be heard from beyond, so she supposed it led to the Academy.

Matilda scrunched her lips. How could one strike another for pleasure?

Males were such odd creatures.

She headed up the narrow staircase, arriving at a lantern-lit first floor.

An open door opposite revealed a pleasant dining room, and so she supposed this floor to be the living quarters, small but well maintained, covered by fresh paperhangings with the latest chinoiserie patterns and sumptuous rugs of Turkish design. She turned, as Betty had directed, to the left.

A wide closed door of mahogany confronted her, but as she put hand to handle, a voice bellowed, "Higher."

Mr Hawkins, if she wasn't much mistaken.

A muffled reply.

Then a thump.

With brow creased, Matilda opened the door and gazed into a middling-size ballroom.

In the centre, Mr Hawkins stood...naked.

Well, almost naked anyhow.

Solely knee-length breeches and a white loose shirt clothed his powerful frame, those colossal hands raised whilst a slender young man in much the same attire twirled on his toes and batted Mr Hawkins' open palm with his bare heel.

Matilda closed her mouth.

"Better," he called. "You'd never be able to use this in the ring, but it's a handy technique to have. Now, put it into sequence."

The pair took up a stance similar to the drawings Matilda had studied, but only the young man jabbed out his fists, bare feet dancing soundlessly upon the wooden floor. Mr Hawkins ducked and dodged, his Herculean shoulders straining the cotton seams of his shirt, rolled sleeves displaying bronzed forearms and rippling sinew.

No actual hitting appeared to be taking place, merely fists brushing as though to measure distance and reach.

Skin glistened, Mr Hawkins' shirt allowing a slab of tanned muscle to peek through.

And weren't his lower legs hairy?

Matilda blinked.

In 1813, she'd visited Burlington House with her parents to view the marble artefacts purloined from Greece. One frieze had displayed a centaur fighting a disrobed man – all defined muscle and grey-veined, hairless skin – and since then Matilda had thought herself *au fait* with a male's components.

Yet...

What the frieze had failed to depict was the grace of movement, the sheen of exertion, the harsh breathing and heaving chest, the hairy legs and–

The buttocks were the same though, and her new employer also sported a fine *pectoralis major* with a prominent–

Matilda removed her glasses and wiped them clear on her skirt.

Then promptly replaced them.

The young man twirled and stabbed out a foot, his fluid agility a sight to behold, but Mr Hawkins caught the foot before it could clout him on the chin, his shirt front pulling to reveal–

Matilda dropped her reticule.

Bright hazel eyes twisted in her direction.

The foot tumbled from Mr Hawkins' grip – no effort whatsoever to cover his unseemly dishabille, and he strode towards her, retrieved her reticule from the floor and offered it with open palm.

"Ah, Miss Griffin. I thought you might be early." He stood

so near that she knew not where to place her eyes, so settled upon his – irises the hue of brown earth with flecks of fresh leaf.

All that manly exertion had bewattled her senses.

"I apologise if my early arrival has discommoded you," she murmured, tentatively taking her reticule by the top ribbon.

Mr Hawkins' lips parted to reveal a smile of pure white. Shouldn't a pugilist be left with mere gums?

"I am rarely discommoded." He peeled down a shirt sleeve, concealing the golden skin. "But first I must introduce you to my daughter."

Matilda held her own smile in place because she knew precisely what was to be forthcoming.

With a graceful flick of a broad finger, Mr Hawkins reached down and freed the silky blond plait tucked down the back of the young man's shirt.

A scowling face snatched it back – feminine lips thinned and fair eyelashes framed a narrowed gaze.

Mr Hawkins simply grinned. "Meet my daughter, Chloe." And he swivelled. "Chloe dearest, your new governess."

Through sheer willpower and a strict upbringing, Matilda's smile did not waver.

But, oh dear heavens, Miss Appleton had not prepared her for this.

CHAPTER THREE

"Do we wish our pupils to think?"

Private Education: A Practical Plan for the Studies of Young Ladies.

Elizabeth Appleton. 1815.

There existed some days in a lone parent's life that one dreaded.

This was one of those days.

Seth paced his bedchambers on the second floor, knowing his daughter would enter as the five evening clangs from the St James's Church bells resounded their last.

On many occasions in the basement, he'd practised this little speech for Chloe and yet it never seemed easier to his mind – he'd blather on, bumble his way through and no doubt bugger it up.

She'd have…questions.

A strident knock and the door opened a crack.

"Are you decent, Pa?"

He peered down at himself.

Best silk dinner breeches and finest muslin shirt clad his frame. He would call that decent enough, yet earlier this morning, Miss Griffin had gazed upon similar and looked set to swoon from the impropriety.

For too long had he been surrounded by blustering company with no sensibilities whatsoever – and that was just Betty, let alone the boxing club patrons.

Tonight at dinner, he must rummage for his manners.

"Come in, petal, and we'll discuss the day."

A bundle of energy since birth, Chloe careered over and bounded onto the bed, creasing the covers and scattering the pillows.

For seven years, they'd repeated this ritual, ever since his wife had abandoned them both one warm Thursday night in June.

He'd trudged to their shabby old home in the dark of St Giles, exhausted and sore from training, to find his daughter hunched on the front step, alone and clutching a letter, tears washing her dirty cheeks.

A mere six years old.

Hell, he'd been so lost. Not knowing how to comfort her, how to halt the weeping...or tamp the tight curl of failure within his own belly.

So he'd brewed a pot of weak tea and chatted of his day, left the letter to one side and asked which waistcoat he should wear for their dinner.

The red, he remembered. Always the bright ones.

They'd not bothered with a stew that night but scoffed bread and butter instead, him nattering about boxing and the club that one day might be theirs.

Chloe's tears had dried so he'd put her to bed, tied her hair in a messed-up, bungled plait and whispered she dream of princesses.

His daughter had replied that dragons were more exciting and promptly fallen asleep.

Then he'd read the letter, sitting alone at the kitchen table…

Now his nearly grown daughter was plonked cross-legged on the bed with dreams of pugilistic endeavour, rosy cheeks to her palms.

"So…" Seth arched one eyebrow.

Chloe arched one back. "Miss Griffin doesn't use any short words, loathes yellow despite wearing it, can't see for tuppence without her glasses and has absolutely no idea how to be a governess."

Seth arched the other eyebrow. "So…"

"I adore her."

He exhaled in a gush.

Having introduced his daughter in their practice room this morning, he'd left the two females to become better acquainted, for Chloe to show the new governess her quarters and for a tentative rapport to build.

Chloe had inherited her mother's open nature and gained his own patience to boot. Not one for tantrums, her only flaw to his biased eye was a laxity for following rules and a too-honest mouth.

"Miss Griffin also, for some reason…" A beady green eye fixed upon him. "Believes you a sapsculled pudding-head. She never actually said that, of course… It was just an impression I got. Lack of books or something."

"I'm hardly a brainbox, Chloe."

"Hmm." The beady eye narrowed to that of a blade of grass.

"Anyhow, it matters not, petal. Miss Griffin will be able to teach you subjects that the vicar's wife and I, as your father, cannot."

"Like?"

"Fork placements and how to back out of a room when wearing a train."

Chloe squished up her face, loose blond hair falling over her eyes. "Do I have to?"

"Yes. You need to learn feminine accomplishments alongside the boxing, thus gaining an all-round knowledge. It's either Miss Griffin or...school."

Mulish lips pursed. For all her adult ways, she now scowled like a child of five years.

This was his chance to raise the most difficult of subjects, whilst she was...quiet.

"Chloe..." He sat on the bed next to her, faffed with the coverlet and hauled a deep breath. "You are thirteen now."

"Fourteen in November."

How could he forget. "I need to talk to you about something."

"Hmm?"

"You must have noticed... Well, men..."

"Hmm?" Her eyes had widened and he was aware the nobility would stay silent on such matters, letting their lambs blunder amongst wolves, but he believed his daughter should be armed with all knowledge in order to negotiate life.

Not that it made this any easier.

"Well, you..." Gads, he was pathetic. "You see, pet..."

A gentle hand touched his shoulder. "I know, Pa."

"You do?"

"Yes. Betty told me."

"She did?"

"Yes, when I turned thirteen."

"Oh, right then." Well, that was a waste of all the recitation and pacing in the basement. Not that he was complaining in any way whatsoever. In fact, as inestimable relief poured through him, he thought to raise Betty's wages. "Although, I also…there's a further matter." This wasn't going to be easy either.

"And now you're going to tell me I can no longer practise boxing in the main academy hall."

How the devil had she known that?

"Well, yes. That was it." Had she been at his tea leaves? "But I'm so sorry, pet. I know you love thumping nine bells out of the straw figures there, and having you nearby brought me comfort, brought us luck when we first started up the Academy, but you're growing up and…"

"I'm a girl in petticoats, I understand, Papa. Lord Hareborough was staring at my bottom yesterday."

"I'll mill his duddering top-loft," he growled. "Then revive the scurvy jackanapes to mill him again."

Chloe rolled her eyes. "He's just being a typical man." She patted his hand. "No offence meant. But I no longer feel comfortable anyway."

"Ah, daughter, I'm sorry." And he dragged her into a tight hug. "You can continue boxing in our practice room, of course, but I'm aware you love to train in the Academy with all its chatter."

"And I can still be the next Stokes if I want to, can't I?"

Seth sighed and drew back to tug a lock of Chloe's hair. Elizabeth Stokes had been a championess boxer some nine decades or so past. Yet had her fame been for her skill or the bloody novelty? Seth suspected the latter.

Most went into prizefighting to claw their way from the stews, a winning purse of ten pounds lending a fierceness to the fist and a vitality to any weariness. Never would he deny his daughter her ambitions, merely wished that at such a young age, she leave every option open. Hence the need for a governess.

"Of course you can. But I also want you to be your own person, Chloe. Not Stokes or a genteel lady or a prizefighter's daughter. Just yourself. Do what you wish."

"I do enjoy it," she assured. "The twisting and balance, how to tackle someone bigger than me and working out where my opponent is weakest. You must have enjoyed that? And the feeling when you won?"

He'd done it for the money. To escape a brutal existence with no end. But... "Partly, but it's not all glory and triumph. It's also pain and blood, and the raw reality of getting your nose broken by Jack Scroggins."

"Well I've never been hit properly, I know." Her mouth twisted. "So if I don't become a championess, how else could I continue doing what I love?"

"I'll set my pudding brains to thinking, pet."

Chloe eyed him with chewed lip. "Which waistcoat are you wearing to dinner?"

"Er...the brown?"

A shake of blond head.

"You choose then."

She pottered off to the wardrobe, her long blue dress now above her ankles. His petal was growing like a dandelion. Nevertheless, he clasped his hands behind his head and settled back amongst the pillows, content with life.

"You should remarry, Papa."

"What?" Confound it, where had that come from? And he stomped to the set of drawers.

"I won't be able to choose your waistcoats forever. And then where will you be? Stuck in boring browns and ghastly greys." She stood hands to hips, then swished back to the wardrobe with a huff. "You're only just one and thirty. Old but not an utter has-been."

Scowling, Seth grabbed a cravat. "I could employ a valet

to choose my waistcoats." He yanked the cloth around his throat, almost garrotting himself. "Wouldn't get half as much cheek either."

"But a valet won't keep you warm on winter nights." She peeked over one shoulder and winked.

It appeared Betty had been quite thorough then.

"Well, since we have a new dinner companion tonight," Seth pronounced, "we'd better flash our best togs. How about the green silk waistcoat?"

"Miss Griffin won't be attending tonight. She was so tired, I sent her to bed."

Oh. That was exceedingly early.

"Isn't ordering a charge to bed without their supper Miss Griffin's duty? The grey then." And Seth unravelled the ornate cascade cravat he'd been creating and settled on his usual barrel knot.

Chloe tapped a lip and then handed him a waistcoat that resembled a painted barber's pole. Its wide collar flapped about and the fob pocket was garnished with clashing green embroidery – a Christmas present from a relative, if memory served. She yanked it straight. "I asked Betty to prepare a little something and take it up to her, of course. She said they could have a natter about your rules for the household."

Frowning, Seth buttoned up the striped monstrosity.

He wasn't aware there were any.

"In my most troubled moments," confided Matilda, looking left then right, "I called my cousin...Arsewood and not Astwood. Only to myself, you understand."

"Lawks, I like that!" Betty chortled and patted her on the

hand as they sat together upon a tasteful indigo-blue chaise. "I didn't think fine ladies knew such words."

"I'm quite well read, Betty, and Chaucer mentions that particular vernacular most prominently in his *Tales*."

"I don't really do books," the housekeeper admitted, puckering her forehead, "but if experience of life were pages, I've read a thousand."

How eloquent and honest Betty was.

No over-elaborate wordage, just plain talk and shrewd eyes.

Never had Matilda been allowed to befriend the servants before – even instructed to keep her loyal maid at a ladylike distance as her parents had foretold of calamity, plagues and apocalyptic disaster should the various English classes fraternise.

Yet no disaster befell her talking to Betty – it was…joyful.

"Experience of life is what I wish to gain, Betty. When I reach my birthday."

"Well, 'tis a good thing yer told me yer problems as I'll keep a squinter out for any lurking viscounts, don't yer worry." Another pat and she rose with a hand to the small of her back. "Now, yer look all done in, so finish yer supper in peace and I'll be seein' yer in the morning. It's kippers for breakfast." And off she ambled, softly closing the door behind her.

Matilda reached for another one-inch slab of cheese from the selection Betty had brought up and sighed in pleasure.

Maybe employment at a boxing academy wouldn't be so awful after all.

She solely had to avoid the boxing, the academy members, the muscles – although those were under review – and any odd conversations concerning whiffles and muffles.

Even this bedchamber appeared spacious for a governess,

with a sumptuous four-poster, mahogany dresser and dainty looking-glass. A sitting room was attached with this elegant chaise, a rosewood writing desk and her very own key for the door, which she could lock if she so wished.

Of late, life with Astwood had become oppressive, forever watched over, bedchamber keys held by the butler.

Yet matters had taken a turn for the worse in the past few days – the servants admitting her repellent betrothed to the drawing room without announcement.

The door pulled shut.

His pouched eyes had greedily devoured her tight jonquil-yellow dress and only her pretence of a putrid cough had kept that fetid tongue at a distance of six feet and not inserted within her mouth. Surely a deed that no woman should ever have to endure.

Matilda shuddered, and with plate in hand, rose to amble for the writing desk by the window with its filled ink well and fresh quill nestling upon a brass stand. A short missive must be sent to her confidante, Evelyn, to halt further communication till August, lest any messenger be followed.

Gazing out the window, the foggy night of Green Park reflected back with her own pale features overlaid upon it, shadowed and tired and...anxious.

For the consequences of her dawn flit.

The servants would no doubt have discovered her absence by now and be sending a dispatch to Astwood – would he snort and debauch some more? Or ride back to London at first light?

What if he located her before August? And dragged her home? After all, as her guardian and owner, he had the right of it.

She was naught but a piece of furniture, inherited with the house, that could be sold for fifty guineas and a new coat.

Narrowing her eyes at the misted dark, Matilda sought her courage and nibbled Betty's wodge of sharp cheese – better the life of a governess with its half-day off per week than the wife of a dissolute mutton monger with no freedom at all.

She would be diligent in her work, study all tomes available and research every nuance of governess-ship, and one day she would be the finest educator of young ladies that had ever existed.

CHAPTER FOUR

"A pun is a poor apology for wit."

Private Education: A Practical Plan for the Studies of Young Ladies.

Elizabeth Appleton. 1815.

The role of governess was more formidable than first assumed – which was more or less what the crabby Miss Appleton had stated.

For upon Matilda's first morning, between the hours of nine and ten, a reserve of patience had been required for the endless conjugation of one French verb.

From ten until eleven, unwavering enthusiasm had been crucial in order to critique twenty-two perfect curtseys.

And from eleven until midday, a certain never-ending joy had needed to be summoned to read Mr Molineux's *Introduction to the Globes,* which upon reflection was as dull as boxing.

Now, after a light luncheon together, Matilda sat at the

schoolroom harpsichord whilst Chloe flipped through her music book to find her favourite song.

At least this room was a pleasant place to work, filled with two desks, a comfortable sofa, shelves of her chosen textbooks, slates and writing implements. A window overlooked lively Arlington Street, allowing today's stodgy light to enter, and a fire flamed blithely on the opposite wall to keep the May chill at bay.

All in all, it could be worse, especially after reading of the cultivated Miss Appleton's challenges, but apart from a roll of the eyes over letter writing, Chloe had been a delight.

Not that Matilda had past experience anyhow.

"I've found the words, Miss Griffin. It's called *The Pious Parson*."

"Excellent. I know plenty of religious songs. Why don't you sing it, and I'll join in on the harpsichord when I recognise the tune."

Chloe stood and drew a deep breath...

"'There was a pious parson,
Who lived in Upper Harding,
That loved his lass.
And another pretty lass.
And cherished his dice and carding.'"

Matilda frowned, fingers aloft the keys.

Chloe drew another breath.

"'The parson went a-courting,
For lasses more he wanted,
He found a trollo–'"

"Chloe, I dislike interrupting such a fine and angelic voice but where did you learn this song?"

"Oh, a club member sings it when he's washing."

"I see. I'm not sure... Do you know any others, perhaps?"

"I know one to the same tune called *John and Susan*. Shall I sing it?"

"No! Er, let's broaden your repertoire a little. Come sit by me, and perhaps we might learn one that could be performed at a musical soiree, for example."

Chloe flopped beside her on the stool. "Are they fun, Miss Griffin? Soirees?"

"Yes, of course. Well..." In point of fact, she couldn't ever recall having *fun* at a musical soiree. They were an obligatory event for a debutante to attend – like eyebrow plucking. "Not always, but one can meet new friends. It's just that we are expected to obey the rules of propriety in selecting songs, and the choice can be somewhat restricted for ladies."

Her charge's young shoulders slumped. "I hope I like being a lady. Pa says I'm not awfully good with rules."

Matilda was well aware that Miss Appleton would now fritter away an hour discussing the need for a young lady to obey without question, to follow the edicts of their betters, yet hadn't Matilda herself defied her guardian's word? Sought, in her own small way, to overturn society's expectation that she give herself in marriage without complaint to an aged libertine who smelled of wet dog and week-old cabbage?

Chloe, she had discovered thus far today, was a girl with a thoughtful nature and intelligent mind yet an outspoken tongue and bold attitude.

Should a governess curb such character and mould it to meek and mild?

"I think..." She made to pat Chloe's arm in reassurance,

but awkwardness beset her at such an avuncular gesture. "I think it more important to be kind to one another than to slavishly follow rules and expectations. We all wish to be accepted, of course, but that does not mean we must suppress our true selves. 'Tis a balancing act that I myself have not yet learned."

Her young charge patted Matilda's arm. "Well, why don't we learn together then, Miss Griffin." A broad smile and Chloe dolloped a forefinger on middle C. "You follow my lead." And she took a deep breath...

"'There was a pious parson,
Who lived in Upper Harding...'"

SOME FOLK MIGHT BELIEVE that to be the owner of a boxing academy, one would merely need a brutish fist and a thick skull, yet other qualities were also required, such as forethought, tact, patience and–

"Lord Cholmondeley!" yelled Seth. "Keep your fists up, man. You're not dancing the quadrille at bloody Almack's."

The young sprig nodded and brought his gloves closer to his hairless chin as he and another lordling sparred within a small chalked circle upon the floor – the restricted space kept their footwork tidy, promoted focus and allowed Seth to fit more members into this Academy hall – otherwise he'd be seeking new premises.

For some reason, now Napoleon had been seen to, there had been an upsurge in new members: returned officers with pent horrors that needed to be dispelled in peacetime, and fledgling fellows who wished to show patriotic pride by milling their closest friend on the chops – a curious trait of the English.

Seth skirted a sweat-clad Waterloo hero punching the hell out of a straw bag suspended from the ceiling, and headed to the main ring, where a small crowd had gathered.

Many a gentry cove arrived to view the practice bouts he scheduled for his young apprentices – to gain inside knowledge of the latest up-and-coming prizefighter and conclude whether to wager on or against him.

And Liam Wheelan was one such fighter – young, raw and tough. Yet…

Seth tapped a member of the crowd on the back. "Excuse me. May I pass?"

Without turning, the earl growled, "Find your own patch to…" He twisted his head. "Mr Hawkins, do excuse me. I'd not realised it was you." And he shifted to allow Seth through while also yanking his companion to the side.

Seth nodded his gratitude and stepped up to the ropes. Raised at a modest height for all to see, the ring was surrounded by this simple hemp barrier, the floor scattered with sawdust for grip.

The hulking Liam landed a nobbler upon the other young fighter's conk, then a plump to the brisket. This was no fancy boxing match with nobs sparring in gloves to protect their delicate knuckles, but the bare-fisted combat of prizefighting with few rules.

"You've got a winning lad there, Hawkins," pronounced some duke to his side, before clapping a hand to his shoulder.

Hmm.

The two apprentices circled upon bouncing feet, the younger displaying his agility with a sharp dodge to the right. Yet Liam showed no mercy for effort, and with a swift, determined settler to the jaw, his opponent hit the floor.

Seth waited as the crowd dispersed for other pleasures of London, then narrowed his gaze as Liam smirked at the defeated lad, who gamely sat up and attempted to shake hands. With slack wrist and disinterested eyes, Liam barely brushed palms, and the younger lad slunk beneath the ropes with a grimace. Seth grabbed his arm. "Your technique is good. Keep practising, get some meat on those bones and you'll get there." The lad nodded before heading to the changing room, and Seth twisted back to Liam.

The seventeen-year-old victor reminded Seth of himself at that age – rough and hungry, his eagerness built upon a need to escape a vicious life as the crisp whip scars upon Liam's back attested to.

All essential ingredients and yet the lad lacked two fundamentals…

"I'll be ready for a proper fight soon, won't I, Mr Hawkins? He were a cock robin who tumbled before I'd breathed on him."

Namely humility and patience.

Seth checked his fob watch. Two hours before dinner with his daughter…and the new governess.

Not the only development at No. 25 Arlington Street.

The scent of wildflowers now haunted the hallways.

A graceful laugh echoed behind a closed schoolroom door.

Buttercup silk flashed around a corner.

All reminding him that a woman now lived in his house.

A pretty woman with eyes of sherry and skin of cream.

A pretty woman who thought him a beef-witted muttonhead.

Heaving a breath, he swung a leg over the lower rope and

ducked the upper one to step into the ring. Seth shoved off his unbuttoned waistcoat, hauled his shirt over his head and flung it to the corner post.

He sponsored many a boy from the Rookery, lads like himself who craved a way out, and Liam was good, but anger and arrogance would be his downfall.

"Yer opponent today, Liam, was two stone lighter and twelvemonth younger. If yer met an experienced fighter in the ring, he'd mill yer before yer could raise a fist." Seth lifted his own, the damaged knuckles and hardened skin speaking their ferocious past, reminding the boy of Seth's background, of who he truly was. That when all was said and done, prizefighting wasn't for the nobs and swells that followed their wins, but for common men who needed coin and food to survive.

"I could take anyone on," the lad muttered with a shadowed gleam to his gaze.

"Take *me* on, then, for one round. Yer've fought m'other lads, but you and me have only scuffled."

Liam tilted his head and narrowed his eyes at Seth.

If the lad cared to make use of those eyes, he'd see an ex-fighter in good form, but one who'd ceased brawling professionally four years past. A man with just over three decades who might have grown lax hobnobbing with fancy coves.

"M'pleasure, Mr Hawkins."

They bounced upon the spot to loosen, weight forward, fists raised, until Seth nodded and the young lad, with no assessment of his opponent's stance whatsoever, stabbed out a blow to Seth's noggin.

A simple shift of the neck and the blow flew wide.

Liam growled and attempted a plump to the ribs, but Seth danced to the right and it glanced off with nigh a brush.

Another mill, but too wild, and Seth pitched up a forearm to meet the force, his wide stance enabling his balance.

A further fist jabbed out, this time catching his ribs, but Seth's chest was not a weakness, cushioned as it was by muscle and sinew, and he was easily able to withstand the impact, to tarry until…

Proud of his blow, Liam advanced, too fast, fists pelting, and Seth took advantage to hook his heel around the back of the lad's ankle and sweep him from his feet.

"And the round is over," Seth declared, hauling a sullen Liam from his arse.

He rested hands on the lad's shoulders.

"Liam. Use yer brains. I know you 'ave them under all that temper. Look at me. What are m'weaknesses? Where are m'strengths? Did yer even think before blundering in? Where in the 'ell was yer defence? I could 'ave 'ad yer as soon as yer missed that first rattler, but thought I'd wait till yer sealed yer own fall."

Liam glowered but began to rake Seth with his wolfish eyes.

"Yer've a stocky build, Mr Hawkins, which keeps its balance well. A chest that can take a fist. And yer've bleedin' light feet that can move like a doxy at dawn. But…" His black gaze perused. "Yer've a shorter reach, and I don't mean no cheek, but…" A smile shimmered – the boy within. "Yer ain't no raw buffer, Mr Hawkins, so yer stamina won't be up to much."

"Better. Whereas yer've a long reach, are young and can bide yer time. Wait, punch from afar with power, and I might go down like a Spanish ship in the Armada. Think, Liam, use yer noddle. You ain't fighting no lowlife gutter rats in the streets, but real men with hard lives, rent to pay and babes to feed."

Liam gave a mulish nod.

"And don't be so damn cocksure. Learn from others, and one day, the world might be yer oyster."

"Right yer are, Mr Hawkins. Can we have another bout?"

Seth glanced to the clock upon the wall and grabbed his shirt from the corner post.

"Tomorrow at nine, lad. I've got a dinner to tog up for."

CHAPTER FIVE

"A book may be the ruin of innocence; the prop of virtue; the comfort of the weak; the terror of the strong; the polisher of a mind; or the depraver of a heart."

Private Education: A Practical Plan for the Studies of Young Ladies. Elizabeth Appleton. 1815.

Matilda paced, poked the fire, peered out the window and then paced some more whilst awaiting her employer.

Never having been one for a protracted toilette, she'd washed with the pitcher of water left by the maid, donned the brighter of her four yellow gowns – after all, it was to be dinner – and then…twiddled her thumbs to knots in this stylish drawing room.

Customarily, if worries assailed or nerves seized, she'd read a novel for distraction or a poem to still her thoughts, and although, as requested, Mr Hawkins had supplied the necessary volumes for the schoolroom, she'd found nothing further.

Plays? Sonnets? The latest scurrilous romance novel? The back of a Fortnum and Mason biscuit tin?

She'd perused the shelves – not one book.

Examined the mantelpiece and behind the tray of decanters – devoid.

Poked around the plant pots – barren.

Huffing, she tapped a lip and gazed into the gilt mirror that hung over the fireplace, the drawing in of dusk obscuring the reflected corners of the room not lit by the elegant sconces.

Without fictional fancy to settle her mind, she'd end up mad as a March hare, be found burbling insanity around Green Park in solely her petticoats.

The window seat caught her eye in the mirror, surely a prime place to read and hence discard a novel, so she glanced at the clock. Still time, and she hurried over, yanking the cushion aloft.

But nothing, and her shoulders slumped.

"You appear…dismayed, Miss Griffin."

Matilda spun, Pomona-green cushion in hand.

Propped against the doorframe was Mr Hawkins, head tilted, that scarred eyebrow raised in query.

Composing her features to pious and patient as Miss Appleton had sourly decreed, Matilda smiled in innocence.

"No, no, I am quite content, Mr Hawkins, thank you, just…plumping." She pulverised the cushion for good measure, as she'd seen maids do, then carefully placed it on the seat at a fashionable angle. "Chloe and I had an exceedingly productive day. She's a delightful girl." And to further divert attention, Matilda deployed her deepest curtsey – one more advocated for noblemen than pugilists.

Straightening from his lounged position by the door, Mr Hawkins sketched an equally profound bow and entered the room.

Matilda's nerves heightened.

Although the door was open, with the maid dawdling in the hall, Matilda had never, not once, been so alone with a man – other than the brief encounter with her malodorous betrothed, but that did not count.

This was a…real man.

All rippling physique and glossy walnut hair, immense hands straightening a perfect cascade cravat with ruby stick pin.

A leaf-green waistcoat highlighted the flickers in his eyes, the material clinging indecently, its collar narrow with two rows of silk-covered buttons climbing his chest like an inviting ladder. Lower, his whipcord thighs – powerful and strident – were encased in a black silk which complemented his jacket.

Matilda's gaze dipped to the rug as she recollected a book concerning male plumage: how any subsequent delight felt within a female of the species was an instinctive response and nothing at all to do with one's own inclinations – the book had in fact been concerned with the mating habits of pelicans but surely explained the tendrils of pleasure which now coursed.

Attraction was a mere primitive and animalistic reaction to a male in prime fettle.

"And you are not concerned by my daughter's pastime?" he enquired, crossing those burly arms.

Matilda straightened her spine. "I daresay it is…out of the ordinary, but Chloe's manner is respectful, honest and fun. I see no harm, and it appears to give her an unusual agility and poised balance for even the most arduous of curtseys."

Mr Hawkins' lips twitched as he prowled with lupine grace – and yes, that was the only word to describe the manner in which he walked – to the side table. "Sherry?"

"Yes, if I may, but... As Chloe's governess, should I not dine with her in the schoolroom?"

He prowled once more, but this time in her direction, and she strove to recall more of those pelican specifics.

"Chloe dines here with me. Always has."

"Oh." How unusual. "She failed to mention that."

The sherry glass was proffered. Their fingers brushed.

Pelicans.

Of course, an arousing cologne of leather and musk was not generally associated with that genus of water bird either, although the glands of a deer were used to create musk, so perchance it was also a mating attractant and hence the explanation for her olfactory pleasure.

He cocked his head. "Did you not dine with your parents?"

"Not until I was fifteen and had something worthwhile to communicate. I dined in the nursery till then." Put into words, that sounded appalling. She'd adored her parents but until her mind had been that of a fully functioning adult, she had remained unseen and unheard at mealtimes.

"With your governess?"

"She only came for five hours a day. Then it was solely me and my books." If she had to discern his expression, it was pity. "I was quite content," she assured. "Within those pages, I could visit a forest or volcano, watch a play of tragedy or friendship, debate philosophy with myself, or feel sadness and...and love."

The hue of Mr Hawkins' eyes shifted to that of sedimentary rock and swirling kelp pools, and she swallowed. He had stood somewhat closer than proper to pass the sherry and her skin had prickled with an agreeable awareness.

She reminded herself that this type of human behaviour was commonplace beyond the *Ton* world, that maids and footmen did dine together, and persons of both genders sat elbow-to-elbow in stagecoaches – all without coming over slightly peculiar.

"I am sure you are correct, Miss Griffin," he murmured, "in that books can convey the very essence of a writer's soul, emotion and experience."

Matilda nodded. "And if I had allowed myself to be married off, I've a feeling that sadness would have been my sole experience."

FOR ALL HER DEBUTANTE INNOCENCE, Miss Griffin was likewise as worldly as a society matron.

Many young misses would have acquiesced with their guardian's choice of husband, not understanding what their future life may entail, yet those observant sherry-tinted eyes and that astute mind had watched, cogitated and decided upon a different path.

She was all Seth had hoped for in a governess to his daughter – a lady with manners and poise, but equally not one who would seek to curb Chloe's free spirit with orders of obeyance.

The sole curious aspect was...did not a governess habitually sport blending brown frocks or unobtrusive greys? A layer of invisibility within their employer's household?

He'd supposed the moulding buttercup yellow from yesterday a remnant of her previous status, yet when he'd first entered the room this evening to discover her investigating the window seat, it was to be confronted by Miss Griffin's gilded posterior, a golden beige that outdid the flaming fire, dress molten against her curvaceous form.

Now, she faced him, and he noted that the silk's hue matched her glasses, caused a lustre to her smooth skin and contrasted with her hair, deepening it to midnight.

He cleared his throat, straightened the green waistcoat that Chloe had chosen and thrust a finger inside his new cascade-style cravat, which quite frankly should come with a warning that it may throttle one's breathing route.

And where the hell was Chloe?

"Shall we await my daughter in the dining room?" Seth extended a forearm as though to escort a lady at a genteel ball – which surely was all wrong.

Earlier, he'd instinctively bowed in response to her elegant curtsey. Then wondered if that was correct procedure. After all, she was his employee, but the etiquette books he'd read in order to fit in with the swells who frequented his club hadn't covered this little scenario – the lady governess and the low-bred pugilist.

"And I am sure you are correct, Miss Griffin, concerning your betrothed. Marriage should be based upon love and respect. Sadness is inevitable in life, but there is no reason to walk into its embrace, if it can be so helped."

A tentative gloved hand reached out and rested upon his sleeve, but surprised eyes surveyed him. "How eloquently put. And a sentiment not widely held within the *Ton*, where money and title rule. It sounds as though your marriage was a happy one. I'm sorry for your loss."

Seth's eyes flickered, had not considered his words could be taken as such, so merely nodded as they passed through to the dining room.

Seating her in a walnut Chippendale chair, he watched as she inspected the walls, table and curtains.

No doubt this room was meagre compared to her former residence, but he'd personally chosen the paperhangings and commissioned a table to seat four but extend should the need arise. He loathed attending some event where one had to yell to be heard by your supper companions.

"Is all to your comfort, Miss Griffin?" he asked, placing himself opposite.

"I was just thinking what a pleasant room this is. Intimate and cosy, although..." A crease appeared between her brows. "I don't wish to persuade in any way but...the rooms could do with some books, perhaps? Just a few to cheer the shelves and so forth...but I understand they are expensive." Miss Griffin pushed her spectacles up. "I've not visited, but I believe there's a little shop on Pendle Street which sells them..." She lowered her voice. "Second-hand."

Seth grinned and–

"Sorry I'm late," Chloe gushed, then halted her step, steadied her balance with palms flat and curtsied with the previously unseen grace of a queen, despite the gown revealing her ankles. "Betty needed help with the meringues."

"That's fine, pet. I was about to ask Miss Griffin how she sees your timetable proceeding."

Chloe plonked herself left of Seth as the maid staggered in with a soup tureen. A swift grace was vowed before they both lifted their heads to Miss Griffin.

"Well..." With eyes wide as acorns, the governess coughed elegantly and gazed to the ceiling as though the timetable was written in the ornate plasterwork. "For the mornings, a selection from: Astronomy. French. Grammar. Maths. Painting. Classical Studies. Geography and so forth. All sectioned into one-hour slots. Then for the afternoons…" She breathed deep. "Etiquette – at balls, soirees, musical events and suchlike. A lady's accomplishments, naturally. Sewing. Recitation. Pianoforte. Bookkeeping. Netting and so on."

His daughter gaped.

"That's most…" Seth floundered.

"I'll be as old as eighteen once I've learned all that."

"I studied much the same as a child," Miss Griffin declared. "Chloe, your elbows…"

"But…" His daughter's elbows retreated from the table. "When did you go to the park? Or play hopscotch with friends? Or Battledore?"

Miss Griffin's spoon whirled in the soup, her brow furrowed. "I was sent to the museum twice a sennight with a maid."

"Not the park?"

"Well…" His governess gave a fleeting smile. "I do remember a brief visit to the Serpentine in Summer 1806."

"To feed the ducks some bread?"

"It was more presented to me as studying the environmental habitat of the domesticated mallard. No bread that I recall."

Seth winced, for it appeared his governess's childhood had solely been devoted to studious endeavour. Worthy enough but somewhat lacking in fun and friends.

Not that he hadn't made many a mistake with Chloe, but he'd always sought to bring cheer to her life, to make up for what they lacked.

One long ago winter's night, they'd run out of candles when he'd not the coin to pay the tallow-chandler's bill, but he'd claimed it was akin to All Hallow's Eve and they'd chortled over ghost stories in the pitch dark.

And now he understood why, at the interview, Miss

Griffin had mentioned how she wished to experience life, to no longer be shielded from either its blessings or perils, and an absurd desire to aid her cause arose within.

To escort her to Vauxhall Gardens and watch her gasp at the miraculous cascade, to partake of an evening at Astley's Amphitheatre and laugh at the clowns, or just a simple picnic in the sunshine surrounded by jovial company.

In lieu, he filled her wine glass with the finest claret that his Academy members' money could buy.

FEELING PLEASANTLY MELLOW after Betty's superb main course of pigeon pie, stewed hare, ragout of vegetables, roasted duck and a jug of gravy, Matilda allowed her spine to meet the chair back and proceeded to sip her pudding wine.

Cousin Astwood employed a certain *Monsieur Porcher* as chef, who although could do wonders with a lone asparagus spear and a thimble of *jus du frisa,* was inclined to leave his diners hungry.

Those mealtimes with her cousin had involved silent stares or ignoring his rants on a woman's duty to submit.

Here, Matilda listened in as Mr Hawkins chatted to his daughter about a certain young Irishman who wished to be a prizefighter, and although Matilda hadn't the foggiest about plumpers or whiffles, she enjoyed the rapid movement of his calloused hands, the rasp of his voice.

Perchance the husky squawking of male pelicans had a similar effect on the females?

"Do you like boxing, Miss? Or know any moves?"

Matilda blinked. She'd no wish to insult anyone and end the day by being disemployed but... "Generally, a lady is not exposed to the...sport, so our opinion is not qualified or taken note of."

"Hmm." And her charge nodded.

Content with her diplomatic response and with the likelihood of disemployment lessened, Matilda continued, "Indeed, from the little I know, it appears most gruelling and with my small stature and paltry strength, I doubt I would be capable."

"'Our doubts are traitors…'" murmured Mr Hawkins.

Matilda frowned. *'…And make us lose the good we oft might win, by fearing to attempt.'* She slid her confused gaze across the table, noted those rough fingers caress a fragile glass stem with care and serenity. Those words of Shakespeare spoke her very thoughts at times: fear for her future struggles as governess and the treacherous doubts that crept in when alone in her bed.

But where had he learned these quotes?

"Did you attend school, Mr Hawkins?" She didn't mean to be rude but…

Chloe filled her mouth with meringue.

"Only on Saturdays at the local charity school. My father was a coal heaver and I followed in his footsteps. No time for learning."

"No, of course." And she supposed a man whose profession involved pugilism would not have need of reading material – walloping and thumping being learned through experience.

"Do you…" She bit her lip. "Do you know if a circulating library happens to be nearby?"

Mr Hawkins leaned back with levelled eyes that could pierce diamond. "Are we lacking in something, Miss Griffin? Do you require more books for the schoolroom?"

What could she say? It was just that she missed them, by her bed and in her palm, like dear friends surrounding her, the touch of smooth paper, the smell of bound leather. When she'd awoken at night, afraid and alone in the nursery, a book had soothed her, tales of the tropical Molucca Islands and its native birds lulling her back to sleep. One day, she'd travel there...

Mathematics and grammar were all very well, but rather dry.

Oh, why had she not filched just one book of poetry from her bedside table?

Pride, she thought dejectedly. Not wanting to take anything from Astwood.

However, now she led a working life and could not expect possessions of her own. Perchance when she'd saved some wages, she could dash to Hatchards and buy a small volume, just for herself.

Never should she have brought up the subject, as surely it appeared ungrateful – she had wonderful food, a warm bed and agreeable plumage to look upon.

"No, 'tis fine. Please forget I mentioned it, Mr Hawkins." And Matilda endeavoured a smile.

Her employer frowned, a puckering that appeared foreign to his brow, then dropped his serviette to the table. "I shall expect you in my study at the hour of ten on the morrow, Miss Griffin. We will discuss it then."

Oh botheration.

CHAPTER SIX

"A prudent young woman will pause, therefore, on words, before she utters them to men, and will regulate her action by unconstrained dignity."

Private Education: A Practical Plan for the Studies of Young Ladies. Elizabeth Appleton. 1815

"What do you make of the new governess, Betty?"

Seth checked his fob watch – a quarter before the hour of ten – tugged down his errant cuff and tidied his aquamarine silk waistcoat before straightening an illustration of himself with Mauler Mike on the study wall.

A snort answered his question, so he swivelled. "You don't like her?"

Blue eyes flashed with mirth and her lips smirked as she tidied the coffee pot away, so Seth tapered his gaze in sternness, despite knowing it would not make a blind bit of difference.

When his wife had left them all those years ago, their

Rookery neighbour, Betty, had taken up the reins, cooking them meals and letting down Chloe's dress hems every fortnight, her husband Mick assisting with training and schedule.

A few years later, with enough money in his pocket from a championship win, Seth had left the Rookery, persuading them to come with him, and Mick now looked after the day-to-day running of the club whilst Betty still looked after the lot of them. They had a neat little house not far away on Haymarket and spent every August on the coast.

"Yer Miss Griffin is refined, honest and has a noggin big as Dorset. But she's also hardy as old boots, and I like her very much, even if she don't exactly use words that trip off the tongue. A bit wordy, like."

"Well, that's…good. Thank you, Betty."

With a wink, she ambled out, and Seth hemmed and hawed, waiting for the clock to chime ten.

Despite scarcely passing time with Miss Griffin, he had discerned much over dinner last night.

Firstly, as Betty had so eloquently described, her intelligence was obvious, French words bandied about with *savoir faire.*

Secondly, compared to that prospective governess who'd reassured him at the interview she'd have his pugilistic daughter beaten for such 'unnatural inclinations', Miss Griffin appeared understanding of Chloe's interests.

And thirdly, for all the society events the lady must have attended, she appeared utterly oblivious of her own beauty and radiance.

His wife had known the price of her smile and sea-blue eyes from an early age – to get out of trouble…and into it. Had known how to cadge an apple with a pucker of lips or receive a free ale with a suggestive cock of hip.

Miss Griffin seemed unacquainted with feminine wiles, quite unaware of how her exquisiteness could drag a man to his knees.

Indeed, if he had to summarise the lady, it would be honesty in all matters. She'd revealed the truth at the interview, and when Chloe had asked a difficult question at dinner concerning meringue etiquette, she'd not fibbed or brushed it off with excuses but acknowledged her ignorance and replied they'd research it the very next day.

So many people pretended in these times, even himself with his accent and manners. He'd spent countless nights learning aristocratic diction, mimicking the swells' mannerisms and airs, so that nowadays it was second nature. Only in the company of a fellow fighter did his veneer of respectability melt like mercury, displaying the warrior beneath.

Yet Miss Griffin's character was as natural and clear as breathing.

The carriage clock chimed and he faffed with a letter to look busy.

On the eighth bell, a knock sounded.

"Come in."

Nankeen-coloured cotton, more suited to a picnic by the Serpentine, garbed his nervous-looking governess, black hair severely pinned and lips bitten rosy red.

"I hope, Miss Griffin, that I am not interrupting your morn with this?"

"Not at all. I have left Chloe practising her singing, an accomplishment in which she is entirely euphonious."

No, he had no idea either, so…

"After your comments last night, I thought I would conduct a small tour of the house. It was remiss of me not to do so on your first day."

. . .

A RUSH of air left Matilda's lungs that she felt quite sure had been held in since last night.

In fact, she'd been irksomely bothered by inexplicable dreams of Mr Hawkins all night through. He'd been sternly reprimanding her, nude except for those snug black breeches. Not so irksome, some might say, but then a magnificent pair of feathered wings coloured in gold and red had sprouted upon his back. Within a clear blue sky, he'd soared aloft, dipped and twisted before, with a fiery gaze, he'd swooped down upon her, rough hands encircling her waist and–

Then she'd woken up.

Inexplicable, as she'd said.

Matilda cleared her throat and took refuge in cool courtesy. "That would be splendid, thank you." And she attempted a swift bobbed curtsey, aware she only knew sweeping, elegant forms. Maids appeared able to bob in all haste without nigh falling over. "I also wished to ask a…favour."

Eyebrows raised, that enigmatic scar wrinkling. "Tell me on the way." And he waggled his forearm.

With some hesitation, she laid her hand on the indigo superfine, sensed his muscles tense. "Of course…Sir." That being the correct address, she'd concluded late last night, as he was her employer…and it was less protracted than *Mr Hawkins*. And in any case, the maid did it.

They departed the ground floor study and he pointed to a black-painted door opposite the kitchens. "The only area out of bounds," he stated, "is the basement as it's for club members and my own use."

Matilda shuddered. What on earth did males do down

there? Was it some kind of fighting pit where barbaric combat was enacted…or a changing abode where taut thighs or unclothed musculature might be glimpsed?

She breathed deep – that kind of wild imagining was the result of not having any novels to occupy her.

"I will avoid it at all cost, Sir," she assured fervently.

A smile shifted his lips – lopsided and disturbingly attractive – hazel eyes twinkling, aquamarine waistcoat complementing his olive-toned skin. Delicate flowers were embroidered upon the cotton, which in no manner detracted from his masculinity, and a single row of blue buttons tempted one's gaze to follow upwards…or downwards.

He appeared young and carefree this morning, and it occurred to her that Mr Hawkins had looked most tired last night. "Does the Academy take much of your time?"

"It is lessening now the membership is stable, but in the early days it was unending – accounts, shows, exhibitions, let alone the classes. I have assistants, equally capable, but most members only wish to learn from the champion prizefighter, not his assistants." He guided her up the staircase. "On the first floor, you are familiar with the dining and drawing rooms, and you've seen the ballroom we use for our personal sparring practice, but there is also a small salon with a balcony here."

They wandered left and into a pleasant, light room with sofas, no books, French doors and walls decorated in muted colours. Which reminded her…

"The favour, Mr Hawkins… I-I wondered if I might request…" This subject was vulgar in the extreme, and her parents would turn in their graves, but needs must… "Might I have an advance on my wages? It's just that Cousin Astwood replaced my entire wardrobe with yellow and I am aware it is hardly proper governess attire."

He twisted, his gaze settling on her nankeen skirts. "I did wonder. Although I have to say that while your cousin may be an oaf, he does have exquisite taste. The colour adds a sheen to your skin and intensifies the coal silk of your hair… if you don't mind me saying so." He fiddled with his cuff.

No, she didn't mind at all. No one ever complimented her. But then yellow was nature's attractant, the flowers in spring blooming that hue for the early insects.

"I'm afraid that in order to forge ahead in my profession, I ought to dress suitably. I would only need a small advance…I think." Shamefully, she had no idea. She could recite Hamlet and yet had no inkling as to the cost of a simple brown frock.

Mr Hawkins unlocked the French doors and they wandered onto the balcony that overlooked the garden and hence Green Park. By day, their lush neighbour appeared tranquil and not scary at all.

Grey clouds hung low and heavy with ominous rain as they had done most days this year, a scant breeze gusting cologne of leather and male.

"The dressmaker is visiting next week as Chloe likewise needs new clothes. She could fit you at the same time."

"My requirements are simple."

"As you wish." Mr Hawkins urged her back inside as she shivered in the crispness of the hour. "And as for wages, I also need a…favour, and if you agree, it will pay for these dresses."

Matilda pursed her lips and crossed her arms.

What would a widowed virile man ask of his female unchaperoned governess?

Rampant images from a Greek vase she'd once viewed startled Matilda – disturbing and altogether indelicate. "What exactly do you wish me to do?"

He swivelled from the French door. "It's my turn to host our Annual Champions' Dinner at the weekend, and as you are here, I wondered if you could act as my hostess? Conversation, menus and suchlike."

Oh.

But...

She thrust her shoulders back and drew her short stature up as high as it would go, stepping close. "Mr Hawkins, although I may lead a working life now, I still do not consider it proper for a lone woman to oversee a dinner full of solely male...pugilists." She glared. Honestly. Men. They had no idea! "If it should ever become known that I did so, my reputation as a custodian of innocent girls would be forever ruined, my future career in tatters. Employers would consider me a lightskirt, a blowsabella they could call upon at any time to–"

"Miss Griffin." Her fluttering fingers were captured within his hands, coarse and strong. Then they tensed and were swiftly drawn away. "Even pugilists manage to marry, you realise. Often quite successfully as well. Most of the fellows will bring their wives, except for a scant few who remain bachelors, or like me are widowers, and Nobbler Nick always brings his sister to these events. We are quite...civilised."

Matilda bit her lip and closed her eyes.

What a nitterwit.

"I can only apologise for my presumption, Sir."

"A not unnatural one." He grinned, displaying those white teeth. "I should have worded my request better, and I am sure this will hold no trepidation for a lady such as you. After all, you must have attended many a society event."

"Yes, but I... I tended to keep to the edges."

. . .

SETH GAPED. "Never say you are a wallflower, Miss Griffin. I shall not believe it."

"More like a cauliflower, Mr Hawkins. Rather bland – only the head is of interest and liable to stunted growth." She sighed. "My parents did not attend a plethora of society events and so only when I acquired my guardian was I obliged to. But Astwood's acquaintances were all whiskerless cubs in silly coats or aged libertines with gout, and my talk... bored them. I apologise for this coarseness but believe my prospective betrothed solely wished to marry me for my plenteous bosom."

A strangled grunt left Seth's lips, but employing all restraint, he did not lower his gaze.

"I'm sure other attributes appealed," he bit out. Many came to mind but he desperately needed to change the subject. "Do I have a deal – new dresses in return for a hostess?"

She held out a hand as though a wagering lord. "You do, Mr Hawkins. I believe men handshake their accord before a fight. Shall we do the same?"

Her skin was ice-cold but soft as silk within his own; not the *same* in the slightest. "They do indeed. And now for one last room."

Ushering her from the salon, he then strode for the ornate door with stout ironware at the end of the passageway. Miss Griffin trailed behind – the brush of skirt and scent of flower.

"This was once the music room but it's been converted." Seth twisted the worn handle and swished an arm for her to enter.

He followed, closed the door and collided into the back of her as she'd halted not two steps inside.

A gasp... "A library! But...what a library. Oh!"

Seth strode to the circular reading table with its leather baize and tray of liquors to shut the book he'd been reading last night after dinner, shoving it to the shelf beneath.

"How do you like it?"

"I thought..." Eyes that rivalled the brimming decanters glimmered. "It's beautiful, Mr Hawkins."

"Most of the books just came with the house." He downplayed it, yet 'twas one of the reasons he'd bought the place, in truth. Noblemen had libraries as old as their lineage, collected over decades, so such a treasure for a man like Seth was not to be missed. "But they were scattered willy-nilly amongst the rooms, stacked beneath table legs and holding doors open. I decided to collate them."

He himself was not able to invent stanzas of metred perfection, spin tales or write of jungle adventures, but Seth appreciated and savoured every written word, and indeed, he'd dreamed of a library when young.

Miss Griffin moistened her lips, and his jaw twitched, an involuntary tremor coursing within.

"May I?" she asked.

At his nod, she took a run for the nearest shelf and brushed a finger reverently over the book spines.

Seth shuddered and watched as her lips unconsciously curved in utter delight.

Those gold-rimmed spectacles highlighted her sherry eyes, and her skin shone pure against hair so intense a black, it drew you in like a cloudless night. Her retroussé nose wrinkled as she removed a volume of poetry from the shelf, flicked through the pages and paused...

"'I wandered lonely as a Cloud
That floats on high o'er Vales and Hills,'"

Miss Griffin grinned, and he could not resist continuing…

"'When all at once I saw a crowd,
A host, of golden Daffodils;'"

She twitched an eyebrow and he cleared his throat.

"My mother's favourite," he excused in a deep voice.

With a suspicious eye, she nodded and wandered over the rugs.

His daughter also enjoyed this library but remained too young for many of the writings – philosophies, histories and some ancient bawdy plays he'd unearthed in a trunk. All these treasures he'd piled here when the construction works for the Academy had taken place, and only when those had been completed had he sat with a cabinet maker and pencil, sketching designs and scouring library plans.

Central to one wall was a magnificent oval window overlooking the park, allowing plentiful light to fall upon the chesterfield reading sofa. Slanting away and protecting the contents from that same light, shelves of chestnut at differing heights were crammed with books.

The cabinet maker had stated that locked glass doors were all the dash, but Seth could not contend with the idea of thrusting books behind barrier and key, as though too precious to touch and read.

Miss Griffin perused the shelves with an enchanted eye, until turning. "May I…borrow this one for my chambers? I promise not to damage it."

His eyes flickered to the book clenched tightly in her hands as though he might wrest it from her at any given moment.

"Certainly. Take anything here you can use or read."

"Thank you. I…I do believe, Mr Hawkins, that serendipity herself was guiding me when I wrote my application letter to you. I'm so glad its verbosity gained me an interview."

He opened his mouth to explain that actually he'd been as desperate as a flower girl with a cart full of blooms at six of an eve, but Miss Griffin beamed, book now pressed to her bosom.

Serendipity indeed.

CHAPTER SEVEN

"What could be more interesting than an elegant and unaffected letter?"

Private Education: A Practical Plan for the Studies of Young Ladies. Elizabeth Appleton. 1815.

"Do you think my pa handsome, Miss Griffin?"

"Er…" Matilda had vowed to respond to all of Chloe's questions most truthfully but hadn't been forewarned of this one. "Miss Chloe Hawkins, please concentrate on your letter writing."

The grouching blond mop of hair fell upon the paper once more, ink smudging the edges, table, fingers and floor.

Matilda sneaked a peek at Miss Appleton's tome for some ripe advice, but there was naught as regards awkward questions about handsome employers.

Ink blots, however, were a severe wrongdoing and to be punished with a sharp reprimand.

For two days now, they had followed the routine laid out in this book, plodding through Mrs Trimmer's *Ancient History* – which even Matilda had discreetly yawned at – and reading aloud *Grammar of Geography*, which certainly imparted no lust for travel. The spine of Salzmann's *Elements of Morality* remained unbroken and Matilda had considered poking around the library for more edifying material.

Lessons on one's deportment had proved more successful as Chloe was a graceful girl with a cheerful disposition, despite having rehearsed another fifty-six curtsies.

A knock on the door and Betty bustled in. "Elevenses, me darlins. Sponge cake with vanilla cream, gingerbread, Oliver biscuits and a pot of tea." Betty flumped on the sofa, wiggling her toes in the air. "Phew, me aching feet. How's the lessons goin'?"

"We are practising the art of letter composition this morning, and Chloe is writing a missive to her friend. Are you ready to read it aloud, dear? Then we may have tea."

The quill was all too keenly thrust down and her charge breathed deep.

"My dearest acquaintance Modesty–"

Betty snorted. "That poor girl. It ain't decent to burden yer child so."

"My dearest acquaintance Modesty," Chloe repeated with a glare, *"no doubt you will anticipate the purport of this epistle–"*

"Piss wot?" Betty whispered, eyes gleaming.

"Epistle," bawled Chloe, *"which is to ask..."* She glanced up. "I think this next bit flows better...*do you fancy melting a bob on a jaunt to Bullock's gaff next week to see the stuff snaffled from Napoleon? It'll be a lumping great jape and Pa might buy us ices. Love Chlo. P.S. There's even Napoleon's own carriage...with a bed in it!"*

Matilda briefly closed her eyes.

Thus far they'd only covered the opening pleasantries of letter composition as the entirety could not be taught in a single morning. But the remainder showed creative promise.

"A carriage with a bed in it, are yer sure?" Betty quizzed, swiping a slice of gingerbread.

"Yes!" cried Chloe. "And it's bulletproof!"

Matilda shook her head. What a vivid imagination.

"Have you visited Bullock's Museum before, Miss Griffin?"

Well, no.

That particular museum had opened its doors before her parents had died but her father had considered it vulgar – a harem-scarem collection of goods shoved together in order to titillate the public without any academic relevance whatsoever. The ostentatious Egyptian Hall in particular – although never actually viewed – had been disapproved of.

Yet she knew it held Birds of Paradise specimens from the Moluccas…

"No, but it does sound interesting. I hear it also has an armoury, a collection of Captain Cook's treasures and many preserved mammal exhibits from Africa."

"Go on with yer. Sounds a bit lifeless to me," declared Betty, dipping her fingers in the sugar bowl to extract three lumps. "But yer should ask Mr H to take yer both soonish, as Mick says they've a busy one next week, and then yer'll be stuck in reading Mrs Tiresome's tedious toes till Judgement Day."

"Tomes, you mean?"

"I know wot I said."

"No time to waste," wailed Chloe, flopping on the sofa next to Betty. "But which one of us should ask him?"

Two pairs of eyes lanced in Matilda's direction. She peered behind. No one else there.

"Me? But... Mr Hawkins would be far more amenable to you, Chloe."

A shake of the head, her young charge's mouth crammed with biscuits, crumbs cascading, and Matilda debated whether she herself had the tenacity for this type of employment.

"Yer'll have more chance of success, Miss Griffin," Betty cooed. "It needs a governess's stern touch. He's in the Academy's main room." And she winked.

Winked?

"Well, maybe I'll ask at dinner."

"He'll have made plans by then, Miss Griffin," lamented Chloe.

"In that case, I shall attempt to find Mr Hawkins at luncheon."

Shaking her head, Betty poured the slopped tea from saucer to cup. "He'll be in the basement then."

"Well I..."

"Have no worry, the Academy'll be empty at this time of day. All the nobs are busy shopping for horses, Hessians or whores."

Matilda was fighting a battle of decorum doomed to fail in this household.

The housekeeper wafted a silver teaspoon. "And as me da used to say to Ma when he fancied a jig, 'No time like the present.'"

Matilda was fairly sure that a *jig* was not the Celtic dance she was familiar with.

"If you think so..."

Two heads nodded in utter complicity.

"Shall I fetch a shawl though? Saffron is rather–"

"Perfect," said Betty with a grin. "Yer look like an egg yolk."

Trusting Mr Hawkins would not scramble her wits, Matilda stalked for the door with determined intent. It was true that Chloe had worked hard and deserved a day out, but snooping over her shoulder she noted the troublesome twosome sharing a satisfied nod.

She'd been outmanoeuvred by a sly-boots of a housekeeper and a girl of thirteen.

Some days, she was a woeful governess.

RIGHT, left, left, right...

Seth found the repetition of walloping the stuffing out of the pads nailed to the Academy wall quite soothing.

It appeased his frustration over Liam, who'd punched a fist through an ale-house window, punctured the ire that had expanded when Lord Dunton had broken the weighing machine by using it as a swing, and placated his worries over the packed schedule for this week.

Although a laborious time of it was in fact welcome, in order to distract his thoughts from the tempting trail of scented buttercups about the place.

A faint "ahem" came from behind.

"No tea, Betty. I'm busy."

Then again, when had Betty ever cleared her throat in a delicate ladylike manner to claim his attention? Which could only mean...

He twisted and sherry eyes widened to the rims of her spectacles.

Not surprising, as solely loose breeches clad his body –

no shirt or cravat. And though as a prizefighter he'd fought in this same garb before a braying crowd of thousands, he felt as naked as a shorn sheep in February.

"Miss Griffin..." He stalked to the clothes peg in the corner, wrestled into a shirt and wiped his brow with a towel. "You should not be here."

"Betty and Chloe said..."

Hmm. Did they now. "Well, if you prefer, I can dress first?"

But she'd rediscovered her governess mien, shoulders rigid and eyes cleaved to the ceiling.

"No, no. I just..." Her stare arrowed to his face. "Chloe would like to attend Bullock's Museum and I concur that the idea is a splendid one, enabling a better understanding of French carriage workmanship." She allowed a lone blink. "According to my educative guide, museums promote a shared experience without which..." His governess waffled on, her eyes watering from the strain of their fixed position. "And although books are essential for one's learning, a museum places feathers on the drawings, so to speak." She twisted her hands in a dress of saffron. "So, you see, we wondered if you might escort us." Miss Griffin breathed at last.

Seth considered his week: meetings with investors, two new fighters to initiate, Liam Whelan to sort out, two dukes and an earl who wished for individual sparring sessions with himself, and Prinny now desired an exhibition of pugilism for some nob from Spain in under a week.

"It would be my pleasure. Any particular day?"

"Tomorrow at ten?"

"Fine."

"Good."

"Good."

She peered with concern at the bars upon the walls,

frowned at the empty ring and blinked at the broken wooden A-frame which supported two seats for weighing purposes.

"Do you wish to view the Academy whilst no one is here?"

"Oh, would you mind?"

Yes. No. He'd no idea. Only that she plucked his wits like a crow at the gibbet.

"Certainly not."

They paraded the Academy as though strolling Hyde Park – admiring the ring in place of the Serpentine, the boxing gloves in place of the roses and the drawings of disrobed fighters in place of preening stallions on Rotten Row.

She grimaced at some, peeped at others and gawped at most.

"I am in awe, Sir. All this built from nothing. You have worked so awfully hard. I hear the love in your voice for this Academy, see the pride in your eyes. It is all quite splendid."

A prickling warmth seeped within.

Blood, sweat, tears and his heart had gone into this club.

"When I first envisaged it, I did not want a dingy backroom with sawdust on the floor and peeling paint, but an open airy place that the flash swell– er, aristocrats would enjoy practising in. I wanted flawless carpentry and exclusive patronage."

He gazed around – at the brown velvet curtains draping oblong windows, the immaculate washing tubs and the pristine dumb-bells positioned in their racks.

All those evenings he'd sat alone while Chloe had slept, he'd sketched, then resketched, the most practical layout and the luxuries with which he would furbish it, and with his prizefighting money, determination and a little investment, it had all come to fruition.

. . .

"AND IS YOUR PATRONAGE EXCLUSIVE?" Matilda asked. "I should imagine so with this level of exquisiteness."

Mr Hawkins stretched his fingers wide, doubtless to ease the aches amassed from toiling all those years. "It began slow. Merchants and gentlemen who'd seen me fight, but then my name became synonymous with focus of one's mind when sparring, and, as you say, the craftsmanship of the decor. That in turn encouraged the higher echelons of the *Ton* to give it a try. They never left."

Synonymous.

Echelons.

Such a broad vocabulary for a man who declared he'd not had time for learning.

Set to become a coal heaver, her employer had instead built a fine Academy with dedication, resolve and, no doubt, quite a few sleepless nights. All whilst raising a delightful daughter alone.

Mr Hawkins, she was beginning to realise, was quite a man…in every which way.

To her shame, she had observed him for quite some time as he'd thumped that set of pads, the stark hue of his olive-toned skin in contrast to a gentleman's pallor, the brawn of his back rippling and tensing – as barbaric and savage as she had ever imagined, but also innate and sensuous.

Then he'd spun.

Carved marble turned mortal flesh, but with a sprinkling of dark hair. Almighty shoulders and that *musculus abdominis* – so flat and toned.

Once she would have bemoaned the heroines of a Gothic novel who melted at the sight of a masculine forearm, but Mr Hawkins' torso was surely deserving of some slight puddling – a natural reaction to a prime male displaying his feathers.

A mere biological response.

"Well, thank you for the wonderful tour. I am most impressed but should return to the schoolroom and tell Chloe the good news about Bullock's."

Mr Hawkins twisted to her with gaze serious. "Your cousin is not likely to be lurking at the museum, is he? Or any of his set?"

"Unlikely, unless as a stuffed exhibit in Room 3, Cabinet 6, labelled *Lacklustre Specimen of Viscount*."

Laughter gushed forth, that lopsided smile emerging, and Matilda felt inordinately pleased with herself.

"Miss Griffin, I cannot believe you ever thought yourself a bland cauliflower."

"I may well look like one at Bullock's too, as just in case, I'll wear a veil with my white bonnet to obscure my features."

"I had thought to take you all to Gunter's confectioners afterwards, but ices and a veil sounds a calamitous mix."

"I've never attended Gunter's. Mother considered it plebeian." She slammed a hand to her mouth. Why did she keep insulting her employer – it did not bode well for her future. "Oh, I didn't mean..."

"Sweet strawberry ice with flecks of mint, Miss Griffin. Does that not appeal?"

Her mouth watered and corset groaned. "It sounds divine," she admitted, licking her lips.

"Then tomorrow, we shall visit."

"That would be most agreeable." She fiddled with her saffron skirts. "Well, thank you for your time, Mr Hawkins. I know you must be busy."

"Not at all, Miss Griffin." And he swept a short bow, shirt ties slack and parting to reveal that well-defined chest.

Attempting a swift bobbed curtsey, Matilda tangled her feet and almost tumbled akimbo, but with a nonchalant air, she swept from the room, feeling more breathless than when she'd watched Mr Hawkins hit things.

How curious.

CHAPTER EIGHT

"Conjure not up ideal misery, but strive to do your duty, and cultivate a contented mind."

PRIVATE EDUCATION: A PRACTICAL PLAN FOR THE STUDIES OF YOUNG LADIES. ELIZABETH APPLETON. 1815.

Silence shrouded their little group as they lingered on the pavement to absorb the splendours of Ancient Egypt plonked in the middle of Piccadilly.

Matilda peered through her veil at the highly decorative frontage and mused that Father may have been correct regarding the academic relevance of Bullock's Museum after all.

Red-brick buildings of a more conventional nature crowded either side of the white-painted museum like wallflowers harassing the diamond of the season.

"Do you think, Miss Griffin," said Chloe with a scrunched nose, swinging her skirts, "that Egypt looks like this?"

"Not in any pictures I've seen, Chloe. And there is usually more…sand."

"Magnificent columns though," commented Mr Hawkins, looking inordinately handsome with his clean-shaven jaw and ruffled hair.

Flanking the museum's entrance door were white fluted pillars with bulbous heads and lotus bud capitals supporting a cornice which jutted forth with splendour. Above, upon a plinth, stood two fifteen-foot-tall stone statues with haughty glares, gods who'd seen cities rise and fall and obviously found Piccadilly rather a bore.

Tall oblong windows either side were filled with octagonal leaded glass that glinted in the sunlight, surrounded by stone inscribed with ancient script. Pediments above protected the carvings of winged suns unable to take flight in their solidity.

"Who are the statues of, Miss Griffin?" enquired Chloe. "They must be nippy in this weather without togs."

"Isis and Osiris, I believe." She tipped her head further back. "And those are sphinxes above…and then a scarab beetle."

It was garish, tasteless and possibly the most enthralling place Matilda had ever seen.

A fierce gust blew down the street, the never-ending construction works to the east gilding the white paint of the museum in a layer of London's subterranean dirt.

"Shall we?" declared Mr Hawkins, holding both arms out, and in utter exhilaration, Matilda and Chloe squeezed tight and dragged him forth.

. . .

Heads of Hathor loomed atop fake columns like menacing gargoyles, metal serpents coiled up railings and signs of the zodiac crowded the ceiling.

Seth gaped.

This was merely the hallway which preceded the main exhibitions, and his governess likewise shifted foot to foot, veil swishing left and right.

"Do you...like it?" he enquired politely, aware that such garish Egyptian decor was equally fashionable for the swells' pads in Mayfair.

"Well..." She tapped her foot. "It's not at all reminiscent of the drawings in *Description de l'Égypte.* Perhaps Mr Bullock has taken artistic licence?"

He'd certainly taken something.

Whilst Seth had procured the tickets and catalogue from the booth, Modesty had arrived, and it had been decided that it might be prudent to first view the infamous carriage of Napoleon before the crowds of London descended.

An elaborate sign ahead indicated Exhibit Room 1, a wide archway presenting the backs of bonnets and beavers, gowns and boots. A crush of colour...and of people with the same idea.

"Maybe we should come back la–"

Gleaming wheels flashed in a gap between the buckskins and gowns, and his daughter shrieked, grabbed hold of Modesty and tore off at quite a clip.

"Chloe!" Miss Griffin called. "No running in the..." But it was too late.

"No matter," offered Seth as the girls charged towards Napoleon's magnificent blue carriage as though invading Russia. "We are not young for long."

"But as governess, I should–"

"This morning is time off for us all, although I must apologise that ices at Gunter's is not possible afterwards. A meeting has cropped up, but I'm sure we can all visit at the weekend." Her lips curved behind the veil…at least he thought so anyway. "Are you interested in the spoils of war or something else? There are upwards of fifteen thousand natural and foreign curiosities, antiquities and productions of fine arts."

"You read that in the catalogue."

Seth merely winked and placed a steadying palm to her shapely waist as hooting bucks and their doe-eyed counterparts galloped past, the back-up calvary late for battle.

Truly, he'd never seen such a confounded cannonade of bodies, and as they approached the archway, he wondered what his members who'd survived Waterloo must think of all this clamour.

A pink-bonneted matron scratched the dark-blue carriage door for proof of its supposed resistance to bullets, a grey-haired gentleman with monocle frowned at Napoleon's supposedly gilded coffee pot and a young buck stuck his nose in Napoleon's supposedly gold chamber pot.

"Rather than the carriage, may we see specimens of the Birds of Paradise?" asked Miss Griffin, wincing as Chloe and her friend scrambled aboard and up to the coachman's seat. "I'm not sure which hall they are in though."

Seth ushered her from the archway to a quiet corner and studied the museum plan, turning it this way and that, while Miss Griffin consulted the catalogue, only to find the two bore no relation to one another whatsoever.

Instead they wandered at will, studying curiosities from the South Seas in gleaming glass cases and speculating as to their uses. Miss Griffin, as one might have guessed, was knowledgeable yet without pretension. She simply...knew stuff.

A mock-medieval hall housed a gruesome armoury of spikes and chains, and classical art lined the walls of a Roman gallery.

This William Bullock certainly was a showman – Egypt, Italy, Polynesia and Africa, all contained within No. 22 Piccadilly.

"I believe the Pantherion," he directed, now examining the plan upside down, which seemed to make more sense, "is where you may possibly find your birds. Take the left door here to pass through Exhibit Room 6, where, and I quote, 'a wondrous exemplification from Scotland can be found'."

The veil granted him a nod and marched onwards, but the spectacle of Exhibit Room 6 halted their stride.

Bizarre basaltic rocks lined the roof, walls and floor, a lone torch casting an eerie flickering glow to this...cave, for want of a better description.

Those raucous bucks from the carriage melee lurked and sniggered whilst their ladies prodded the strata.

"The catalogue states," Seth murmured, "this is Fingal's Cave on the Isle of Staffa."

Miss Griffin's veiled face twisted left then right before she raised the material, tucking it into her bonnet, and at last her tawny eyes gleamed in the torchlight. "Having never been to Scotland, I cannot naysay Mr Bullock, but I believe a cave may be somewhat cooler. It's hotter than Satan's lair in here." She peeled off her gloves, wafting them around while studying the strange hexagonal-cut walls.

A hoot of laughter from the corner, and Seth raised his head, noticed a grinning buck sidle up to the torch, lift a hand and...

Darkness smothered the cave, followed by disorientating doe'ish shrieks and a buck's chortles.

"Miss Griffin? He thrust out a hand, caught silky material and then…let go. He could be grabbing anything. "Do not be afraid."

"Oh, good grief," he heard her mutter after another feminine shriek. "It's a fake cave in Piccadilly, not ghostly Green Park at dawn."

"I believe one of those bucks snuffed out the torch for fun."

"Fun! Honestly, the male species has some strange ideas. Where are you? I have no wish to fall." And fingers descended upon his chest, firm and pressing.

"You've found me," he managed to bite out as her hand wandered.

"Hmm. Is that… I hope that's your *pectoralis major*. It certainly feels like it, most defined and…broad. I've never felt a real one before. Only marble."

Breath stuttered to a halt as Miss Griffin's touch now spread across his chest, vanilla and flowers scenting the air, all other noise forgotten. It was suffocating, the dark, the heat and her caress, entombed lust roaring to life.

He covered her hand with his own.

MATILDA GASPED, her bare fingers trapped between the heated silk of a waistcoat and the calloused skin of an immense palm.

Her nails dug. A faint rumble juddered.

The cologne of leather, the rough edge to Mr Hawkins' breath, and the silk-clad muscled indentations beneath her hand provoked an awfully strange rumpus within, coiling and decidedly unstudious for a museum attendee.

"Yes, Miss Griffin," she heard him state huskily at last. "You do appear to have found my *pectoralis major.*"

Oh.

Maybe the bucks had the right of it and a darkened cave did have its amusements. The clandestine nature of it all compelled her hand to continue its wander – purely to steady herself of course. Mr Hawkins' palm pressed firmer, his fingers interlacing with hers. "Do you think I could–"

Torchlight flickered anew, and in that moment, their gazes met.

Mr Hawkins' features held no amusement.

In fact, his jaw was tight, pupils cast to Stygian black, lips thinned. Bare restraint and...more that she did not recognise held sway, but it both terrified and thrilled in equal measure.

The light slanted away, their hands dropped and her swift exhale was echoed by his.

"Well..." She puttered with her veil. "It appears a new torch has been procured."

Mr Hawkins spun to inspect the walls. "Indeed," he murmured.

All at once, a sinking sensation pervaded her as Matilda suspected a proper governess should never mention chest muscles – especially if they belonged to one's employer.

With a rustle, Mr Hawkins twisted back, arm proffered. "Shall we continue, Miss Griffin?"

She noted his expression had returned to amiable and considerate, and so resolving to never again mention his rather magnificent pectoralis, she took his arm and they followed a short passage, turning a tight corner to reveal...

A colossal room, light falling from a circular dome in the roof upon a mishmash of items crammed in cheek by jowl. The high walls were decorated with armour, shields and pistols, whereas lower down, cases of glass contained legions of stuffed animals eerily staring out.

"The Pantherion," she whispered.

Central to it all, and guarded by an armoured medieval knight for some reason, was a roped-off display of statuesque animals from Africa – an elephant, zebra and giraffe, plus a few creatures she'd not a name for. A slack palm tree shaded the sight, a huge stuffed python coiling around its trunk, and upon another branch were blue peacocks – which she thought came from India not Africa.

"A mite macabre for my tastes," Mr Hawkins declared.

Matilda sauntered amongst the cases, peering in at lifeless crows, motionless woodpeckers and less than magnificent plumed pelicans, until at last she found her Bird of Paradise.

But…

Its tail drooped and some of the feathers had fallen off; a vagrant leaf could not disguise the stitching. It looked…sad.

The adjacent case helped not – the Black-bodied Bird of Paradise had faded to grey and it was missing an eye.

"Oh."

Peculiar and sinister, and she so wished to hear their song. More birds squinted down from branches, but without life, their magnificent tails curved downwards not upwards, their demeanour stilted and unnatural. All useful, she supposed, for study, but the drawings she'd viewed held more emotion and…motion.

"Not what you hoped for, Miss Griffin?"

All night, she'd been so excited at the prospect of seeing these birds, had dreamed of them in flight, their tail feathers brushing her face.

"I…" The next case held a Golden Bird of Paradise – the one she'd wished to see most of all – but the gold had tarnished.

A fierce sadness enveloped her – for the lifeless birds and, pitifully, for herself.

Never would she view them in the wild, had been dreaming foolish dreams when she'd talked of voyaging to the Molucca Islands.

Her scattergood of a cousin had destroyed that hope – by squandering her parents' money and the dowry that would have been hers in August.

Yet here, at least, Matilda had thought she might imagine the birds in flight, share their exotic life and be dazzled by their colour...just for a few short moments.

"No. Not what I expected. Although perhaps I expected too much."

A robust hand took her own and she gazed at Mr Hawkins. His eyes appeared brighter than those of any creature here – kind and strong and full of soul.

Today, a handsome burgundy waistcoat with fine gold buttons adorned his person, its high collar accentuating his firm chin, delicate embroidery his broad chest, while jet-black coat, buckskins and shiny top-boots completed an effortless poise and immense power.

"Why do you like these birds so much?" he enquired.

"Many reasons – their colouring, grace, feathers and so forth, but also flight. I oft yearned to be a bird when young. To feel the sky rushing about me, to escape whenever and wherever I wished, to see the land so far below. I have lived a life based on theory rather than experience thus far, and to be a bird would be to experience...everything. To travel anywhere."

"'Unpath'd waters, undream'd shores.'"

Matilda winched a brow. "From another discarded theatre print, Mr Hawkins?"

His lips twitched. "Litter, Miss Griffin, is the very menace of London."

They sauntered the room, but Matilda's mood struggled to lighten, not even when Chloe and her friend arrived, arms windmilling about and cheeks as red as roses, having discovered the bed in Napoleon's carriage.

"It's beneath the coachman's seat," Chloe gushed. "There's a bedstead of steel and a writing desk, a gold booze case and a hand basin – all with a big *N* inscribed, in case he lost them."

"Which considering they are all housed in Piccadilly, he most certainly did," said Mr Hawkins wryly. "Now, I believe Gunter's ices are in order. The girls, I'm sure, have worked hard at their lessons." Chloe nodded; Modesty's eyes darted to her toes. "And Miss Griffin…" Matilda glanced up. "Needs a little cheer."

"But your meeting?"

"A duke can wait, Miss Griffin, but strawberry ices melt." And he cast her a wink.

A curl of joy seeped through Matilda's doldrums.

No one had ever been thoughtful of her feelings or aware of her mood. Her confidantes considered her shrewd, level-headed and never one for succumbing to wayward emotion; her parents had purely been interested in her tutelage and Astwood viewed her as a commodity to be sold.

But Mr Hawkins had sensed her sadness…and sought to alleviate it.

A muscled ex-prizefighter he may be, but solicitude and quiet perception underpinned his nature – a man as deep and unfathomable as the hieroglyphics in the Egyptian Hall.

THE SILVER SPOON lifted and tilted to rosy lips, strawberry ice teetering, and then, as Seth's governess consumed the sweet, she sighed her pleasure.

He shifted uncomfortably and leaned as near as he dare in a tea shop. "How is the ice, Miss Griffin?"

Those lips curved, which was all he could see with the veil covering to just below her nose, a tantalising glimpse of forbidden fruit.

"Not plebeian in the least, Mr Hawkins. I'd say positively patrician."

Seth chuckled, but caught a glimpse of his daughter watching him with a thoughtful expression as she licked her spoon, so he nonchalantly drew back.

As luck would have it, this little place on Berkeley Square was relatively empty for once, and they'd managed to nab a table in the corner. No perusal of the menu had been needed for Chloe and her friend, as in the past they'd plundered all the ices and now had their favourites. Miss Griffin, however, had spent an inordinate amount of time dallying over each option, asking questions as to sweetness and acidity.

She'd plumped for the strawberry with mint flecks.

Seth himself had solely ordered a cup of strong coffee in order to fortify himself for an irate duke. Yet he still couldn't find it within himself to regret this visit to Gunter's – helpless to do otherwise after he'd listened to Miss Griffin tell of her love for the birds, her wish to view them full of life...and then her sudden awareness that she may never be granted such a wish.

He'd seen dreams, both minuscule and immense, shattered before: respected fighters who'd lost their last chance at a championship; wives whose soldier husbands had not returned from battle. Even the starving dogs that slunk from the butcher's back door when they realised there would be no bones that week.

No matter the circumstance, wealth or poverty, everyone had dreams. And Miss Griffin's, he realised, were to travel – to see the birds she so adored. Foolish dreams, some might claim for a genteel lady turned governess, but no dreams were foolish – as that was rather the point.

Yet when one thought a dream might no longer be possible, a sadness eclipsed the joy in life, a loss that had no reality.

He remembered losing a fight when Chloe had been young. Recalled trudging home, certain his dream of the Academy was an absurd delusion.

Betty had taken one look at him and shoved a beef pasty in the ancient range oven, and Chloe, with that innate knowledge of a child, had hugged his knee. Betty's husband had arrived to debate his defeat and how to strengthen for the next fight, and his old friend, Kian, had barrelled through the door with a keg of ale.

And with their good cheer and optimism, the future had brightened, his soul had arisen and all of a sudden, everything had seemed possible.

Dreams may fade, new ones arise, they may evolve or stay ever constant, but they made life worth living – be they others' or your own, trivial or ambitious, serious or foolish.

All dreams should be treasured.

"Thank you, Mr Hawkins. I've had a wonderful day."

And Seth turned to smile at his governess.

CHAPTER NINE

"For birds are like men in their contests together."

PRIVATE EDUCATION: A PRACTICAL PLAN FOR THE STUDIES OF YOUNG LADIES. ELIZABETH APPLETON. 1815.

"Do you think Miss Griffin pretty, Pa?"

"Er..." Seth had once vowed to respond to all of Chloe's questions most truthfully, but he sensed a trap left as wide as a barn door on a summer's noon. His daughter dallied by the wardrobe, her innocent green gaze concealing devilish intent, and his own eyes narrowed. "Chloe Maggie Hawkins. Dismiss any tomfool idea rattling around that attic of yours this instant or I shall be forced to add the quilling of tea caddies to your lesson plan."

His daughter merely grinned. "So, you're not denying she's pretty."

"Waistcoat," he demanded with outstretched hand. Then flinched. "A bit garish?"

"I prefer to call it *burnished,* and the gold highlights your eyes. Perfect for an 1811 Champions' Dinner."

Shrugging it on, he made for the mirror to attempt a coachman's knot for his cravat – the cascade style was too much of a faff and made him look like a lace fountain.

"I think Miss Griffin finds you handsome."

He rolled his eyes...and ignored the frisson to his gizzards. "I'm your father. You're supposed to think everyone finds me handsome. It's obligatory."

"Miss Figstone certainly finds you handsome. Is she coming tonight? I saw her from the landing last time she came to dinner – she bats her lashes at you and thrusts her dumplings."

"Language, Chloe. Yes she's coming and no she doesn't." Actually she did, but that was by the by.

"Hmm. You stay alert, Pa. She's got plans."

"So have you, it appears." Seth completed the cravat knot with a flourish, straightened it, and donned his jacket. "Is Modesty here yet?"

"No. She's arriving at seven, and if there's no rain, her parents are taking us to see the tight-rope walker at Vauxhall Gardens."

Once a fortnight, Modesty's parents took the girls out for the evening and so they'd arranged tonight to coincide with the dinner – preferable to having his daughter earwig from the landing.

"Well, keep close to them at all times." And he bussed her forehead. Not that he had to worry with Chloe's pugilistic skills.

"Of course. And...maybe you should wear the amber stick pin."

"Amber?" Odd choice, but he rootled in the bottom of the drawer and held it to the light. "Why amber?"

"It matches the waistcoat." He peered down. So it did. Chloe tweaked his cravat to crooked – apparently it gave a rakish air – then saturated him with Spanish Leather cologne. "Perfect." She nodded. "Go slay 'em, Pa."

BIRDS OF PARADISE in the flesh, Matilda reflected.

Except these were no flighted warm-blooded vertebrates from the Molucca Islands, but the wives of the Prizefighting Champions who flitted about the drawing room for pre-dinner sherries in silks, feathers and lace.

Matilda felt an alliance with the stuffed specimens from Bullock's Museum – tired, rather moth-eaten and out of their habitat.

Late into last night, she had reacquainted herself with the schoolroom's copy of *Miss Pikesworth's Guide to Etiquette.* Within paragraph five of the chapter entitled 'Faultless Entertainment', Miss Pikesworth had pointed out that a hostess should greet her guests with a cordial nod and an enquiry regarding the weather.

But all the guests had appeared to be on familiar terms and so introductions had been a flurry of hugs, kisses, manly handshakes and sturdy backslaps.

No one cared to lament the rain.

Seventeen persons had crowded into the drawing room, a devil of an odd number to later sit for dinner, but nevertheless eleven gentlemen and six ladies now mingled, gulping sherry and scoffing lobster patties.

Paragraph eight of the 'Decorous Dining' chapter then dictated that in order to avoid embarrassing silences during drinks, the hostess should preserve a flowing conversation via a wide range of topics – the latest music from Vienna, the latest turban fashions from France or the latest silk styles from India.

But this assemblage required no such guidance.

They discussed their children or friends and their professions since retirement, nattering over each other and swapping gossip more adroitly then the Almack's patronesses.

Matilda made her excuses and left the svelte Mrs Medley chatting to a dapper Mr Belcher about Benjamin Brain's tripe shop and instead attached herself to a group discussing Wifflin' Willie, who had ventured to Wales for a 'milling-set-to', never to return.

It meant nothing to her. Should she steer the conversation to Vienna?

Matilda disattached herself without anyone noticing, pottered to the decanters to check the sherry was replete and then silently lurked in the corner like the cauliflower she'd pronounced herself.

She pondered whether her lacklustre performance as hostess would be sufficient to earn her a bundle of brown governess gowns at all and then cogitated how long it would take to bury Miss Pikesworth.

The book, of course.

"I do adore your golden frock, Miss Griffin. Is it genuine silk?"

She twisted to a lady in lustrous lilac, tall with ringlets the hue of morning sunshine.

"Thank you so much, I believe so..." And all of a sudden, Matilda became horribly aware she could not remember the voluptuous beauty's name. "Have you come far?"

Although she was certain the surname had begun with a *P*...or a *D*.

"Cheshire, actually. A little market town called Altrincham."

Matilda blinked. "Goodness, 'tis a long way to travel for a dinner."

Mrs Pewhurst? No. Dalworth?

"It gives us a chance to visit the London swag shops, and Tim's never missed a Champions' grub-up."

"Tim?"

Tim…?

"Mr Dewhurst, my husband."

Phew. Faux pas averted.

Matilda nodded sagely. "The gentleman in the black jacket?"

"That's Giles. Mine's the one in brown."

Incompetent nitterwit.

"And your husband won a big…mill?"

Mrs Dewhurst's lips twitched. "Three Commons titles, actually. Wimbledon, Worcester and Epsom. Tim the Turfer, they used to call him. Previously a butcher, but now we have a little farm." She twirled a glove-clad hand. "I don't miss the fight days but I do miss the friends we made. Many of us have not seen one another for an age as we all live in various parts of England now, although Nobbler Nick and his sister still live at their old Marylebone address." She leaned near, tuberose perfume wafting. "No doubt we'll all be nattering till the early hours."

Dear heavens.

Although that was unkind as Mrs Dewhurst was truly delightful. They all were. It was herself who was the odd one out – Matilda the Mopsey.

"And Nobbler Nick is…?"

"Oh, Mr Nick Figstone, the buffer in bottle green talking to Giles. And his sister is chatting to Seth."

A headache loomed from all the names, but through the throng of guests, she surreptitiously surveyed her employer, who loitered by the French doors conversing with a stunning female in plumage of scarlet with eyes that ran over his splendid torso like ants on a nasturtium leaf.

"*Miss* Figstone?"

"That's the one."

Narrowing her gaze, she noted the lady more or less rest her sumptuous bosom upon Mr Hawkins' forearm.

Not that the sight affected Matilda.

In the least.

As long as she ignored the curious ruckus that tipped her belly inwards – probably the lobster patties.

This night, her employer exuded charm and masculinity, a waistcoat of burnished gold highlighting his eyes and bronzed skin. An exotic paisley pattern in a darker shade overlaid the gold and its pockets were outlined in sinful black. A rakish air hung over him as he laughed at some doubtless droll remark of Miss Figstone, his relaxed mien and well-tied cravat holding her eye.

"So why are yer enchanting ladies hiding in this corner?" a Scots drawl enquired, and Matilda twisted to be confronted by a tall rangy fellow with the bluest gaze she had ever encountered. A dab older than her employer, grey hair stippled his temples and fine lines crinkled beside his soulful eyes.

At least she could remember his name as he'd arrived early and without a companion, hence making her table numbers odd, and he wasn't a fighter at all, but an acquaintance of her employer.

A Mr Kian Finlay.

"We are discussing Miss Figstone," whispered the lady, "and her intentions towards Seth."

What? No, they weren't.

And Miss Pikesworth had stated that such clandestine tittle-tattle was not to be encouraged by the hostess.

The Scotsman perused. "She's not a chance. He likes his women with a bit more up in the belfry than in breast."

Matilda's toes faintly curled at such wordage, and she could only hope her own personal failure as hostess would not affect her employment as governess in any way.

"Although," continued Mr Finlay, "not a lot wrong with plenty o' both."

An odd sense of anxiety rose from her slippers and wobbled her knees. Any hostess worth her salt should guide the conversation to Vienna and yet it was careering away faster than a hare in open grassland.

"I..."

"Giles the Grinder is less fussy," replied Mrs Dewhurst with a laugh. "But then that milling cove had all the nous dubbed out of him by too many whiffles to the cannister."

The headache materialised and Matilda held a hand to her wrinkled brow. "I... If you will excuse me," she stuttered. "I must go to the kitchens and check all is prepared."

Mr Finlay bowed. "Of course, Miss Griffin."

After a swift curtsey to them both, Matilda dashed for the door, crossed the hall, put spine to wall, closed her eyes and despaired.

She was hopeless. Knew not what to say. She could read all the books that a library held but none of them would help with this.

When her parents had held dinners, they'd always been quiet scholarly affairs, adhering to every word of Miss Pikesworth. Astwood's were unsavoury events that she hid in her room from, and her friend Evelyn, before her abducting duke, had lived in an attic, so not had sufficient room for entertaining.

"Wot yer doing there, girlie?"

Matilda kept her eyes closed. "I'm useless, Betty. For all my wordage and reading, I don't understand their language. They are all so spontaneous, sociable and beautiful and I feel…dim-witted and small."

Skirts rustled. Gentle hands descended to her shoulders. The scent of fresh bread and kindness. "Yer silly goose. They know each other, 'tis all. They've scrapped together since they were nippers and got leg shackled as youths. Bit unfair of Mr H to ask yer, I think, wot with yer being an unmarried miss and not one of them, but men never understand stuff like that."

"But I've been to dinners with unknowns before."

"Not as hostess, where yer supposed to have the upper hand. Now, tell Betts wot the problem is."

Matilda breathed deep. "I don't know what milling coves are. Or whiffles. Or muzzlers. The guests are all so attractive, exuberant and uninhibited – chatting about bosoms and suchlike."

A snort erupted. "Were that concerning Miss Figstone, perchance?"

"She's wearing beautiful scarlet and making Mr Hawkins laugh."

Matilda hadn't meant to say that and opened one eye.

Betty's bilberry eyes gleamed, her cheeks covered with flour. "Pah. Have no worry there, but…as to their lingo. If yer dunno something, how d'yer learn, girlie?"

"Read a book."

Betty sighed and rolled her eyes. "And if there's no books?"

"Ask someone who does know."

"There yer go. So ask. Start with Ribber Rufus. He's a handsome bachelor and would love to tell yer all about it."

"Well, yes, I suppose I could. I'd not wish to appear dim though."

"Do yer think I'm dim cos I dunno where El Dorado is?"

"Not at all. Although I don't believe anyone does."

"Well, then. Nobody is dim-witted, they just haven't learned stuff yet."

How sage and insightful Betty was. She viewed life in a wholly different way – forever optimistic, never judgemental, and Matilda wished there'd been a *Mrs Havistock but call me Betty* in the Griffin household when she'd been growing up.

"And as for the other…" Betty shook her head and tutted. "Go in there, tell 'em grubs up and feel proud of who yer are. Yer wanted experience, didn't yer?"

"I did, Betty. I do."

"Well, this is it. So enjoy it, relish it and ask questions till yer head's brimmin'. Yer a bright, pretty girl who's taken the bull by the horns in life. Now go ride it."

Maybe that was getting a dash carried away, but Matilda knew exactly what Betty meant, and bussed her on the cheek. "Thank you, Betts. You are a wonder."

"Away with yer. And be the gracious lady yer are with Miss Figstone – she's a nice girl. Merely scratching up the wrong tree, 'tis all."

Matilda ought to clarify her interpretation of that phrase but she got the gist.

THE '1811 ENGLISH COMMONS PRIZEFIGHTING CHAMPIONS' Dinner' had been an unmitigated success, but Seth nevertheless scowled as the clock chimed midnight and another giggle drifted from the sofa where Miss Griffin sat between Ribber Rufus and Giles the Grinder, her after-dinner glass of Madeira wine kept precipitously topped up by the attentive buggers.

Telling himself that he was merely protecting his governess from any inappropriate propositions from Giles or Rufus, he gave his excuses to his friends and sidled towards the decanters…via the rear of the sofa.

During pre-dinner sherries, he'd been worried for Miss Griffin, had noticed she appeared harassed and rather glum, a false smile plastered to her lips, and when she'd vanished from the room, it had taken all his social graces – which were few – to extricate himself from Miss Figstone's attentions.

His guests all knew each other too well and so took liberties, running tame about his house, pouring their own drinks, rearranging the chairs, shedding shawls, language was…ripe, and Nobbler Nick couldn't read so the hostess's elegant calligraphical script on the menu was rather pointless.

He'd cursed himself for being such a witless dolt and had hunted her out, only to find Betty, who'd called him a witless dolt.

But when he'd returned…

Miss Griffin, with a true beguiling smile, had announced dinner was served, leading the way to the dining room like a golden lantern.

Not the slightest discontent had creased her brow when, despite the placement card proclaiming it Mrs Dewhurst's seat, Miss Figstone had dropped herself next to Seth. Instead, his hostess had swiftly rearranged the cards with a calm dexterity.

During the feast, a rowdiness and merriment had emanated from the far end of the table causing all eyes and ears to seek its source – Miss Griffin, who'd held her companions in thrall, and Seth had lamented not being able to view her amber eyes as they'd lightened with laughter.

After-dinner port had been swiftly guzzled by the men, eager to return to their ladies, and once again, Miss Griffin had been a mesmeric flame that he'd been unable to turn away from – beguiling the champions with questions of pugilism, complimenting the ladies on their style, flitting from group to group and captivating them all with her honesty and eagerness to learn.

She'd likewise captivated Seth with her competence, fluttering fingers and joyful vitality – all held within a golden dress, which scattered his wits and melted his control.

Casually, he leaned against the sofa back and earwigged in.

"So pray tell, then," Miss Griffin enquired, "if a snorter to the snout is a blow to the nose, what is a rattler to the rails?"

"Jab to the teeth," Rufus responded with a broad grin, proving he'd been able to dodge that particular blow during his career.

"And an ogler in the gaslights?"

"In the eye," crowed Giles to her right with a salacious wink.

"A nutcracker? No, don't tell me." She shoved her spectacles up, ebony ringlets bouncing upon her silken nape. "That must be a severe blow to the head."

"Near enough," drawled Ribber Rufus, who then leaned so close she must have been able to feel his breath. "And how about a...famble in the dandle, Miss Griffin?"

Her hand lifted to her lips and she...giggled.

Scowling anew as Seth realised she had no need of his rescue, he continued to the decanters, where Kian also lurked.

"Well," his old friend began, "yer governess is causing a sensation."

"Hmm."

"And Rufus has taken a shine to the bonnie lass."

"Hmm."

"A canny idea to have her as hostess."

"Hmm." Actually, no, it wasn't. Rufus did indeed appear smitten and for some reason, Seth found that quite irritating.

"Ribber Rufus is particular when it comes to the ladies," his friend wittered on, "and he looks enamoured…and she also."

Seth swivelled. "It's her job as hostess to be attentive."

Kian held up a palm and grinned.

A trill of giggles, a rumble of fierce laughter and Seth gritted his teeth.

"Does yer lass Chloe like Miss Griffin?"

"Very much."

"Hmm."

"What does that mean?" he groused.

"Och, Seth, yer a mite tetchy tonight. Have another wee brandy."

He glared at the poured liquor and its shimmering burnt amber hue.

Indeed, he'd enjoyed this evening but vexation prickled his neck, and seeing all his friends had also brought old memories, both good and bad, to the fore.

"Seth?" a seductive female voice whispered at his side. "You promised to show me the ballroom?"

His gaze lifted from the brandy and stretched across the room to settle upon Miss Griffin.

That molten gown, which would blend perfectly with his own waistcoat, highlighted her flushed cheeks and creamy décolletage, tendrils of dark hair brushing her gilded bodice.

Gold and black – riches and sin, the beautiful day and wondrous night, enticing him like no other.

She glanced up and their eyes collided.

Noise ceased.

Desire surged.

To stride over and…

A hand pressed to his shoulder. "Seth?"

Miss Griffin twisted away.

The moment moved on; the jabber of friends resumed; Kian scrutinised his liquor.

"Yes, Miss Figstone?"

"The ballroom?"

He blinked. "But of course." And he swivelled to proffer an arm, aware he was walking in the wrong direction.

CHAPTER TEN

"Every man feels a respect and an awe in the company of a virtuous and lovely woman."

Private Education: A Practical Plan for the Studies of Young Ladies.

Elizabeth Appleton. 1815.

"I do hope you'll visit us in Cheshire. You'd be most welcome."

"Thank you, Mrs Dewhurst," enthused Matilda. "I've never been north before."

The lady and her champion sauntered into the rainy night, and smothering a yawn at the lateness of the hour, Matilda waved until they ascended the hackney.

Mr Finlay remained the last guest, still nattering to Mr Hawkins in the hall, and she fidgeted, desiring her slumber post-haste. Mercifully, her employer strode to the stand to collect the Scotsman's hat, cane and gloves, so Matilda took her chance. "Mr Finlay, I must bid you good night."

"And to yer also. Never have I had such an agreeable

dinner at Seth's roost. All due to the bonnie hostess, I reckon."

Matilda blushed beneath his scrutinising blue gaze and–

"Ahem."

She turned to her employer, who prodded Mr Finlay none too kindly with his accruements.

Mr Hawkins loitered with a distinctly rumpled demeanour. Fine lines of strain etched his brow and a tinge of stubble darkened his jaw. Sans jacket, his linen sleeves were rolled back to the elbow revealing muscled forearms, that burnished waistcoat half-unbuttoned, gold fob watch peeking from his pocket and cravat dishevelled.

Handsome and rather dangerous looking.

"Miss Griffin?"

She shivered. "Yes, Mr Hawkins?"

"I would appreciate a moment of your time if you are not too fatigued? We could convene in the library? I will be but a moment."

Matilda nibbled her lip. If she'd been in attendance at a society ball and such a request had been made, worry would have beset her – a rake of the Season set to seduce in the library, but this was Mr Hawkins.

And doubtless he'd already done his seducing for the night with Miss Figstone.

Not that it mattered.

In the least.

He was her employer and nothing more.

"Certainly," she replied, disguising her yawn.

A tight nod and he spun to Mr Finlay, who, for no good reason she could fathom, winked at her.

She meandered up the staircase for the library, a curious assortment of emotions churning within – pleasure at the success of the evening, to be sure, but also its opposite.

Regrets and a lingering sadness had intruded as she'd bid farewell to their guests.

Perchance the laughter, after so much concern for her future, had brought other, deeper emotions to the surface. For the occasion had reminded her of all that she'd lost, of all that she would no longer have.

As governess in future households, she would be expected to play an invisible role, speak only when spoken to, be on her best behaviour at all times and never laugh too loudly or distract a gentleman's attention.

A woman of two worlds – servant and society – yet not fully accepted in either.

She was spoiled within this household, where *Ton* rules did not hold sway. Befriended by the housekeeper and indulged by her agreeable employer and his charming daughter with ices, museums and...companionship.

Two lanterns still bathed the library in a golden glow, the open cabinets of books welcoming her with their warm-coloured bindings and scent of leather. No quarter was given to sculpture or art, though one lone mirror did hang over the fireplace reflecting the velvet curtains of green drawn firm against the sodden night. She ambled to the round mahogany reading table to peruse a small volume, its pages laying open.

Whenever she had visited the library, be it morning or night, a different book had sat waiting as though its reader had not a moment since departed the room.

And not books that she supposed most gentlemen would read of an evening – on carriage maintenance, angling or pistol polishing – but novels and poetry by Rousseau, Byron or Scott.

Tonight it was Edmund Spenser's *Faerie Queene*.

She roamed to a chestnut bookcase and caressed the ornate spines for bedtime reading.

Byron? Too romantic.

Blake? Too sad.

Her hand faltered upon the essays of Michel de Montaigne – an antique leather-bound book, and she removed it from its slot, breathed in the pages and brushed the golden gilding.

Father's favourite.

After dinner, he'd oft recited these philosophical essays in the original French, Mother listening intently to his deep restful tone, herself flicking through drawings of the Molucca Islands.

She'd been sheltered, certainly, in her upbringing, and many a night she had wished to be elsewhere, exploring an exotic island or in the trees with her birds, yet now Matilda wished she'd relished those peaceful hours with her parents, taken from her all too soon. Philosophy had not been her own inclination, but she missed their presence and guidance and…

She missed *them*.

"Miss Griffin? Are you…"

A pristine white handkerchief was thrust before her and she realised that two fat tears were trundling down her cheeks, that her employer had silently stalked into the library. "I… I am quite well, Mr Hawkins. Merely tired, I think."

"I apologise then, most sincerely, for keeping you from your bed."

Twisting, she took the handkerchief from his hand and dabbed at her face. Mr Hawkins' eyes were narrowed in concern – intense and striking.

"No, not at all. I'm unsure sleep would be forthcoming in any case." And Matilda made to replace the book.

A broad hand stayed her own for a moment. "Have you a taste for philosophy?" Then let her slide it home.

"Not really, but it was my father's favourite."

"Ah, I see." And she had a feeling he truly *did* see. "It was remiss of me not to enquire before, but I assumed your parents died long ago."

"Three years this autumn," she replied, holding the handkerchief out to him.

Mr Hawkins accepted the soggy bundle with nary a frown. "Not that long at all. I am so sorry. Was it illness?"

Matilda swallowed, never having spoken at length to anyone about her parents' death.

"No... I do not wish..." Her words trailed off, unsure what she wished for.

"If you do not wish, Miss Griffin, then that is your prerogative, but I cannot abide seeing my governess in such distress. So if at any time you wish to share, I do have broad shoulders."

Matilda gazed to those shoulders, as mighty as Atlas' to bear the world. Forever she had assumed to be self-contained, taught to restrain emotion, but tonight, she...she hurt.

Her gaze flicked up to his face, half-shaded in the lantern light, rough, stubbled and with that scar, but also calm, sincere and with that kindness.

Cousin Astwood had shown little care for her parents' death, the vicar had advised her to bear the grief with stoic valour as such was the transience of life, and one great-aunt had declared it a blessing they'd at least gone together...

Maybe.

But it hadn't felt like a blessing to Matilda.

The wind gusted outside, a swash of rain pelting the velvet curtained window.

"I... I always..." She bit a lip to prevent a tremble. "Why do the days you most want to remember – full of joy and fun – evaporate in one's memory like a summer's cloud, and yet days you wish never to recall – ones of grief and tragedy – cling like a bitter and befogged winter's night?"

He released a long leaden breath. "Perchance, to remind us that life is short? So as not to take it for granted?"

"Yes, that might be true." Matilda rubbed the heel of a hand to her chest. "I lost my whole world in but a moment. Everything. My parents, home, future. I tell myself that such is fate, yet...why must fate be so cruel?"

Mr Hawkins shook his head. "I wish I knew."

And she was aware that sadness was not confined to her alone, that her employer had also lost a beloved wife.

"My parents went to Kingston to attend a lecture. I merrily waved them off and hurried back inside, dare I say, gl-glad they were gone so I could return to my atlas of the South Sea Islands, but..."

The handkerchief returned to her cheek, caressed in silence.

"There was a collision with a racing phaeton and they... my parents perished at the roadside. I was told Mother died swiftly, but Father... He was gravely injured by shar...shards of wood." Whenever possible, she suppressed the visions that such recollections caused, but tonight she let them sorely flood over her – her delicate mother crying out, her gentle father in so much pain, tended to by strangers as their life ebbed from them in a dank Kingston lane, and she prayed once more that God had taken them with all speed.

"Miss Griffin... Forgive this forwardness," he whispered as his broad palm lifted to cup her jaw. "And I know words can never be enough but... I am so deeply sorry."

She tipped her head, gazed into his eyes and nodded her

gratitude, drawing comfort from his sincerity. "I believe I've never fully…felt their loss, never been given *time* to feel their loss. Astwood took over with undue haste, clearing my parents' bedchamber before it was cold. I removed all their personal diaries to the attic, and one day I hope…I hope to retrieve them."

"You need only ask and I would help you with that."

Through blurred eyes, Matilda surveyed his firm lips but gentle regard. "I do not know why I feel like this tonight. I apologise, for I had a joyous dinner and your friends are all so charming."

"Memories," he murmured, "can seize one at the strangest of times – a scent, a picture, your father's book or seeing old friends. You have both my utmost sympathy and… understanding, Miss Griffin." A soft sigh escaped his lips.

His hand still lingered and although the impropriety of their closeness was beginning to intrude, she found she didn't much care for once.

Miss Pikesworth's Guide to Etiquette had been wrong about everything else, after all.

Instead she faintly rubbed her cheek back and forth in his rough palm, not knowing whence her boldness had come from.

For a brief moment, Matilda thought she saw a flash of intense…fire flare within Mr Hawkins' eyes, but then it extinguished and he drew away.

He ran that same hand across his own jaw, the rasp noticeable over the soft patter of rain outside, before he turned to survey his books. "I asked you here as I wished to express my thanks for all your hard work tonight. It was not an easy task that I requested of you." His fingers brutally tugged at his hair. "And you were…perfect."

A shroud of pleasure wrapped her inner sadness. "Oh,

thank you, Mr Hawkins. If truth be told, I was a little nervous."

"You'd no need. Also..." Spine rigid, he fiddled with a bookend upon the shelf. "Rufus... Not knowing your situation with family and suchlike, Rufus asked me as your employer if he may call upon you, but I replied you were your own woman for asking, and that what you did on your free days was your own business."

Rather stunned, Matilda spluttered. "Well, he's awfully nice but..." Indeed, no curious sensation of any kind had overcome her in his attractive company, no desire to rub her cheek upon his palm or share her deepest sorrows. "I'm not drawn to him in that way."

"Because he is an ex-prizefighter?"

"Not at all." She frowned at the back of his gold waistcoat, the lacing accentuating his slender hips. "I like him of course, but..." How best to explain it? "I do not feel the same attraction which you evidently have for Miss Figsto–" She bit her tongue. "Not that it is any of my business."

Mr Hawkins twisted to her and tilted his head. "You believe myself and Miss Figstone to be entangled?"

"Well, I noticed you did disappear together." Matilda's gaze slunk to her feet, spectacles sliding down her nose. "She's a beautiful lady."

"She is indeed, but I took the chance tonight to tell her that although I enjoy her company, I do not feel we would suit."

Matilda's eyes flicked up.

"Miss Figstone..." Tugging at his cravat, he sighed. "To be truthful, she reminds me too much of my wife."

"I see." Except Matilda didn't, and she nudged her spectacles back up.

Seemingly aware of her confusion, Mr Hawkins ambled to the decanters and poured two glasses.

"Perhaps this witching hour," he said softly with a resigned smile, "promotes in us confession. For my wife, you must understand, Miss Griffin, deserted me for a highwayman."

It carried the air of a comedic play, yet her employer's shoulders were taut, lines bracketing his lip, no amusement to his profile.

She'd conjured images of a loving marriage, her employer so very content, a wife easing his fighting pains and cheering him on, only to succumb to the lung disease or a tragic accident like her parents.

"Is she…is she still alive?"

A shake of head and he prowled towards her, proffering the glass. "No. One year after she left us, Bow Street caught up with the highwayman; there was a pistol exchange and she was caught in the crossfire."

"I-I'm so sorry." She took the glass and sipped, its burn gliding down her throat to aid the cold in her chest.

His lips curved to a grim smile. "I mourned her the day she died just as much as when she left me. Does that make me a fool?"

"No!" And without thought, Matilda laid a hand upon his bare forearm, felt heated skin, wiry hair and the thrum of muscle. "It makes you faithful and constant, and any woman would be blessed to have such devotion."

And she meant each word.

Ever since her first day of employment, she had considered Mr Hawkins a balanced, secure man, one satisfied with life. But she supposed everyone had their sorrows – it was just that some were better at hiding them.

"My wife left us while I was training. Abandoned a six-year-old Chloe with a letter and a penny doll as substitute."

"How awful."

But Mr Hawkins shook his head and rubbed his nape.

"I grew up in the Rookery, Miss Griffin. A cruel place where fists rule and the only law is survival." He grimaced. "Being a fighter who'd won a few minor contests, girls paid me attention, but Samantha was like a bright star within that squalor – yet didn't she know it, knew how to twist the lads around her finger with a wink. In the throes of raw youth, I pursued her, and she gave of herself freely, but I was the one caught. You think your *Ton* world strict? Try explaining a kiss away to an Irish mother with an iron skillet."

"You married?"

He shrugged. "At scarce seventeen, neither of us knew any better, quite frankly. And we were both...browbeaten, for want of a better word. Maybe I could have refused, but..."

"You loved her."

He nodded, gaze flat and empty. "I loved her vivacity and generous nature. I loved her beauty and she made me laugh. I wanted her and so I had her. Samantha was fond of me enough, said she loved me." The contents of his glass were slugged in one. "I promised her I would get us out of the Rookery. Together."

Matilda's hand tightened upon his forearm, and he abruptly stared down as though unaware she was still clutching him. He'd been lost in a far-off world – of youthful dreams and a future all planned.

With a soft inhale, Mr Hawkins gazed up. "But... We hardly knew each other in truth. Samantha... She viewed the fighting world as excitement and roaring crowds, medals and adulation, whereas for me it was a way out. I wished to save every penny, she wanted to spend. I needed to sit in at night and recover from my busted ribs, she yearned to dance in the ale-houses. I was dead with exhaustion and she was so full of life."

"You are making excuses for her."

"Perhaps. But we just saw life so differently. Each time I took a fist in the face, I thought of our poverty, of how we had to escape. Then Chloe came along so soon, and I fought for us all and yet... Samantha still seemed to think the glory more important. That we should be celebrating when we won meagre coppers. I fought more matches and trained harder to get us out. I can't say that as a young man I didn't enjoy being with the lads on fight days, the adulation of the crowds, but then I was never home and..."

"And then she left you..."

"Yes, she left me. She left us. The worst is that I could see it coming, the end of our marriage. It was like a lingering illness, so the loss of Samantha wasn't a sudden end for me. It had been happening for months. The slow tearing off of a limb, leaving nothing but sorrow for a piece of me lost."

Matilda caressed his forearm, swallowed the lump in her throat. "Your wife chose her own path, as we all must do. And you have Chloe – for comfort and purpose. You've raised a fine girl, Mr Hawkins, who will become a fine and genteel lady...if she so wishes. She worships the ground you tread."

His hand covered hers, a smile that bespoke his pride and true joy.

"You do realise Chloe adores you also."

"Really... Oh. I've never been adored before."

An inveigling warmth spread through her, dissipating some of the sadness within, but equally a fire spread up her arm and Matilda peered down – no sign of her slender fingers beneath that broad smothering hand.

Permit never clandestine attachment – Miss Appleton's words insidiously whispered within Matilda's ears but the lady was doubtless correct.

"Well," she began, gathering her governess mien, "I should retire now, Mr Hawkins. My governess compendium has some strict instruction on unmarried persons being alone in a library at such an hour. Not respectable at all."

"Why is that?"

Erm. "Well… The employer could… The governess might… They could…"

He raised that eyebrow with the scar; she wondered on its cause.

"Well, they might…kiss or something," she blurted, pulling lightly to liberate her hand. It would not budge.

"How utterly dreadful," he murmured, and his grip shifted to her wrist, drew her forward – so close she observed a gold rim encircling his pupils. His lips parted and her heart thumped like a tribal drum for the Saharan rains.

So she tattled on as she usually did when in a dither. "Well, it is. I was kissed once before, and it was truly dreadful. I wouldn't wish it on anyone."

Matilda startled at the violent emotion which slipped through Mr Hawkins' eyes – twisting the easy brown and submerging it beneath irate green. She could see the pugilist…

"Who kissed you to make it so awful?" he demanded.

"My betrothed. Lord Sidlow. But it matters not. It won't happen again."

"You're damn right it won't," he muttered. "I vowed never to use violence outside of the ring, but I could make an exception."

"That won't be necessary, and in any case, you must think me foolish. People kiss all the time, after all, without making a fuss."

He released her wrist but only to clasp her fingers and draw them upwards, to brush firm dry lips upon the back of her hand in a perfect gentlemanly kiss. Many a man had done the same and yet never had such scintillation journeyed up her arm and then prickled in so many places.

Mr Hawkins sketched a bow. "As I once said, no, I do not think you foolish at all. I think you a brave lady and an exceptionally good listener to boot, who commands my utmost respect." He stretched to the shelf behind, reached for the elegant Michel de Montaigne book and placed it within her fingers. "For you. A keepsake. And I know your parents would be proud of the lady you have become. Brave and...enchanting."

No one had ever called her that before – bluestocking, dull, glass-eyes, to be sure, but not brave and enchanting... "Thank you for such kindness, Mr Hawkins. I shall treasure it always." She gave a watery smile.

"Good night, Miss Griffin." Those elemental eyes flickered with gold fire once more before they dampened. "'Valour is strength, not of legs and arms, but of heart and soul.'"

She dipped a curtsey. "Good night, Mr Hawkins." And turned to depart the library with a broad smile.

For she knew from whence those words had come: the very book clutched in her hands.

Such a rare and gallant gentleman.

CHAPTER ELEVEN

"Life is short; employ it honourably; do what good you can: you need not want for opportunity."

PRIVATE EDUCATION: A PRACTICAL PLAN FOR THE STUDIES OF YOUNG LADIES.

ELIZABETH APPLETON. 1815.

"I don't know why you continue to work for that scoundrel, Kian."

"That *scoundrel* is yer principal investor."

Shrugging, Seth drained his tankard and dumped it to the kitchen table. True enough, and he perused his friend as he replenished their ale from the jug Betty had left out for them. Fortnightly, they convened to sluice their throats before leaving for a local ale-house, but Kian appeared tired tonight, shadows creeping across his pale skin and grey misting his black hair.

Mind you, Seth likely appeared similar.

Since the Champions' Dinner three days past, he'd focused all his hours upon the Academy in order to distract from the lure of Miss Griffin. A lure she seemed so unaware she held.

But she was his daughter's governess...

So each evening at dinner, he would compel himself to ignore the manner in which the candlelight caught a flash of blue in her midnight hair.

Quash the recollection of her moist sherry eyes and tender words in the library that night.

Bludgeon the desire which lurked stormily beneath his skin when he recalled her silken cheek against his calloused palm.

Trample the thought of how he had so nearly kissed his genteel lady governess...

He rubbed his nape, exhaled heavily and supped his ale.

"You should come and work with me, Kian. We'd be a good team."

"Aye, but I earn more at the Prince's in a night than yer'd pay me in a sennight."

"I'll have you know I upped the members' fee. I do very well."

"My wage is three guineas...a night."

Hell, that was rather a lot. "You can pay for drinks then, alth–" Seth's nostrils twitched. "Do come in, Miss Griffin."

"Oh, I shouldn't mean to... I'd not realised you were here, Mr Finlay. I merely wished to reheat my tea. I let mine go cold, you see, whilst reading."

Miss Griffin shuffled at the kitchen door and looked left then right, eyes big as hens' eggs at the sight of them.

He supposed they did appear like bloody gruff barbarians, both having done away with their stylish daytime rig for loose neckcloths, rough breeches and grubby boots. The sole nod to elegance was Seth's emerald-green silk waistcoat – Chloe's choice, of course.

Kian, ever the gentleman that he wasn't, stood, then bowed with a glint to his blue eyes – the rogue.

Seth sprang to his feet. "Please, come in. The range is still hot. So why not brew another."

His friend insisted on handling the kettle and enquiring of Chloe's lessons, complimenting Miss Griffin on her honey dress – which was saffron, not honey – and rooting in the cupboard for the Oliver biscuits.

Seth gritted his teeth, despite knowing full well that Kian's heart solely beat for one woman alone.

"How did you know it was I at the door, Mr Hawkins?" his governess asked, leaning against the range and warming her palms.

"The scent of an English garden in June." The words tumbled out before his lips could put a leash to them.

Kian vainly attempted to smother a smirk.

Seth cleared his throat. "Betty always smells of flour, the maid of lye and Chloe of lavender. It could only be you – meadows in sunshine." The intimacy of recognising a woman by her scent was not something a gentleman should confess to, a breach of delicacy too far, but that scent surrounded him by day...and haunted him by night.

"I'm rather indulgently still using my last bar of Andrew Pears' soap. It must be that."

Images of an entirely debauched nature assailed him, ones he'd successfully bridled over the past days but ale had clearly slackened the reins... Miss Griffin soaping herself in a slipper bath, all creamy skin and loose, damp coal-black hair, teasing his eyes with glimpses of heaven.

Without question he remained alone in this tormented passion as she twisted away to boil tea, leaving Seth to stew.

"And what do you do, Mr Finlay? I did not have the time

to enquire on Saturday," she said apologetically, bustling from the larder with a jug of milk.

"Dinnae worry, yer were well occupied with Ribber Rufus." He grinned at Seth. "I work in...protection and security for the Prince."

"Gosh." She dipped the teaspoon and stirred. "At Carlton House or–"

"Not that Prince," Seth interrupted, winking at his governess. "*The* Prince."

Ebony eyelashes batted behind spectacles in confusion, fingers tapping her fragile china teacup.

Kian yanked out a chair for the lady to sit. "He owns a few gambling hells. Got an exclusive one on–"

"Pall Mall?" she squealed, looking hesitant but then plonking herself down anyway. "Cousin Astwood lost two hundred guineas, his gold watch and a mistress at that place. I was amused for days."

"That'd be the one." And with the lady seated, both ruffians allowed their arses to hit the chairs anew.

"Goodness. And you work for the owner?"

"Aye."

Seth kept quiet. The Prince had a shady reputation, not one a lady should acquaint herself with, and he watched as she merrily interrogated Kian about gaming hells, their female attendees and the mathematical odds of winning.

Many a gentlewoman would've had a fit of the vapours and be in need of the smelling salts by now, alone with two scruffy low-class rascals in the kitchens, yet Miss Griffin was formed of hardier stuff.

With fortitude, she'd survived her parents' horrific death, outwitted her malicious cousin and braved governess-ship at a boxing academy.

"I wish to travel, Mr Finlay," she was now saying into her

teacup, "but I think it an unrealistic dream. This may sound selfish, having grown up surrounded by wealth, but all my experience of foreign lands was through books and study. I led a sheltered existence and these two weeks as governess have been a revelation. I realise a working life can be arduous but there is also immense satisfaction." She bit her reddened lip. "For that, I have Mr Hawkins to thank, for giving me this chance, placing his daughter within my care and showing me...life."

Miss Griffin abruptly glanced up, eyes gleaming her gratitude, that dimple revealed, and Seth's innards twisted with yearning to show her yet more life, to show her that a kiss from a lover was not to be dreaded but welcomed, begged for and pleaded never to end.

Yet respect and circumstance tamped his passion, as it had done so in the library. He was her employer, she a lady and a governess, and who knew what the future may hold. With that keen intellect and exquisite beauty, a duke might sweep her off her scanty feet or some dotty old aunt may bequeath her a fortune.

He owned a boxing club and still dropped his H's when he'd quaffed a few ales.

Kian tutted. "I canna understand keeping daughters beneath lock and key. My wife grew up amongst sailors as her Irish father was a sea captain and she never came to no harm. Adored the grog as well."

"Do you know," Miss Griffin stated, peering at their drained tankards with pursed lips. "I've never even drunk beer."

"Well, might yer come with us then. To the ale-house?"

What! Seth's head shot up. *No.* There was experience of life and then there was...grubby benches, suspect meat pies, roving doxies and bosky poltroons.

"Oh, how exciting!" she declared. "I've never visited such an establishment before. But no, I couldn't. Could I?" She sucked a lip into her mouth, eyes wide. "Just one beverage might be acceptable, purely for anthropological reasons as I believe species of people inhabit those places whom I've never even met."

Yes, and Seth would keep it that way. "Miss Griffin. You are governess to my daughter and as such should not visit an ale-house. It is no place for a lady."

Hell, he sounded like a stiff-rumped surly boots, and with shoulders drooping, she sipped her weak tea, eyelashes as wilted as the tails on those damn museum birds.

Never had he felt such a shabby blackguard.

Miss Griffin wished to experience life; he could understand that. Yet this was no smart dinner or respectable museum outing but a mucky ale-house where a fight could ensue or a lady could be...importuned.

"Come now, Seth," his friend grumbled with a glare, "I no took yer for being such a stickler. Yer ma supped aplenty in the Old Goat ale-house, and Chloe used to come with us when she were a wee thing. What's wrong with yer? Let the lass have some fun. We could try The Red Lion." He grabbed Seth's coat sleeve, blue eyes so grave. "Life is short. Yer know that."

Yes, he did know.

For Kian had married that beautiful Irish daughter of a sea captain and they'd loved each other as turtle doves, but nigh five years ago on a bitter Tuesday morning, she'd taken a chill; by Wednesday she had a fever; and on Friday she'd passed to the angels, Kian clutching her in despair.

His friend had never recovered, in truth.

Still, it was downright blackmail. And he'd not fall for it.

CHAPTER TWELVE

"Let us look at vice, naked, stripped of every trapping of birth and fashion, and we shall only feel horror ourselves at the sight."

PRIVATE EDUCATION: A PRACTICAL PLAN FOR THE STUDIES OF YOUNG LADIES.

ELIZABETH APPLETON. 1815.

"Down the hatch," Mr Finlay toasted, clunking Matilda's stationary tankard with his own.

She squinted at the pewter vessel that had been placed before her on the table, a brown and exceedingly murky liquid sloshing, clouds of beige froth drifting.

Matilda's gaze sloped back to the two men sitting opposite, both watching her with rapt interest and no small amount of concern.

In order to experience a flavour unknown, she had chosen the popular Porter Ale, which her confidante, Evelyn, had once declared tasted of horse blankets dipped in pond water. But reasoning there must be some explanation for its fame, Matilda sipped, maintaining a watchful eye upon the precipitous froth.

Smoky, bitter, deep.

As she swiped a top lip with her tongue, she noted Mr Hawkins follow the movement: doubtless it had been vulgar, but no serviettes were provided.

She sampled again. Silky and full. A gulp. Toffee and roasts.

"We can get yer a pale ale if yer prefer?" prodded Mr Finlay. "'Tis a dab sweeter."

"No..." She took a further gulp and the two sets of eyebrows opposite ascended. "I rather like it. The beverages for ladies are oft too sweet for my palate. I appreciate the bitterness."

Mr Hawkins' gaze remained hooded in the nebulous light, but Mr Finlay nodded in approval and once more clunked her tankard in what she assumed was some sort of maleness ritual.

Feeling inordinately pleased with herself, Matilda sat back as best one could upon the bare wooden bench set against a stone wall that she'd been shepherded to when they'd entered.

Beneath blackened beams, tables and chairs were spread in no discernible pattern, the patrons ranging from rough to refined, a tangled room of class and accents.

No doubt the scabby Miss Appleton would clout any governess with her three-hundred and twenty-six page book for being so audacious, but so much life could be viewed within an ale-house, and how else was Matilda to teach the evils of immorality if she knew not its forms.

Being a lady of the *haut monde,* she now realised, was similar to a fragile china tea service. Kept in a cupboard until genteel company called, made to do one's duty, granted a delicate clean and then put away again, watching whilst the hard-wearing pewter tankards were used each day with love and purpose.

Rather purple prose, to be sure, but this evening, Matilda wished to be a tankard...

Still, it was dreadfully improper to be sitting here, and the thrill of it shook her to her very boots – ones that rubbed as they belonged to Betty, her own mustard kid-leather footwear having been rejected as too elegant for an ale-house.

In addition to the boots, Father's ancient cloak concealed her saffron gown and one of Chloe's old caps her hair, so she felt toastier than Icarus. But that had been the strict condition laid down for this adventure, hence she wrapped the cloak tight, not wishing to give her chaperones any excuse to send her home.

"Another, Kian?"

Goodness.

Matilda glanced to their empty tankards and realised that while she'd been whimsically wool-gathering, they had been studiously supping.

A nod, and Mr Hawkins rose, stripping off his jacket in the convivial warmth.

At the bar, a small flock of males greeted him: back slaps – that would knock her to her knees – traded for manly punches to the stomach.

How peculiar a male's social interactions and habitat, which perhaps explained why he'd not been overly effusive at a female's presence here.

"Why the sigh, lass?" Mr Finlay stared with those soulful blue eyes from the seat opposite. A handsome man, yet his striking raven plumage affected her not.

"I believe Mr Hawkins would prefer I wasn't here."

Mr Finlay chuckled. "We've been friends since we were whippersnappers, Miss Griffin. He has an easy-going nature on the surface but beneath there's a will of iron." With a wink, he leaned close, inducing no pleasurable prickling whatsoever. "Seth wanted to be a prizefighter, and so he was the best. He wanted a club, now he has dukes squabbling in a queue. If he dinnae truly wish yer here, Miss Griffin, yer'd be safely tucked up in bed dreaming of ribboning yer bonnet. I'd say he's merely on edge cos he's worried for yer welfare."

Matilda surreptitiously surveyed that callipygian figure of Mr Hawkins once more as he roamed at the bar. Even in rougher garments he manifested power and magnificence, and personally, she felt as safe as a nugget of gold in the Bank of England.

He returned and sat with a stern air, causing an awfully wicked rumpus within. White sleeves billowed from his finely tailored emerald-green waistcoat with oval frontage, his neckcloth loose enough to expose his throat, stubble stippling his jaw.

"So, Miss Griffin, what do you think of your first ale-house?" Mr Hawkins settled back.

"Well…" She glanced to the left, then to the right.

The patrons at the bar were gesticulating merrily, tankards airborne; a table of slouched gentlemen played cards while two young women prowled at their periphery wearing bright dresses and worn smiles; and a grey-haired couple sat munching pie by a smouldering fire – hardly a scene of Hogarthian debauchery. Indeed, from the outside it had not even resembled an abode of beer, but a normal terraced house tucked in a tight alley, yellow bricked and slate roofed with three storeys.

"It's most cosy," she admitted. "Like Betty's kitchen."

"As it should be," Mr Finlay concurred. "'Tis an old alehouse and the best in the area."

"It's rumoured," her employer added, "that with St James's Palace opposite, King Charles and Nell Gwynne used to meet here in the basement for trysts."

"How…romantic," she fibbed. To the best of Matilda's knowledge, basements were inclement, with rats and mould.

"'Ere yer go, Seth lad." And Matilda goggled as yet more brimming tankards landed on the table enclosed by a set of vast swollen hands. "So 'ow's it with the flash set? Milled any dukes o' late?"

Peeking at the newcomer, she noted a clean apron surrounding a broad girth.

Moving upwards, she observed an open white shirt which struggled to contain a mountainous chest. Further was a neck the size of her waist and lastly came a physog belonging to the veriest villain that had ever breathed – unshaven, an eye patch and a grin that appeared to be formed of merely three teeth.

Which, before her interview, was more or less how she'd imagined her employer would look.

"Tonks!" Mr Hawkins rose to the villain and Matilda shrank to the wall.

"And who's this cub with yer, Seth?" growled the villain. "A new fighter? Bit of a bantling if he ain't even finished his Porter."

Matilda glared, her half-full tankard clutched close.

"Bloody 'ell." He whistled, that one eye drifting over her face…then lower. "Got yerself a flash piece of trol–"

"Tonks." Mr Hawkins stepped between them, his firm fingers gripping the villain's shoulder before he bent to his ear and whispered something.

"Oh. Gottcha. Bloody 'ell." And the villain whistled again.

Matilda glanced to Mr Finlay, who winked. Was that supposed to be reassuring?

But her employer moved aside and swept an arm as though a Master of Ceremonies. “Miss Griffin, meet Mr Tomkins. The owner of this ale-house and an old friend. A champion in his day, he won the 1810 Moulsey Hurst.”

Gosh.

Unsure of the etiquette in this establishment, but quite sure a curtsey would prove problematic, Matilda rose from the bench to thrust out a hand. “Pleased to meet you, Mr Tomkins.”

A Goliath’s palm swallowed hers – snug and benign. “Likewise.” He jerked his head towards her tankard. “Me missus can make yer a tea, if yer like?”

“No, no. I quite like this Porter juice.”

“Right yer are. So yer teaching little Chloe stuff.”

“I am. She’s delightful,” Matilda said seating herself again.

“Still boxing, is she?”

“Yes, daily.”

“Never rests,” added Mr Hawkins. “And still talks about your win against William of Whopping.”

Matilda was astounded to view a blush of colour rise in Mr Tomkins’ cheeks. “I got lucky, ’tis all. But, aye, never had a day like it. Me. Tonks Tomkins. Champion.” He shook his head. “I were a street orphan, Miss Griffin, never thought I’d see me twentieth year, but though I never knew me letters, I could scrap me way outta anything.”

“Congratulations, Mr Tomkins. And now you own this fine establishment.”

“I do indeed, but me wins were nothing compared to our Seth ’ere. And yer should’ve seen him last year, parading before the Prince Regent and all them flash nobs that arrived after Waterloo; then there’s dukes bickering over his club membership like doxies after a sailor. He's done right rum good, Miss Griffin."

Matilda tilted her glance to her employer, who fidgeted from foot to foot. "How impressive, Mr Tomkins, he's never said. And which particular championships did our Mr Hawkins win?"

"Well 1811 were his big 'un. Fred the Footman – on accounts he were a footman, see – versus Seth the–"

"I don't believe Miss Griffin wishes to know all this." Mr Hawkins folded his arms in front of his waistcoat and appeared most stern.

She gazed from one to the other. "I do. I really do."

"He dinnae like his moniker, lass," Mr Finlay explained. "His first sponsor named him and it kind o'stuck."

Matilda waited with bated breath. What could it be?

"Seth the Smasher?" she guessed all of a sudden.

"No."

"Scuffler Seth?"

"Nope."

"Seth the Stallion?"

Mr Finlay chuckled for some reason. So obviously not.

"Seth the…Stupendous?" She was quite enjoying this. "Or Seth the–"

"Scholar," Mr Hawkins interjected, obviously having had enough of her guesses. "My sponsor caught me reading before a bout." He unfolded his arms and grabbed his ale with a grouch. "And that was that."

"Another theatre print?" Matilda questioned rather tartly.

He tipped his tankard. "Exactly so, Miss Griffin. Exactly so."

. . .

"AT ONE TIME," slurred his swaying governess, "I thought pugilism quite savage, but I'd be most interested to attend a contest now…" She hiccupped. "Purely for studious endeavour, you understand."

Seth frowned. They never should have allowed her that third tankard, but she'd insisted that a spree of Madeira wine with a friend had caused no ill-effects of any kind, so what could be the harm in Porter Ale to a hardened drinker such as herself?

Miss Griffin was as hardened as a waxen ballerina in hell.

Kian tapped his fingers upon the table. "Well, me and Seth are off to a prizefight the day after next."

Hell and damnation. Kian had a loose trap tonight.

"Really?" she said, swiping her pink tongue over that froth-coated top lip. "Do you suppose I could–"

"No," pre-empted Seth, shifting in his seat. "Women do not go to fights."

"Untrue," countered Kian beneath his breath.

"*Ladies* do not go to fights," Seth amended.

"We could hide her beneath a cloak and muffler, a wee lass like this."

"She'd look like a nefarious footpad on the prowl."

"Dress her up as a lad then? Like we used to do with Chloe."

A tankard slammed to the table. "I am *not* wearing breeches," Miss Griffin stated haughtily, cloak flapping. "Honestly, *men*… I've heard tell of some dissolute ideas whilst soused but…" Her lips maintained their movement but no more than mutters came forth.

Kian smirked. "We'd best be stirring our stumps before midnight." He rose and stretched his long limbs. "I'll settle the bill with Tonks."

"Miss Griffin," implored Seth, "if any harm came to you, I

would never forgive myself. A prizefight is no place for a lady, even dressed as a nefarious footpad. It does not involve gentlemen strutting with gloves on but bare knuckles and brutality."

Removing her spectacles, she gazed at him – haughty eyes softening while she placed flushed cheeks to palms.

"I would have liked to see you fight, Mr Hawkins."

That would be the Porter Ale talking, but nevertheless, as they stared at each other, the rope of lust tightened ever further betwixt them. He knew it for what it was, but he wondered if the innocent Miss Griffin did.

"You're a lady. You shouldn't even be here, an–"

"I've had the loveliest of evenings."

So had he.

Indeed, he could not remember the last time that a woman had held him so enthralled.

An itch could be scratched but it was his empty soul that cried out for company when Chloe had gone to bed. His skin, likewise, yearned for touch, not for one night but for all nights – intimate and profound.

Being a prizefighting champion had brought many women to his door, but he never opened it – too bruised, too particular or just too damn tired.

Yet this scant snip of a female made him crave once more.

"I could get a taste for this ale," she admitted, draining her tankard.

"'Tis strong and potent, you realise."

"Like you, Mr Porter." She scrunched a brow, blinked. "Erm, I don't think I meant..."

"Time to depart, methinks." He stood and raked the bar for Kian but caught Tonks' eye instead, who held up a coin and nodded towards the door.

Kian had left them.

With a sigh, Miss Griffin straightened her skew-whiff cap, flapped her cloak, shuffled along the bench, rose with palms pressed to table and then lumbered around the edge, peering for the door.

"Very well, Mr Hawkins."

Seth captured her wrist as she veered off course, her cap falling, breast brushing his arm, desire rendering him speechless.

A jug-bitten patron made to rise, understandable as such beauty was rarely seen here but one glare from Seth and his arse hit the seat anew.

"'It provokes the desire…'" Seth murmured.

"'But takes away the performance'," she finished, yanking her cloak straight. "Does that pertain to actors who over imbibe?"

"Yes," he said hoarsely.

Because Shakespeare was wrong, honesty wasn't always the best policy.

CHAPTER THIRTEEN

"Retreat instantly; you have not a moment to lose. Virtue impels you."

Private Education: A Practical Plan for the Studies of Young Ladies. Elizabeth Appleton. 1815.

"Jab. Jab, jab." Matilda missed. "Jab, wallop," she tried for variation, fists flying in front of her.

Why had she never tried Porter Ale when worries had bitten at her heels? Any troubles wafted away upon a cloud of brown froth.

"Because tomorrow," a male rumble answered, "your head will feel like Thor's hammer is beating a staccato rhythm upon it."

Had she said that aloud then? And how well-educated Mr Hawkins was. No wonder his moniker had been Seth the Scholar.

"I do have an extensive library."

She paused as they exited the tight alley that led onto Pall

Mall. Apparently, her thoughts were being voiced. Porter Ale truly was a wonder.

"Jab," she tried once more, punching out with her fist to the shadows.

A firm hand settled at her waist, another on her wrist, and she lost her breath as Mr Hawkins' colossal broadness loomed close.

"You will fall if your stance is not correct. You need to spread your le..." He breathed deep. "Your feet should be a little more apart. Good. Now, palm flat and roll your fingers towards it. Keep it tight and..." He eased her thumb out. "This curls low on the outside or you will break it upon contact. Perfect."

"I wish I'd known all this previously as it gives one a certain confidence. Do you know, I received quite a scare wandering the empty streets at dawn on the first morning of my employment."

"Who scared you?" He glared with fierceness in the yellow glow of lamplight.

"Leper ghosts."

She sensed his confusion and witnessed his shake of head. "You shouldn't have been out there at dawn, and I was probably awake and in the basement, so you ought to have knocked. Now, wallop me instead of ghosts."

"What if I hurt you?" *And what did he do in that basement?*

"That is rather the point. And you do not need to know. Pretend I'm an attacker and give me a peeper in mourning."

Matilda bit her lip. "A black eye?"

"You're catching on."

She jabbed out, but his head shifted to the side and she stumbled forward, flattening herself to her employer.

What a wonderfully strong chest.

"Thank you," he mumbled dryly somewhere into her hair.

"We'd best end the lesson there and resume when you are less...tired. Now, despite only being around the corner, we must hail a carriage or I'll be carrying you home."

To be truthful, Matilda wasn't quite so befuddled as all that.

What she felt now was a merry contentment – a freedom as she sauntered the shadowed London streets with a handsome ex-prizefighter, both protected and at liberty. Better than any frowning *Ton* ball or constrained soiree.

She wished Mr Hawkins would indeed sweep her into his arms and carry her home. Theoretically, she could pretend to swoon in boskiness but coquettish wiles had never been her strong point.

Or indeed a weak point.

"You have made me happy, Mr Hawkins," she revealed. "And I *did* mean to say that aloud. Thank you for tonight. I know you were ear bashed into it."

With the gaslight to his back, his expression was now hidden in silhouette. "It was all my pleasure, Miss Griffin."

A hackney carriage appeared at last, rattling down the Pall Mall cobbles, and Mr Hawkins thrust up an arm and let out a yell.

It slowed to a halt and the driver peered down, his face demonic yellow in the muddy light. "Where to, Guv?"

"Green Park. The back of Arlington. Only around the corner."

A sucking of teeth ensued as though they'd asked to be conveyed to the highlands of Scotland. "Been an accident on St James, yer realise," he griped. "Four bleedin' phaetons, three lost geese, two ale carts and a drunken lordling. Only missin' the five gold rings. We'll have to go via Haymarket." He wiped his nose. "Cost yer double though. Especially this time o' night."

Mr Hawkins rolled his eyes but nodded, so Matilda yanked the door open and flumped onto the seat, a strange odour of damp grass assailing her nostrils. "Have they had a horse in here?"

"Straw on the floor," he explained, climbing in and shutting the door. "To soak up…spillages."

"Oh, how interesting. Like what?"

He folded his arms. An action, she'd learned, which meant he would avoid her question.

"Haymarket shouldn't take too much longer this late."

See.

A yell and the carriage jolted into motion, darkness engulfing as they departed the pool of gaslight.

And abruptly Matilda felt…peculiar.

It wasn't the ale which still pleasantly hummed in her veins but a prickling awareness of Mr Hawkins lounging opposite, of the masculine scent of his cologne – leather and herbs – the rustling of his coat and catch to his breath.

He cleared his throat. "Are you warm enough, Miss Griffin?"

"Warm enough to boil an egg. Can I take the cloak off now?" And without waiting for an answer, she flung the apparel aside and fluffed her bodice.

She heard him grunt. In disapproval of her attire, perhaps?

This evening had been another marvellous experience, one she wished would never end. Good company, exciting places, chatter and…Mr Hawkins' strong calloused knuckles to look upon.

Besides the spectre of Astwood ever finding her, the sole grey miasma which lurked in her belfry was the memory of her betrothed's kiss. At times, she awoke with the taste of him still on her lips: day-old fish with stale tobacco in addition to that same body odour which dogs attracted after three days in the rain.

"I was wondering…" she murmured, but her attention meandered as they rattled past a mansion with lamps strewn across its façade, their glow highlighting blood-red window frames and a doorman the size of Wales, sparkling laughter floating from within. "Is that the Prince's?"

"Yes."

"Could we stop off and–"

"On a list of 'Undertakings That A Lady Should Never Contemplate', ale-houses and attending a prizefight dressed as a nefarious footpad on the prowl are in the top ten, with that gambling hell at number two."

She sniffed and speculated on number one. "I was wondering then…" She bit her lip, knew he could disemploy her for this little request, but nevertheless tonight was her moment to venture into unchartered waters. "W-would you grant me one kiss?"

Silence was not exactly what she'd expected.

Even a startled *No* would have been more appreciated, but instead a shaming hush filled the carriage.

A silence so silent it almost hummed.

Kissing must be number one on that list then.

She'd foolishly thought an attraction sparked between them, but it must all be within her fervid imagination. It had painted false pictures that this compelling man would find her yellow plumage attractive, and an odd despair filled her.

Never had she imagined wanting another's lips upon hers after her betrothed's slobbers or another's touch after his creeping fingers.

Now she did – but apparently the feeling was not reciprocated.

She twisted to stare out at the theatres of Haymarket –

gaudy dresses and lit Doric entrances, gentlemen laughing and dogs barking, laughter and life.

"N-never mind," she stuttered, and fervently hoped that Mr Hawkins had quaffed enough ale to forget.

SETH'S RESTRAINT and self-control remained legendary within the prizefighting world.

Never one for rousing to turbulent anger or succumbing to ploys of provocation.

Yet one plea from Miss Griffin and he longed to wildly haul her from that seat to his lap, to grasp her slender nape and ravenously kiss her until her lips were torrid red, all restraint unleashed.

Silence remained his sole protection, fingers gripping the seat to prevent them from reaching out, his teeth gritted and body taut as before a fight.

At last he allowed his gaze to cover her. A mere shadow in the corner, but passing lamplight caught her features and never had he seen such dejection: lips pressed, eyes unseeing, brow furrowed.

He could not bear it.

"Miss Griffin, I have always deplored arrogant nobles who take advantage of their maids, so what kind of man would I be to kiss my governess in an enclosed carriage when she'd no means of escape?"

He sensed her turn.

"If I were not your governess, if I was simply an independent widow, or a barmaid at liberty, would you have acquiesced to my request?"

"But you are not–"

"Pretend, Mr Hawkins," she said stridently. "What would you have done?"

Seth swallowed. He could lie, say he had no desire for sherry eyes behind golden-framed spectacles, that he preferred the barmaid in The Red Lion, that a pocket Venus was not to his taste.

Yet a bitterness coated his tongue and heart at the thought.

He was an honest man.

"I would have tangled my fingers in your silken hair and ravished your lips with mine till breath ceased for want of one another."

There, that might silence her delectable mouth for once.

"I resign," she said huskily.

"I beg your pardon?"

"I resign from your employ. I wish you to ravish my lips, Mr Hawkins, therefore if my status as governess is the lone reason for your refusal, then I shall resign. A kiss won't take long, will it? And you can reinstate me a few moments after."

The saucy wench.

A kiss could last for hours or whole nights. And her forthright assertion of want melted his resolve like morning mist before the warming sun.

"Why do you wish me to kiss you?" he hoarsely asked, fingers uncurling. Did she solely desire the pugilist for his protection and brawn...or the man beneath?

"Gosh, you do talk a lot. But to answer... Because you are thoughtful and kind and gentle. You perceive...me. The true me."

Naught to do with his brawn there.

"And," she added, "because I wish to feel your mighty *pectoralis major* press against me."

At least it was last on her list, he'd take that, so he hastily lifted himself, hunching in the close confines and twisting to sit beside her.

She squeaked as he removed her spectacles and cupped her cheek, the motion of the carriage nudging their bodies close, then closer. He brushed a thumb across her skin – silken and warm.

This was an exceedingly bad idea.

"I accept your resignation, Miss Griffin," he murmured nonetheless, slanting to her, the scent of flowers in his nostrils, head and heart. "And you must call me Seth."

The carriage lurched and their lips neared, breaths mingling... His entire body suffused with blistering desire and–

A finger pressed to his lips. Soft but undeniable.

"Just one matter."

"Yes?"

"Without tongue, if you please."

Speechless, he stilled.

"When my rancid betrothed attempted to kiss me, you see, he inserted his tongue. I later discovered he had a French grandmother, but being Anglo-Saxon, I assume you will refrain. However just in case–"

"Why don't you reserve judgement, Miss Griffi–"

"And perhaps you ought to call me Matilda," she gabbled on. "And perhaps I ought to–"

He kissed her.

Keep it gentle, he scolded himself, *don't scare her,* despite her lips being sweet temptation and bitter joy, hops and meadows, spring and summer.

Thus he maintained the kiss at tame and exploratory, their mouths merely caressing, brushing and tasting.

As he'd so wished to do since Matilda Griffin had marched into his study with her bold plan, he slipped a hand into her sleek hair, scattered pins and drove her nearer, breasts teasing his chest as the carriage jolted along the cobbled street.

All might have been fine; it may well have ended there; he would have drawn back.

But her hand clasped his shoulder and then climbed till her fingers twisted in the short hair at his nape, nails lightly scratching, yanking him close and crushing their lips together.

Ferocious need erupted, spiralling his control and grinding it to dust.

He hauled her tight, a hand to her curvaceous rump so that she half-straddled him, a scalding heat upon his thigh, and he kissed down her neck, nipped her throat, the shadows a colluding partner to his endeavour.

Guilt should have arisen, but her gasping breaths and breathy moans urged him on.

"Seth…"

And likewise, he growled her name against her skin as those small hands explored his chest, tugging at his neckcloth.

She was a twisting flame within his arms and he claimed her mouth once more. Her lips parted and without heed or thought, he thrust his tongue, tasted.

Then cursed as she stiffened.

Then groaned as she softened, allowing him in.

Slender fingers kneaded his chest, stroked his throat, and somehow her fulsome breast came to be in his palm, but no resistance was offered as he caressed and stroked, only a heartfelt moan and tip of hips.

Heaven help him, he wanted it all. To tug at her saffron bodice, rip at her ribbons, yank up her skirts and pull her fully astride, to sink inside and possess her.

To ravish the proper, passionate and beautiful Miss Matilda Griffin…

So…he slowed his kiss, covered her grasping hands with his own, halted their roaming and instead turned his thoughts to being belted in the mug by Jack Scroggins.

Matilda Griffin had wanted to erase the memory of her previous kiss, he knew that. She'd enjoyed her evening and sought to continue her adventure, but he must now be the one to draw it to a close.

They turned a corner and moonlight stole into the carriage. She goggled, lips moist and eyes wide in wonder, and the devil on his shoulder stabbed him in the groin and asked why the hell he was halting.

"Matilda, I am but a man and such…desire can only lead to…" Unaware of her knowledge concerning carnal matters, his words stumbled to naught.

"I am fully conversant, Seth," she said huskily, "with the mating habits of warm-blooded mammals."

But not of a man with blood ablaze and body primed.

Seth garnered all his scattered restraint. "Then you know why we must stop, Matilda." He found her spectacles and replaced them on her nose. "I reinstate you as governess."

She drew away to the corner and his own body shuddered with the rip in contact, yet he dragged himself to the opposite seat.

"I accept and thank you for reinstating me, Mr Hawkins."

"My pleasure, Miss Griffin."

Yet with that kiss, all had changed – at least for him – and he watched as she attempted to pin her hair with fingers aquiver, sliding strands capturing the moonlight.

He knew not where this may lead, or even if Miss Griffin desired further adventure, but he would pursue it nonetheless – this passion and like-mindedness.

In truth, they'd known each other scarce weeks, and he still recalled the pain of a tattered heart, sliced open by the wrong choice. The wound had knitted through time but like his scarred eyebrow, a faint ache endured, forever reminding him to act with caution.

He would discover more of her dreams and fears, and equally he would divulge more of himself.

"You must think me brazen, Mr Hawkins," she murmured, catching his eye.

"No, Miss Griffin. I think you a bewitching lady."

And therein lay a part of his dilemma.

The lady and the pugilist?

It sounded like the title for some lurid tale of absconding lovers, wicked nobles, romantic dinners, threatening relatives and a chase at the finale.

He'd revealed a little of his past, but not enough – the violence which had driven him, the brutality he'd endured in order to achieve his dreams. He had nigh ten years on Miss Griffin and a daughter to boot.

But perchance, there was one way he could show her his life. A stage on which was portrayed his background, the struggle and the years gone by.

"Miss Griffin," he drawled low, "have you ever dressed as a nefarious footpad on the prowl?"

CHAPTER FOURTEEN

"The diseases of the school-room are, principally, indolence, carelessness, sluttishness of person, fits of grandeur."

Private Education: A Practical Plan for the Studies of Young Ladies. Elizabeth Appleton. 1815.

"Jus' have some hot crumpets," Betty soothed, thrusting a plateful across the schoolroom table.

Blobs of butter liquefied into the crumpet holes, and Matilda closed her eyes to the sight.

Mr Hawkins had been in error last night. The god Thor wasn't beating upon her head with a hammer. No, he was trudging about her belly in hobnail boots, roiling her innards and causing perfectly wonderful crumpets to be scarcely beholdable.

"Thank you but no." Matilda drew a deep breath and pushed the plate towards Chloe, who sat beside her. "You have them, dear." She clasped her fingers together. "I don't know how people can drink ale. It causes a terrible upset within."

Betty shrugged. "Well, ale's cheap, cleanish and Ma fed it to me as a babe, so I s'pose me belly is used to it, whereas yer were a virgin last night."

Quite.

And still was, as far as Matilda understood the parlance.

But somehow her ale-house excursion had become known to all and sundry, despite her tip-toed progress up the stairs upon their return.

"So..." Betty mumbled, helping herself to a biscuit. "Wot did yer want all this crinkum-crankum brought up for?"

They all stared at the "crinkum-crankum" upon the mahogany trolley: a filigree silver tray was laid with the Hawkins household's finest bone-china tea service comprising tea caddy, mote skimmer, hot water pot, teapot, three teacups upon saucers, jug of milk, sugar pot with tongs and three silver teaspoons.

"We are to have an etiquette lesson on how one prepares tea. For if a duchess came to call, for example."

Betty pulled out a chair and seated herself.

"Miss Griffin..." Chloe chewed her lip, nose scrunched. "I've been making tea since I could reach the kettle."

"I know, but society ladies have certain rules that must be adhered to. Now," Matilda daintily grasped the silver mote skimmer and held it aloft. "This has many uses, but one is to place the tea leaves into the pot." And she carefully measured out two spoonfuls. Then added another – strong tea cured all ills. "Next we add the hot water with a steady hand, ensuring there is no uncouth gurgling. Replace the lid. Then the hostess leaves it to steep whilst she and her guests converse upon a pleasant subject."

They all looked at one another.

Pursed their lips.

Stared at the teapot.

"So did yer have a rollickin' time of it last night?" asked Betty. "Yer look a dab peaky."

Matilda twisted to Chloe. "The weather being a suitable subject."

"Bit dull though," bemoaned her charge. "Can't we talk about last night and–"

"I believe the tea has steeped sufficiently for the purposes of this demonstration." Matilda leaned forward to grip the pot. "I shall serve my own and then you may duplicate my action. The tea is always poured first. Balanced and slow to maintain the leaves at the bottom of the pot and to prevent drippage upon the saucer."

Betty sniffed. "But why take yer to a bowsing ken of all places? Thought Mr H had more breedin'."

Matilda scrabbled for the mote skimmer once more. "Now, any leaf remnants can be removed with this, hence the fine holes. And then milk is added afterwards. Without exception afterwards."

Chloe peered into the cup. "I like to add the milk first. Did Pa behave himself?"

Matilda swooped upon a stray tealeaf. "Adding the tea first warms the cup so one does not serve it cold. However, too hot and it may crack the bone china. 'Tis a delicate balance."

"So Pa didn't behave himself then?"

Narrowing her eyes at the innocent smile of Beelzebub's progeny, Matilda folded her arms. "Now, if one requires sugar, one should use the tongs and never, *never* fingers."

Betty sniffed again. "The maid next door said it were gone midnight when yer returned."

"Now, let us see you pour the tea without spillage."

"And that yer hair were a bit...windswept."

Enough was enough.

"To correct any misapprehensions, it was my own request to attend such an establishment in order to study the detrimental effects of liquor and to apprehend its behavioural consequences. Any...peakiness is entirely due to the ingredients within Porter Ale, which I am convinced does not merely contain barley and hops. During the course of the evening, needless to say, my coiffure...loosened, a natural outcome of the humid atmosphere within an abode of beer. And furthermore," she declared, "Mr Hawkins was the perfect gentleman throughout."

Chloe nodded. "Good. And of course, you would've been a perfect lady. No doubt about that."

Matilda swallowed.

No one is wicked all at once; but becomes so, step by step. A favoured juicy adage of Miss Appleton, but had not Matilda been wicked all at once?

She'd desired Mr Hawkins' kiss, yearned for his touch – to experience the strange sensation of both freedom and protection he evoked.

And what a kiss.

A torrid heat rose in her chest as she reminisced... The exquisite moment his lips had altered from tentative to forceful, the manner in which he'd dragged her aloft, those hefty hands snaking through her hair, calloused grip caressing her waist, the feel of him beneath – sturdy thighs and robust chest.

And she couldn't even begin to describe the moment he'd pressed with his tongue.

Well, she could, actually. Silken, intimate and...needful.

But then he'd halted.

Most men, she assumed, might have taken advantage, and

doubtless if she had responded to her betrothed's bungling kiss – and now with the benefit of comparison, she realised it *had* been bungling – she would have been flat on her back behind the potted palm.

She shuddered anew, and Betty patted her hand. "I'll cook yer up some tripe tonight, that'll put yer to rights. And mebbe some stew. Ma always swore that a good dose of Porter Ale in a stew softened gristly meat within the hour."

Matilda narrowed her eyes at the troublesome twosome as Chloe's lips jiggled and Betty innocently batted her lashes.

Then laughter and hugs erupted between the three of them, shared and teasing.

Such closeness this family had, such *joie de vivre*. There may be no expensive butler or footmen trimming the candles, but happiness and love filled their home.

Wiping mirthful eyes with her apron, Betty rose from the sofa. "I'd best be off. Mr H is in a rare mood this morning. Keeps whistling."

Chloe nodded. "And he chose a fine blue waistcoat instead of his normal day-wear brown without my guidance."

Two pairs of eyes impaled Matilda but the churning of her stomach prevented a flush to her cheeks, so she smiled with Betty-like innocence.

"Perhaps, Chloe, he is merely looking forward to reading your thousand-word essay entitled 'The Quilling of Tea Caddies: Theory and Practice'. Or perchance, Betty, he is merry in anticipation of tomorrow's fulsome breakfast picnic being readied for our departure at seven of the morn?"

Chloe groaned, Betty groaned, and Matilda sipped her perfect tea.

SETH WHISTLED. Then caught himself.

In no way should he be so joyful. His weighing machine remained broken, Liam was to be stood before the magistrate for brawling, and the bloody awful weather this year was costing a fortune in coal for the boiler.

Indeed, nothing had altered just because he'd ruthlessly kissed Miss Griffin.

On the other hand, everything had.

She'd invaded his dreams for what had been left of the night: astride him in that bloody carriage, as dark as the cave in Bullock's Museum, her fingers wandering at leisure, lips pleading for more against his bared *pectoralis major*.

At dawn, he'd descended to the basement for an hour, which had vaguely woken him for the day but–

The five chimes of St James's faded and the door handle twisted.

"Pa?"

"Come in, Chloe."

She pottered over, but her shoulders were rounded, lips glum. This wasn't his girl.

"What's wrong, pet?"

She clambered onto the bed, crossed her legs and looked grouchy. "I've been punching the straw figures you set up for me in the ballroom but…. All I could think was…for what? All this practising I do. What's it for if I don't end up being another Stokes?"

"Ah, Chloe." He sat alongside and gave her a hug, yet a thought had been lingering for a day or so… "You can be whoever you want, of course, and this may seem an odd suggestion, but… You remember the Duke of Rothwell?"

His daughter nodded, jutting out her lower lip.

"Well, he mentioned the idea of an academy for ladies, with the focus on defence."

Her blond mop cocked to one side. "What do you mean?"

"Well..." How to explain? "What would happen if two villains accosted you in an alley?"

"I'd squeal and pretend to be a weak-kneed damsel, then when they were close enough, slam one a poke to the belly followed by a mitt to the sneezer. The other would see stars after my nobbler to the noddle and a stamp on the old dew beaters. Then with a culp to the lughole, I'd scarper. After maybe a clicker to the gob."

"Excellent, although a clicker to the throat might have downed one quicker and required less force."

She nodded. "Hmm."

"Now, what would your governess have done?"

This idea had coalesced after Miss Griffin had mentioned that the simple knowledge of how to protect herself imbued her with more confidence, and Seth of all people knew that was half the battle. If you scuttled through the streets in fright, the cats came out to play. If you stalked chin high, they may just think better of it.

Chloe tapped a lip. "Miss Griffin would end up with her skirts over her head. Most likely her throat slit. Which would be a shame, as I adore Miss Griffin."

Seth winced.

"Indeed... So, she needs someone to teach her how to defend herself. I cannot do it, propriety and all that, and in any case, many women would not be comfortable with a man demonstrating."

"But it's not ladylike."

"No. It is not seen as such, but I suspect in private that many, like Miss Griffin, would very much like to learn some basic techniques."

"Hmm. Do you think I could?"

"Of course you could. But it also depends on your

aspirations, Chloe. This would not be in a public arena with applauding masses, medals and prize money, but for personal satisfaction, passing your knowledge on and helping other women. Not only with defensive techniques but also the focus of one's mind. All similar to what I do in the Academy, I suppose."

"I've never taught anything before."

"You are only thirteen–"

"Fourteen in November."

"Quite. And this is merely an idea at this stage for when you're older. But if you wished to try teaching, then I suggest you begin with Miss Griffin. Just some basic essentials for escaping a ruffian in the streets."

"With thumping?"

"With the most effective incapacitation for a sharpish scarper." And he winked.

His daughter giggled, doldrums shifting as fast as Hopping Ned's toes. "Yes. Yes, I think I could teach that. I'll ask her if she'd like to attend a lesson. Now, which waistcoat are you wearing for dinner?"

"I can't, pet. The chap's coming to fix the weighing machine." The mood swung to grouchy again. "But we are all going to the prizefight together on the morrow."

"But *you* told me..." She stabbed him with a governess glare exactly akin to Miss Griffin's. "That ladies do not attend fights."

"Your governess won't be attending as a lady but as a nefarious footpad on the prowl. It was all Kian's suggestion to take her, anyhow."

"Ah." Chloe nodded sagely as though all was explained. "And I suppose she couldn't refuse him. Not with those blue eyes of his."

Seth scowled and crossed to the wardrobe to throw on a

loose jacket. "And I suppose mine are a boring brown?"

"I asked Miss Griffin today what colour she considered your eyes, and do you know what she said?"

"I have no wish to know." He'd learned with Chloe that if he wanted to know something, it was better to deny it.

"Oh. I shan't tell you then."

Perhaps he'd done it too often. "Daughter of mine?" And he produced *that* look of fathers.

Chloe grinned. "She said they were a mysterious mixture of spring's nature and autumn's earth."

Seth scratched his chin. "Is that good?"

His daughter rolled her eyes. "If we notice, we notice. If we don't, they are mere brown."

"Oh, I see." He didn't.

His daughter sighed that ancestral sigh of generations of womenfolk...and tutted for good measure. "What colour are Miss Griffin's, Pa? A mere brown?"

"Gads, no. An elegant mixture of brandy and sherry and...my amber stickpin." Oh, he did see. "Chloe, you are frighteningly perceptive when you want to be."

"Hmm. I obviously didn't inherit that from you."

Cheeky blighter, and she shrieked as his cravat landed on her head, whilst deep inside Seth, a glow kindled.

He'd avoided Miss Griffin this day, not seeking to crowd her, not wishing to know if her memories had been drowned in Porter Ale or if her request had solely come from an impulse for adventure.

Yet with Chloe's disclosure about his eyes, surely she felt...something.

MATILDA FELT RATHER DREADFUL.

Yawning, she plodded up the stairs with feet like dumb-bells and legs of lead weights, the late night and Porter Ale having, as Betty had succinctly put it, "done her in".

Dinner had been a quiet affair with just Chloe, although Matilda's appetite had returned, and they'd tucked into Betty's finest chicken and peas.

With such weariness, however, thoughts of wretchedness now prevailed…

Last night in the darkness of the carriage with ale and life coursing her veins, asking one's handsome employer for a kiss had seemed *such* a good idea.

Yet in the light of day, it seemed *such* a bad idea.

He must think her a harlot. One who had the responsibility of teaching his daughter morals and virtue.

Truly, she must strive to remember her chosen vocation and not become distracted by caring fighters with crooked noses and fiercely carnal hands, eyes and chest. And lips.

Mr Hawkins had acquiesced with her request for a kiss but never had he spoken of a need for anything more profound within his life, and so she should not expect further adventures.

Once Chloe no longer required a governess, Matilda would surely continue in her profession. By then, she'd have references and be retained by some aristocratic family as she'd always hoped… With starchy butlers and silent dinners, miserable servants and condescending noblemen.

Wretched thoughts indeed.

Arriving at her bedchamber door, she noticed a brown paper-bound parcel resting upon the floor, and lifting the neatly wrapped item, she hunted for a message.

Naught.

Frowning, she opened her chamber door and strolled

over to sit upon the bed, twisting the small package this way and that.

Vague tales of governesses receiving gifts of an unfavourable nature from their crop of charges rattled in her head – frogs, worms and suchlike. Yet surely Chloe was not that way inclined.

Miss Appleton would no doubt issue a sour command that the governess refuse such items for fear of bribery but…

Matilda could not remember the last time she had received a wrapped present.

Her parents had ceased gift giving when she'd attained the age of twelve, and they'd instead settled upon reading one another's favourite passages from books for birthdays and Christmas.

Which had been perfectly…nice.

Nevertheless, as she loosened the string, a curl of pleasure coursed. A new quill? A diary? No, too small.

The smooth brown paper rustled and she creased it back to reveal…

Three bars of her beloved Pears amber soap were stacked upon one another, her favourite scent of flowers assailing her.

A card slipped out.

May you never be without your English garden.
S. H.

The gift was forward and wicked, outrageously scandalous for a gentleman, and possibly the kindest thing anyone had ever done for her.

Matilda's eyes smarted as she stared at the simple blunt script of his handwriting.

Mr Seth Hawkins.

A man whose wits she'd considered at the interview to have been most likely knocked out in some prizefighting field. Whereas in fact she was the witless one to ever have judged him as such.

Astute, determined and kind. Those were the words to describe him by day.

Passionate, intense and sensual. Those were the words to describe him by night.

She smoothed a finger upon the transparent glycerine, slick and gentle against her skin, brought the soap close to her nose, inhaled...

Those thoughts of wretchedness faded.

And all of a sudden, she felt rather wonderful.

CHAPTER FIFTEEN

"Society you are not to expect."

Private Education: A Practical Plan for the Studies of Young Ladies.

Elizabeth Appleton. 1815.

High-perch yellow phaetons and rattling antique dogcarts, bakers with wares balanced upon their heads and pie sellers shouting loud. Scruffy lamplighters shoved in raucous collision with silk-clad gentlemen, and Matilda felt as though the world had turned upon its head.

One chock-full of merriment, jostle and noise, but also scrawny lads with thieving fingers, bosky gents clutching bottles of gin, ladies of doubtful virtue flashing their pink petticoats and girls flicking mud with their toes.

Her heart pounded with this rhythm of life. Frantic, as though the now had to be enjoyed before it was all too late.

"Matilda?"

In utter bemusement, she stared up at Mr Hawkins, or Seth, as they'd agreed for their day out.

"Yes?"

"You must stay close and preferably not answer if anyone speaks to you. We cannot link arms as it will appear… peculiar." And he twitched her nefarious footpad's hood to obscure her brow.

For once, she was glad of the muffler and cloak as the day had dawned a bitter blue, although the cold had made no difference to the mob mingling on Wimbledon Common in every mode of dress.

"I shall. But…where did all these people come from? There must be thousands."

He grinned and shrugged. "From all walks of life. We'll return to the carriage to watch the fight with Chloe and Kian, but let's wander the field a little first. I'll show you the ring whilst it's quiet."

Quiet?

Wimbledon Common had been transformed.

A square platform had been erected in the middle of the Common, two feet off the ground and encircled by wooden posts with ropes slung between them, empty but for two boys who scattered wood chips upon the boards.

Outside this platform was a wider grassed area, also fenced from the Common, where groups of men strutted, and…was that not the Earl of Farleigh, whom she'd once danced with at a ball?

Together, they squashed through the hustling mob beyond, towards this fenced area, and she grabbed Seth's coat-tails in order not to lose him.

"Harry?" Seth shouted to a bulky man with a dog. "Can we come through?"

"Well, burn me breeches, if it ain't Seth Hawkins! Always room for you, lad." And the two shook hands, a wooden gate opening for their entrance.

The man peered strangely at Matilda and she peered strangely back.

She'd gone without petticoats so the cloak fell in a straight line to her sturdy boots – the donning of breeches having thankfully not been mentioned anew as surely they must chafe. A muffler covered her mouth, a cap her hair and then the cloak's hood covered the lot.

All in all, she did indeed resemble a nefarious footpad on the prowl.

So she quite fitted in with this motley assemblage of persons.

The fellow sloped off to inspect the posts and Seth guided her to one side.

"That's Harry, does all the ropes, and this area is where the backers, friends and umpires stand. It also keeps the crowd back…a bit. They stay on the outside, but at Wimbledon there's also a paying stand with seats, which is rare."

She lowered her muffler a mite and observed the packed wooden scaffold which supported benches six rows deep. "Why is it rare?"

"Matilda…" And she twisted back to catch Seth's amused grin. "You do realise prizefighting is against the law?"

"What! No!" *Gosh.* "I'm at an illegal event! How thrilling. But what if the local magistrate finds out?"

"You can ask him. He's sitting in the second row of the stand. The bigwig in brown. Fights are never scheduled as such, the time and location spread by rumour so that the shoulder-clappers don't find us."

With eyes wide, she tugged Seth's coat and raised herself on tiptoes to see. "And that's Lord Farleigh, is it not? Next to the magistrate."

"He's the sponsor, a bang-up fellow. It's a hundred-pound purse today for the winner."

"Well, he can't waltz for a sixpence. Trod on my foot thrice."

A snort and they took a turn around the grassed area as though gentlefolk in a drawing room. Many acquaintances nodded at Seth or clapped him on the back, and although he wore elegant clothing, including a pale-blue waistcoat with intricate paisley pattern and bright gold buttons, he fitted in – his breadth commanding respect and his fighting past their admiration.

Clothed in the finest of green silk jackets, a tall black-skinned gentleman warmly shook hands with Seth, and it seemed to Matilda they made a small wager.

Was that lawful at an unlawful event?

The fellow nodded at her, winked, and then strode away with a swagger, his stature cutting a swathe through the mingling groups.

Matilda beamed. "Is that gentleman from the African continent? I would adore to travel there. What part is he from?"

"New York, I believe."

Matilda blinked.

"That's Bill Richmond, a fellow champion who also fought with me before the Heads of State last year, yet he was born into slavery. Took me under his wing a bit when I first started. Told me the golden rule is to focus and not let anger fuel you. An extraordinary man. Retired now but beat Shelton only two years back – a chap half his age."

A finger to her chin gently closed her mouth.

"Prizefighting is open to all ages, trades and nationalities. The sole requirements are being able to fight and having a motivation to succeed." His brow furrowed. "And I'd imagine slavery provides plenty of that."

"You must think me very unworldly, Mr… Seth."

Fingers raised her muffler but then abandoned her skin after the slightest caress.

"No, Miss… Matilda, I think you enchanting."

A coiling warmth dispelled any chill that lingered from the bitter dawn. *Enchanting.* Was she really? The word garnered images of delicate fairies and seductive mermaids, not a loquacious nitterwit who wore yellow.

They strolled on and she gawked at the array of folk gathering at the outer fence – shabby coats rubbing with silks, the beaver hats of the Corinthians bashing the slouched caps of farmers.

Seth abruptly hastened his stride. "Apologies, but we'd best head back to the carriage as the fighters will soon be making their entrance. Then the mayhem ensues."

They retraced their steps through Harry's gate and battled through laughing lordlings and chortling ragamuffins, much like the scrum at a ball for supper, but soon she glimpsed the coaches encircling the melee, folk sat atop for the best vantage point, and even the trees beyond were leafed with lads.

"The followers are called the Fancy," Seth shouted, "be they lackeys or lords, although some say the swells are just the visitors and don't truly belong, that these fights are for the men of the streets and stews."

A gnarled fellow knocked into her, grunting his anger, before a broad-shouldered woman barged past with a bottle, and all at once, Matilda felt a little afraid, her feet stumbling in the churned grass, the crowd pushing and pulling.

Perchance she did not belong here either.

But a strong arm gripped low on her waist and pulled her from the hurly-burly to where the coaches were lined up cheek by jowl.

"I've got you, Matilda. Never fear."

FRIGHT WAS a rare emotion for Seth.

Yet as a ruffian and his bobtail had barrelled into the dainty frame of Matilda, it had clattered his pulse, and he'd asked himself what the hell he thought he was doing bringing a lady to a heathen fight in the middle of a bloody common.

As a rule, these contests began jovial enough, but frequent brawls broke out amongst the Fancy, pickpockets ran rife and the language spoken so ribald, he wished to clamp his hands to her ears.

Yet that was rather why she was here...

To experience his background.

Some said that although these events were illegal, the law turned a purposely blind eye. Better to allow the lower classes to rage without censure, having worked their fingers to the bone all week, than allow that rage to become revolution...*à la France.*

To Seth as a lad, it had all appeared so glamorous and thrilling, and let's be honest, it was better than attending a hanging, the only other event which garnered such a crowd.

"Are you well, Matilda? We can go home, if you wish?" Although they were hemmed in like geese at Christmastide.

"No! No, certainly not. I just...it's all so overwhelming. I've never seen the like."

"Pa!"

Seth twisted at the shout, finding Chloe and Kian

perched upon the coachman's seat of a carriage two up from his own. With gold trim and spanking wheels, this equipage was fit for a king, whereas in fact it belonged to John Jackson, one of Seth's rival boxing academy owners, who tipped his hat at them in greeting.

The bugger would no doubt cajole his daughter into parting with information – good luck with that, as she'd fed Jackson a right clanker concerning their fees the last time he'd tried.

A cheer surged then weaved through the crowd like a gust of wind through wheat, the thud of horses' hooves trembling the earth.

"What's happening?" Matilda yelled. "I can't see anything."

Seth flung himself to the coachman's pew of his carriage and aided her ascent, their hands clasping.

Once up, he grasped her by the shoulders. "Now, Matilda, this isn't gentlemanly or proper in the least, so please don't squeal." And he swept her into his arms – a featherweight.

No squealing ensued but rather she laughed and clasped him around the neck, fingers linking at his nape…caressing.

Bloody hell.

Every nerve and sinew urged him to fiercely kiss her, out here in the open, amongst friends, thieves and family, but she was dressed as a nefarious footpad, so instead with a lunge he flumped her onto the carriage roof behind.

Now she squealed. "I'll fall through!"

"It's been reinforced." He clambered up and rethought his words. "Not that you're heavy at all but it wouldn't have taken my weight. This is where we sit for the best view."

After tentatively prodding about, she settled, feet tucked to one side, propped on an arm yet leaning into him, their shoulders pressed together.

With the blowing of horns and clanging of bells, two

carriages appeared, four prads apiece, the first with a claret red postilion and fluttering silks tied to every conceivable corner. Nipping at its wheels came the second with a postilion dressed in Royal blue, silks strung along the bodywork.

"The combatants arrive in style. Dusty Dan is in blue and Rolls Roy in red."

"Fascinating. And the monikers? Does Dan cause his opponent to eat dust? And is Roy's main tactic to roll his opponent?"

He'd like to say yes as that was rather clever, but… "Dan's a dustman and Roy's a baker."

She huffed and shook her head before they both twisted back to the spectacle, the two warriors shaking hands within the ring whilst their seconds staked colours to the corners.

Then they stripped to no more than breeches, stockings and footwear.

"Oh, my!"

Seth now wished to clamp his hands over her eyes as the two men strutted for the crowd, flexing arm muscles with bare chests puffed. Matilda leaned so far forward she nigh plummeted from the carriage roof to the turf below.

"Enjoying it now, are we?" he grouched.

A mollifying pat of the hand did not mollify, but then she leaned close and whispered, "They are not as magnificent as you."

Which helped.

Somewhat.

"The two of them will come up to the scratch on the ground and take positions," he explained. The combatants bobbed on the spot with restless energy, loosening limbs and cracking knuckles – more for the crowd than themselves.

"How long do they fight for?" she enquired, eyes glued to the ring.

"Each round lasts until a man is knocked or thrown off his feet. Then a half-minute interval and back at it."

The umpire shouted and a roar shook the earth, surely heard from Land's End to John O'Groats.

"The rules are no butting, kicking, biting, gouging or pulling hair, although we still keep it trimmed, just in case. Jackson there," he scoffed, shoving a thumb to the gold-trimmed carriage two up from theirs, "pulled Mendoza's hair to win. The coxcomb."

Dusty Dan loosely bounced, known for his nifty feet, but Rolls Roy, famous for punching first and asking questions later, milled out a fist to Dusty's cheek and–

"Ow!" A bundle of feminine warmth thumped into his chest, hands clasping his cravat.

"Are you hurt?" He grasped her shoulder, afraid a missile had pelted her.

"No, but he hit him! The beast!"

Seth located her ear within the folds of her footpad's cloak, could feel a cold nose pressed to his chest. "Hitting is rather the point of it, Miss...Matilda."

OF COURSE SHE KNEW THAT – so raw and violent – yet caught up in the fervour of the crowd's enthusiasm, she'd forgotten the actual truth of one man punching another.

"How could you bear to be hit?" she asked, lifting her head till their lips were a mere barleycorn apart. Couldn't suffer to think of Seth being hurt in such a manner.

"'Twas worse in the old days, when the style was to merely stand still and get clobbered. Now at least, the idea is to dodge, weave and defend. But I admit, it is inevitable."

She focused on Seth's chin as he twisted back to the action.

Another crescendo of noise erupted and Matilda peeked from beneath the wool hood of her cloak just as Rolls hit the sawdust, blood seeping from beneath his eye, and she bundled her nose into Seth's waistcoat once more.

All in all, if she could stay buried in here for the entire contest, she could quite get to tolerating this fighting lark.

"Tell me what's happening," she garbled into blue silk. "I just don't wish to see it."

His chest juddered in laughter, all growly, and she groaned, burrowing deep.

"Both have gone to their corners. The bottleman looks soused so Dusty's helping himself to the gin."

"Gin! That's ridiculous."

"It helps the pain. Both men are back up to the scratch."

"And?"

She didn't wish to miss a thing. But equally didn't wish to see a thing.

"Dusty's let fly this time, first a brisket, now a rib tickler, but Rolls nips back, no mischief done. A left ogle by Rolls, but Dusty dodges and takes one to the chopper instead. An undercut and, uff, a whiffle to the smeller."

No idea, so Matilda decided to inhale deeply instead – leather, fresh linen and Mr Seth Hawkins.

Splendid.

"Oy, Dusty," her employer yelled. "Mill a plumper to 'is kissin' trap, yer calf's 'ead."

Honestly...

And what had befallen Seth's accent? She often wondered how a man brought up in the stews had come by his *Ton* diction. His accent did not exactly cut glass like a duke or earl's, but it certainly caused a profound scratch with its well-rounded vowels and crisp adroitness.

"Bleedin' 'ell! Dusty's eatin' dust."

Goodness. Was it time to go home?

"And 'es up again."

Botheration.

"And bleedin' down again."

Good grief.

Bursters, clippers, teasers and lots of claret, which could conceivably have been either wine or blood, who knew?

The fight continued and she had absolutely no idea what was happening.

What she did understand was that she liked this side of Seth Hawkins, without artifice and full of good cheer. Masculine, to be sure, yet not once had his arm departed from her lower waist. She enjoyed his rough-edged words and grumbling chest, the way his hand tightened when Dusty was toppled.

"Matilda?" That deep voice shivered her earlobe, if such a thing was possible.

"Hmm?"

"Why don't you try just watching their feet?" And with a gentle tug, he drew her from her burrow. "Focus on their footwork."

She did as requested, ignoring the jabbing fists and grunts of pain.

"Oh, it's like they are dancing."

"Good. And who do you think will win?"

She studied the fighters. Striped Stockings was lighter and niftier, dancing a lot. Plain White Stockings also bounced around but with more economical movement. "Plain," she announced. "Stripy will wear himself out."

"I agree. Dusty has the mettle but he's too raw. He'll learn..."

"Like you did?" And she met his eyes.

"Yes, exactly like I did."

"How many contests did you fight?"

"Too many smaller ones to mention. But like this?" He glanced towards the combatants. "Ten. And many men cannot do more than twelve majors. It...affects things."

"I shouldn't like to imagine you in the ring."

"'Twas my life, Matilda. For a decade." His hazel eyes returned, serious and focused. "To escape violence in my youth. To buy shoes for Chloe. To have food on the table."

"Not for the glory?"

"A man cannot stand before applauding thousands and not feel some sense of thrill, but ultimately no, and..." A roar and she lost him, his fist tightening at her waist. "Uff, Dusty got a mitten to the ivories."

From then on, Matilda concentrated upon the footwork of these men. She still disliked the hitting part but admired their tenacity and whatever drove them to continue.

From the safety of this carriage roof, she could survey the rackety devotees at her leisure.

Mostly of the male persuasion, they flapped hats and bellowed. Two staggering rogues attempted to enter the inner ring only to be whacked back with sticks, and Matilda's eyes widened as a woman was hoisted to a man's shoulders, stockings and more on display for all to see.

No perfumed society ladies sat watching, but upon the carts and carriages a few neat women peeped from behind splayed fingers – mothers, sisters and wives, she supposed.

Another rumble swept the crowd, and she glanced to the ring to see Stripy on the ground, arms and legs akimbo.

"Has he lost?"

"Depends if he gets up." And indeed, the poor man was dragged to the corner, gin splashed on his face and down his throat, slaps delivered to his cheeks. "But Dusty's the local boy, so..."

Disgruntled yells boomed, and the enthusiasts upon the seated grandstand all stood as one in outrage, fists shaking and...

Matilda drew breath as she noted the entire construction wobble, tip and then–

"Seth, the stand!" she cried, kneeling up.

The scaffold gave way, slipping as though built upon reeds, tumbling bodies, one upon another. Cries and grunts.

"Bloody hell," Seth bellowed, clambering down before aiding her own descent to the grass. "Wait in the carriage, Matilda, and don't move. Scream if anyone comes near. Jackson is just there. I'll be back in a jiffy."

Not inclined to argue, she yanked the door and scrambled inside, noticed Chloe being bundled within Mr Jackson's carriage before he gave them a nod, and then Seth and Mr Finlay sprinted to the fallen bodies.

From the window, she was surprised to see a few of the stand's occupants rising to their feet, dusting off jackets and...chortling.

As she settled back into the squabs, Matilda pondered the disparity between this world and that of the *Ton*. Here everyone pitched in when misfortune struck, rushing to another's aid. In society, a mere unintended *faux pas* could see you shunned and gossiped about with malice, the stylish events a perpetual competition, be it for the latest decor, cuisine or duke.

She knew that not all the *Ton* were so heartless, that many good people existed, but within such a stifled world, some lost sight of what remained important. The steps to a dance became more worthy than kindness, the right ribbons more essential than charity, a titled marriage more vital than love...

The carriage door flew open.

"Is everyone safe, Se–"

"Hullo, Cousin." And Astwood seated himself opposite, crossing his legs and slapping the dust from his yellow pantaloons.

CHAPTER SIXTEEN

"For nothing so much shows us our degree of merit as the behaviour we meet with in the world."

PRIVATE EDUCATION: A PRACTICAL PLAN FOR THE STUDIES OF YOUNG LADIES. ELIZABETH APPLETON. 1815.

"I reckon Chloe and myself might head to Gunter's for an ice," Kian declared as they ambled through the crowds and back to the carriages. "Let yer have some time alone with yer bonnie Miss Griffin."

"Not you as well," Seth grumbled. "What's wrong with you all?"

"Begone with yer." Kian halted his stride and cocked his head. "Over the years, we've all seen yer work nose to the grindstone and so deserve some pleasure in life. That lass gives yer a look that could butter parsnips, and I canna help but notice yer own lingering glances, and never have I seen yer in such a grouch when Rufus dallied at the dinner, and then in the ale-house when–"

"I hear you," Seth griped as they continued once more wending their way through the parting hordes with no trouble whatsoever – which was often the case when Kian wore the insignia black feather of the Prince tucked in his hatband, "but you are ignoring the fact that she is a *Ton* lady and I'm a–"

"Successful owner of a boxing academy. With how many dukes clamouring for membership?"

"We will see," Seth murmured, not inclined to continue the conversation. "Didn't you arrive with Jackson?"

"Och, no. I filched a scarlet affair of the Prince's and left it on the edge of the Common for a swift exit."

Jackson's carriage came into view first, gold wheels glinting in the sunlight, Chloe's blond mop hanging out the window.

"Fancy an ice, wee bairn?" called Kian.

His daughter glared. "I'm not wee. I'm not a bairn. I'm fourteen in November." Nevertheless, she tumbled out the door in eagerness.

"Seth'll see yer governess home safe and sound, won't yer Seth?" And Kian flipped a wink as he put an arm around Chloe's shoulders.

"I know he will. A perfect gentleman, my pa." His daughter likewise winked before the troublesome twosome wandered off to be swallowed by the departing crowds.

On the journey this morning, Chloe and her governess had gaily chatted within the carriage whilst Seth had sat atop to take the reins. Now, without his daughter, Matilda could sit up high with him – feel the exhilaration of bowling down the Wimbledon lanes, feel the quickening breeze in her hair, like the feathered birds she so adored.

Seth nodded his thanks at Jackson, who tipped his hat like a gentleman, and Seth strode to his own carriage to tug open the door. "No one was hurt, can you believe? That magistrate was chuckling his pantaloons off."

No answer was forthcoming.

In fact, Matilda had failed to even turn from staring out the far window. Her hood remained drawn back, cap abandoned upon the floor.

"I apologise for leaving you, but..."

She twisted and his guts heaved.

Tears such as he had never seen coursed down her cheeks in silvery tracks, glasses strewn to the seat cushion, hair dishevelled and lips bitten red.

"Matilda! What the hell's happened? Has someone hurt you?" He surged up the step, sat at her side, unsure what to do or if to touch her, but he clutched an arm and she fell into him like a ship to dock, her hands gripping and body shuddering.

Hell and damnation, he never should have left her. Had some ruffian forced his way in? But surely Chloe or Jackson would've heard a scream?

"Matilda?"

"I wasn't going to... But I can't not... And I don't know..."

He enfolded her within his embrace.

"Hold me so tight," she cried. "I beg you."

So he complied, arms clasping her, breasts crushed to his chest. She appeared unhurt but...

"Did someone enter the carriage?"

A nod, and his dread erupted into a dangerous fury. He'd tear London asunder to find whoever...

"Did this person...touch you?"

A shake of the head. "Astwood," she wailed. "He saw me. Recognised my glasses. Followed me. Saw me sit atop with you."

With firm hands, he stroked her hair and lifted her chin. "What did he want?"

She twisted away, sobbed, but he waited.

"He spat I was a whore coming here, thinks I'm your mistress, and that if I don't return tonight and wed Sidlow, he's going to say you were bribed to lose fights, drive away all your patrons and then burn your Academy to the ground."

"Matilda–"

"I couldn't bear it. You've worked so hard. To survive this life and to succeed. You're magnificent. And Chloe too, no harm must ever befall her. I'll pack my bags and leave."

Seth fell still.

Which was all wrong because his fury at Astwood should have surged unchecked.

But...

A blanket of satisfaction had dampened the violent emotion.

Because Miss Matilda Griffin sought to protect him.

Him.

She'd return to that pathetic excuse for a man because she knew how hard Seth had worked to escape this life of poverty. How much the Academy meant to him...

With gentle thumbs, he dried beneath her eyes, clasped her cheeks and kissed her.

No option or thought. Just downright need.

Controlled but insistent, intimate then rough.

He groaned, tugged her close, no notion to cease.

For Miss Matilda Griffin was scratching at his heart, provoking no pain, only thrumming fervour and boundless anticipation. The taste of sober tears, her eager lips, the wild fingers which scratched his nape. She thrust nearer, the scent of her everywhere, yearning and frantic. Intense desperation seemed to grip her as she devoured him, and he could do naught but respond as a gasp escaped her.

And yet…

That gasp alerted his senses and stalled his roving fingers.

Matilda's touch was too turbulent, her kiss too frenzied, as though there was no tomorrow, no time but now to explore their passion.

And then he realised… Realised that Matilda believed this would be their last embrace. That she would be returning to her guardian or marrying Sidlow.

That they would never again kiss like this – with breath seized from their lungs, neither giving a damn.

How wrong she was.

Still clasping her cheeks, he drew away.

"Matilda, you are not returning to Astwood."

"But he'll–"

"I've never lost a major fight, so how could I have been bribed to lose? And my patron was a well-respected earl, a stickler who did not stand for duplicity amongst his fighters."

"But…"

"I have three dukes as Academy members – in fact, four now – who will not leave because some viscount spouts twaddle."

"But…"

"And my principal investor, the man who came to me after I'd won the championship, is the Prince."

"I don't understand?"

"If Astwood dared to lay a finger on my Academy, the Prince would burn *him* to the ground." He shook his head. "Some precautions won't go amiss but what I am trying to convey, Matilda, is that I have allies. Powerful allies in all walks of society." He willed her to believe him with his gaze. "Astwood would not dare touch us."

MATILDA GASPED.

Us.

So short a word, and yet it filled her with a sense of resolve and strength.

As a young girl, she'd been a solitary creature obliged to learn matters for herself, and now, as a woman, she'd been forced to fend for herself against a male guardian who sought to sell her as a commodity.

Seth's utter disdain for Astwood's threats might have belittled and undermined her past struggles, but instead that *us* acknowledged and included her.

"But I am so much trouble to you and your family," she blurted, swiping a hand over her no doubt reddened nose. "I thought I had my future planned but... I wish I were a man some days as a woman's future is forever in someone else's hands."

"No. It is in yours, Matilda. But there is no weakness in seeking help. I could not have built the club without my friends and family." He kissed her hair, forehead and eyes. "Once Astwood is no longer your guardian, you can be anything: continue as governess, join a science expedition to the Moluccas, become a famed actress or marry...whoever you wanted to...if you so wished."

She lifted her lashes, had never seriously considered herself marriageable for her own worth. After all, her dowry was squandered, her conversation dull and this spinster profession chosen. But being held within comforting arms and having a handsome ex-prizefighter kiss you to irrational absurdity sent one's own notions scattering like foxglove seed.

"I…if you are sure I would cause no trouble?"

"Of course I am sure, Matilda, but are you?" He traced the outline of her lip. "This is not the bold and brave governess that I have come to know and…kiss. Why become so missish now?"

Yes, why?

She was acting the pathetic goosecap because…

Not because Astwood had found her or threatened her; those threats she could stomach as she had done so in the past.

No, it was because he had threatened Seth – her mighty and caring Seth – his livelihood, friends and his beautiful daughter.

She'd imagined his Academy up in flames, patrons fleeing like rats.

When had it happened that it pained her more if anything should happen to Mr Hawkins and his family rather than to herself?

And what did it signify?

"You are utterly correct." She wiped her eyes on his cravat and then flapped her fingers on the seat behind to encounter her glasses, before sliding them back on. "Unless he comes with a magistrate, which would surely take some time, he cannot force me to return or to marry."

A nod. "And if that happens, Matilda, then we plan anew."

We.

Not weakened but shored and strengthened. By a man who offered both protection and freedom.

No longer alone.

She evened her breath, reclaimed her spirit stolen by her cousin and beamed up at Seth. "Where's Chloe?"

"Kian has taken her for ices. Heaven help his pockets as she can eat till the waiters weep."

"So... It's just us then."

A smile so wicked the devil must envy it encased his lips. "Exactly so. And now the prizefight is over and Astwood has seen you anyhow..." He unclasped her cloak at the neck and thrust it from her shoulders. "No longer the nefarious footpad on the prowl but the bold and brave Miss Matilda Griffin, governess to the fairly rich and not-so-idle. Ride up top with me? I promise you will gain the wings to feel free as a swift in flight."

"Why yes, I would like that, Mr Seth Hawkins," she replied in kind. "And may I take the reins? I've never done so, you see, and you did say I should not be missish."

"Did I say that?" His eyes expressed mock shock as he descended the steps and held out a hand. "And if so, surely I did not mean taking command of a man's horses. I am undone."

Seizing that hand, she watched his eyes darken to walnut and leaf as she stepped down, witnessed his throat bob. "Something awry, Mr Hawkins?"

"I truly *am* undone," he said gruffly, waving a hand at her skirts. "The sunshine..."

She squinted down. Without her cloak and likewise petticoats, the weak sun shone through her nankeen skirts to reveal the outline of her legs, the material scandalously clinging to her rump and hips.

Shame ought to have descended, a moral outrage at the impropriety; she ought to have scuttled back into the carriage with a dismayed gasp.

Matilda jumped to the ground in abandon. "You promised I'd gain wings. A promise I intend to hold you to."

That feeling...that feeling of life and excitement and

sheer joy surged through her veins. And she knew that it was Seth Hawkins who'd placed it there – with his scalding kiss, his infectious confidence and his limitless fun.

She scampered up to the carriage seat, not caring that her skirts rose to bare her ankles, and she grabbed the reins.

"Care to ride up top with me, Mr Hawkins. I promise to be gentle."

He growled and clambered up next to her, close and pressing upon the box seat. "Miss Griffin." He twisted his head – that lopsided smile sending shivers throughout. "You can be as rough as you wish with me."

Laughing loud, she held out the reins to him, as in truth she had no idea how to handle a carriage, but he placed his broad hands upon hers, kept a firm hold and jerked the leather.

The two rested horses keenly followed from the Common, the trail flattened by boot and wheel, and they departed the tall iron gates. Grass gave way to rutted track, then to lane, and the horses, sensing smoother ground, gained speed.

Trees rushed by on either side, a few blurred men on foot doffed their slouched hats and a fierce breeze ruffled her hair.

Gentle sunshine shone.

And just as Seth had promised, she felt free as a swift in flight.

CHAPTER SEVENTEEN

"I do not conceive a young lady appears to advantage when she is throwing her limbs into contortions and jumping like a rope dancer."

PRIVATE EDUCATION: A PRACTICAL PLAN FOR THE STUDIES OF YOUNG LADIES. ELIZABETH APPLETON. 1815.

It never rained but it poured; the Academy's boiler had malfunctioned, his young fighter Liam had put a foot through an ale-house door, and a marquess had knotted himself in the ropes surrounding the practice ring, which had required them to be cut and rehung.

All the same, Seth whistled to himself as he meandered down the hallway.

Three days had passed since Astwood's threat at Wimbledon, and thus far nothing dire had occurred, but then he'd also hired a man to patrol the gardens, as such menace should never be taken lightly.

He'd kept it hush, not wishing Matilda to feel indebted,

but his daughter had given him that askew look with hand on hip as the burly chap – designed for clouting heads rather than weeding his borders – had lumbered by.

Evenings had been agreeable, with the three of them discussing his day and their lessons over dinner, Chloe playing pianoforte afterwards, yet…

Not that he would ever, for one single moment, begrudge his daughter's company, but could she not stay at Modesty's for an evening this week?

Matilda and he could then converse over a bottle of costly wine and a meal of venison. He would discover more of her tastes and passions, her dreams and wants.

Perhaps he could lurk in the library of a night and hope she might descend for a book to aid her sleep – but that sounded so contrived. And in any case, the intimate surroundings and plush sofas would no doubt initiate a more carnal endeavour.

He banished the prurient images, and as he wandered past the ballroom they used for their practice, the door creaked, moss-green eyes peeping around. "Pa? Can I borrow you?"

"Certainly, pet." He ambled in. "What can I…"

Matilda stood fidgeting foot to foot in the centre of the wooden floor, wearing only white petticoats and…was that one of his shirts? He'd have words with Chloe about that. It drowned her, but nevertheless gaped in all the right places, and he was fairly certain she wore no stays or corset.

"Maybe I shouldn't…"

But his daughter dragged him by the wrist whilst Matilda tugged down the thin veil of petticoats to obscure her bare porcelain ankles.

Too late to save his eyes from the tormenting vision.

"No, no. I need you," implored Chloe. "For demonstration

purposes. I'll stand here and you pretend to be a roving scoundrel who grabs me from behind. You know the move."

Yes, unfortunately for him, he did, and sighing, he removed his jacket and stretched.

They must have practised this a hundred times as it was no mean feat for a slender girl; his lower back had a perpetual ache.

But he lunged and placed an arm about his daughter's neck.

"Wot 'ave we 'ere?" he asked in his most villainous voice. "A helpless little girlie all alone." And he rendered his body lax – it hurt less.

"Oh, Sir," his daughter wittered in her most feeble voice. "Please don't–"

A brutal stamp on his foot threw him off balance, and then with a shove of her backside into his hip, she seized the arm around her neck, bent forward, thrust a hand behind his head, yanked, levered him from the floor and rolled him off her back, letting the wooden boards take his breath.

"Then," she explained to her startled governess, "you can stamp a foot in his talliwa–"

"Mercy!" cried Seth.

His devil-child smirked.

"Do you see, Miss Griffin? It's the element of surprise that makes it possible. Could you do the same?"

"Well, I..." She blinked and pushed her spectacles up her nose. "I could attempt it, one supposes."

Mercy, thought Seth.

"Good. You be the roving scoundrel for Miss Griffin, Pa, whilst I ask Betty for some lemonade. 'Tis thirsty work, all this teaching." And with an exaggerated wipe of brow, she skipped off, closing the door behind her.

Well, he'd been granted his wish of Matilda's sole

company, but seeing him lobbed to the floor by a girl of ten and three years was hardly comparable to intimate dinner repartee and a decent bottle of 1811 claret.

"I apologise," he offered, rising to his feet. "I hope she didn't badger you into learning these methods of defence?"

"Not at all. I think it a wonderful idea and Chloe is patient and enthusiastic. A man teaching me would be too intimidating and…manly. With Chloe's instruction, I feel as though I could succeed. I felt so helpless when my cousin first shook m–"

A blush lit her cheeks, eyes seeking the floor.

"I know he's bruised you in the past," Seth growled. "I saw them on your wrists the day of the interview." He strode over, brushed his fingers upon the baggy sleeve of *his* shirt. "If he ever does that again, I'll rip his arms off."

"Gosh. Could you?" And she grinned.

"You know what I mean."

"I do indeed, but for now, you shall be my villain, and I will try the move as Chloe has instructed."

This sounded like another exceedingly bad idea…

To the back of her, Seth stood – rough and rugged.

Clasped an arm around Matilda's throat – silk and cream.

Breathed deep – meadow and leather.

Whispered in her ear – silent desires.

"Wot 'ave we 'ere?" he purred. "A helpless little girlie all alone."

"OH, YOU WICKED SCOUNDREL," Matilda wittered rather breathlessly. "Please do-n't."

"Wot?"

"I said, *don't*."

"Hmm. I could do…*anything* to yer."

She shuddered at the rasp to his voice. Yes, yes, he could.

"I beg you take your rough, broad, firm, calloused hands off me..."

"I ain't sure," he growled, fingers constricting against the linen of the borrowed shirt, "that had much conviction."

Well, no.

That coarseness of voice induced such a fracas within. Betty had revealed how he'd spent a year learning to speak with perfect diction for his beloved Academy so that the nobles would feel at home, but Matilda adored the harsh edge and swallowed vowels.

Even so, she stomped on his foot.

He failed to move.

Not an utter surprise as, like Chloe, he wore some type of sturdy shoe and she herself was barefoot – similar to walloping a tree stump with a goose-down pillow.

Nevertheless – and not to be seen as a shrinking heroine – she continued with how she'd been instructed, shoving her posterior into his hip, except she missed, stumbled and ended up with her back flat against his rigid torso.

The arm around her neck remained, the other now tethered her waist – tight and altogether more dangerous than any roving scoundrel.

Even in the carriage they hadn't been *this* close; not a poppyseed width existed betwixt them, and she could feel every firm muscle of Mr Seth Hawkins, her sensitive back to his rippled *pectoralis major,* her waist to his flat *musculus abdominis,* her derrière to...protrusions.

"I'm not sure this is a part of the manoeuvre I was taught," she asserted stridently.

"I'm quite sure it isn't," he countered softly. "Now...how yer gonna free yerself from me villainous and depraved clutches?"

This may take some thinking time...

"Erm... Well, I could... No, not that... Maybe..." Savouring the wanton sensation curling beneath her skin, she shivered and arched her neck a dash. "Perchance..."

Seth shifted. "If yer don't think sharpish, damsel, I might ravish yer maidenly body."

Hmm...

"I suppose I could kick my heel back and catch you in the nether appendages."

She slid her bare foot up his leg. He cursed low. At least she assumed so, as it was a short word she was unacquainted with.

Not utterly ignorant of a male's anatomical physique, Matilda understood he was...readied, for want of a better word, and that her own wantonness had ripened to outright waywardness.

Miss Appleton would be shocked to the core.

"You could indeed do that," he murmured, "but please don't. Anything else?"

"I could...bash my elbow in your ribs, twist to the left then wallop you in the throat. Or perhaps wrench your ear and make my escape."

"Excellent. So why don't you?"

Many, many reasons... "I have no wish to be disemployed for rendering my employer insensate."

"You'd be welcome to try, but since I have you helpless within my roguish grip, a question: if we could go on a jaunt for an afternoon, where would it be? You attended the prizefight with me, now I'd like us to go somewhere *you* would enjoy."

"W-without Chloe?"

"Just the two of us...and the maid should it be required... or if you don't trust me?"

Of course she did. Just wasn't sure if she trusted herself.

"Well, I attend a literary salon once a month. Merely a few…not friends exactly but fellow devotees. We discuss a poem or play. I thought to miss this month as it's tomorrow afternoon but perhaps… And I don't believe a chaperone would be required for that."

"Then, Matilda, we shall go. And maybe some dinner afterwards?"

"Why thank you, Mr Hawkins."

"Seth."

"Seth," she repeated, savouring it. No one in the *Haut Ton* had such a delicious name.

"Chloe can spend the night with Modesty. This, of course, is if your host would not mind my attendance at your salon?"

"Not at all. Although if theatre prints are all you read," she said rather dryly, "I'm not sure how interesting it will be for you."

A flicker of lips at her ear told her that he smiled. "But *you* will be there, Matilda."

Gosh.

And she became aware that Mr Seth Hawkins was perhaps…courting her?

Not in the conventional 'waltz and a posy' manner of the *Ton* world but with tender words, a legion of kindness and those ravenous, devastating kisses.

She leaned her head back against his shoulder to gaze up at him.

Sunlight from the oblong windows gleamed on walnut damp hair, his hazel eyes smouldering with undeniable fire.

Not twelvemonth ago, she'd sniggered her stockings off when the hero of a romantic Gothic novel had smouldered.

Yet here it was. Smouldering at its utmost.

His fingers clenched at her waist, material rucking, and

she couldn't help but sink into his form, let her head tip forward, let his lips wander across her nape.

Kissing and sucking the skin to his mouth.

She moaned, hands clutching behind, to buckskin and–

A strident knock and Matilda startled, pitching her head back and causing Seth to yelp as he abruptly released her.

In the doorway, Betty held a tray with three glasses while Chloe clutched a jug of lemonade, her eyes widening in tandem with her gasp. "Miss Griffin!" She pursed her lips. "Well done."

"Oh, I didn't mean to…"

But Chloe nodded in approval. "There's not many that can split Pa's lip with a reverse nobbler to the ivories."

"But–"

"It takes a lot of skill," she commended. "Now, have some lemonade."

Betty placed the tray on a side table and cast a pitying glance. "And I'll fetch yer a cold compress, Mr H…to take down that swelling."

CHAPTER EIGHTEEN

"One reading lesson of poetry in the week is surely enough for children."

PRIVATE EDUCATION: A PRACTICAL PLAN FOR THE STUDIES OF YOUNG LADIES. ELIZABETH APPLETON. 1815.

Matilda glanced to the left, then to the right as she took Seth's hand to alight the carriage.

Beneath the grey clouds brushing the rooftops, this Marylebone street of their literary hostess heaved with noise and folk – bellowing hawkers with sweet buns aplenty, lads waving the latest song sheets, ladies scowling as they yanked their hems from the road sweeper's broom, and straight-backed gentlemen upon elegant steeds bobbing past.

This parish encompassed every class from lower gentry to higher courtesan and all walks in between.

As Seth gave instructions to a groom from the mews, she spied the approach of a familiar rangy figure.

Mr Kian Finlay.

During dinner last night, Seth had revealed that for all Mr Finlay's unrufflable nature and roguish winks, a sadness lurked, eternally in grief for his beloved wife, how he'd never so much as looked at another woman with either intrigue or lust.

Rather a shame for females of the species, as Matilda thought him such an agreeable man.

"What a pleasure, Mr Finlay," she called over the incessant din of hammers, shouts and whistles from a building with no roof. He swished towards her in a voluminous greatcoat of deepest black and, as at the prizefight, a sharp ebony feather was tucked in his hatband – what peculiar plumage. "But what are you doing here? Have you a fancy for Shakespeare also?"

Mr Finlay's soulful eyes creased as he chuckled. "Good afternoon, Miss Griffin. I'm not averse to a play but reading's not my passion. I'm here as a...precaution."

"Oh. How thoughtful. Well, I am grateful. Although I'm sure it won't be necessary. Are you well versed in walloping also?"

"Och, not at all, but I make do with a few wee bits and pieces should the need arise." He unbuttoned his capacious greatcoat and tugged, revealing one side to her gaze.

A cornucopia of knives and silvered objects confronted her. She blinked. Small and sharp, large and sharper, all attached to the interior of his coat with little sewn-on hooks.

"Gosh, Mr Finlay, and I thought you such an agreeable man."

"Yer should see what I've got tucked in the other side."

"I'd imagine you have to walk rather gingerly."

A grin and he tipped his hat. "Yer a fine lass, Miss Griffin."

"Kian!" barked Seth, tapping cane to cobbles. "Stop

dallying with my governess and take care up there. We'll see you in..." He twisted to Matilda. "Two hours?"

"Usually, yes," she replied. "Though we can go on a bit. Where will you be, Mr Finlay?"

"The roof." And he winked before striding off, the three capes of his greatcoat lifting in the breeze.

The roof? Matilda frowned and turned. "Is that a cant expression?"

"No. He'll be keeping an eye out for anything untoward from the rooftops." Seth slipped a hand to her waist as they crossed the road. "As a lad, Kian was a sweep and is happier up there clambering amongst the chimney pots than down here in the streets. I keep telling him he's no longer a fledgling and he'll fall if he doesn't take care..." His brow puckered as they stepped to the pavement. "But I worry he truly *doesn't* care some days. That's the problem."

Matilda patted his arm, the most propriety allowed in a hectic Marylebone thoroughfare, and they paused outside No. 16. A brick terraced house, it had wrought-iron railings with the latest gaslights and four stone steps led to a blue-painted door.

The three o'clock stagecoach turned into the street, mud splattering and horns blaring, and so with all haste, they hurried up the steps and rattled the brass door knocker.

ON OCCASION, Seth had felt envious picturing the swells and their salons – places of literature and learning, with like-minded souls quoting poetry to each other, laughing in accordance upon luxurious chaises of silk.

And he'd been right to be envious because this literary event was splendid, those chaises of silk strewn with vibrant cushions, manuscripts and pallid poets. A table in the corner held a cornucopia of food – pigeon pie, lobster patties and sweetbreads, with every type of liquor at hand. The poets gulped absinthe, the women sipped champagne and all before the chime of four.

Admittance of one's prejudice was a difficult task, yet Seth could acknowledge he'd hitherto misjudged such gatherings, believing he'd be snubbed for his status. At this salon, however, restless merchants mixed with indolent lords, a doctor lectured a naval man upon scurvy and a plump marquess chatted with a hawk-nosed young poet who appeared not to have eaten for a week. Seth felt quite at home within this mishmash of accents and wealth, most attendees having been nothing but cordial, and a few fellows had even shown interest in Academy membership.

The sole gentleman to be rather disdainful was a baronet, but then Seth had often found the lowest titled gentry to be more conceited and pretentious than a ninth-generation duke.

"I hope you are enjoying our gathering, Mr Hawkins?"

He twisted to the hostess, a Mrs Ashby, as she proffered a fresh glass of claret. Pretty, she appeared similar in age to himself, with auburn hair and light-green eyes.

Taking the glass, he dipped his head with a short bow. "Indeed I am, Mrs Ashby."

"I'm so glad. And it is a pleasure to meet you as my brother is a member of the Fancy. I believe he saw you at Chepstow in 1810. The only fighter to ever defeat Invincible Ivan, whom, I have to confess, my brother had fifty guineas on to win."

"Ah. Well, my apologies to your brother but it was a lucky day for me, Mrs Ashby."

"And you are a modest man, Mr Hawkins. Our dear

Matilda told me she is your daughter's governess now? I hope she is...safe within your Academy. She is a treasure which not all appreciate. After the tragedy of her parents' passing, I do so worry for her."

"Miss Griffin is under my protection," he assured, "and is treated as the lady she is. A perfect governess."

Although... Perhaps a governess should not tempt a prizefighter with offers of a clandestine kiss in a midnight carriage or attend fights dressed as a nefarious footpad on the prowl.

But that was what made her so very perfect.

"Excellent." She fiddled with her necklace. "Now, I must initiate our formal discussion before my guests get too soused. Do excuse me."

With a shallow bow, Seth's eyes caught on the saffron skirts of Matilda, who'd been trapped by the belligerent baronet at the punch bowl, and he could tell every muscle in her body was readied for flight, yet etiquette prevented her from telling him to go to the bloody devil.

Miss Matilda Griffin was such a dichotomy. Bold and brave in nature but in turn hesitant and restrained by nurture.

Clenching his wine glass, Seth glowered as the baronet leaned too close, murmured something and then distinctly sniffed her hair.

Coxcomb.

But his bold and brave lady abruptly peered at the baronet as though he were a beetle exhibit in a museum, drew herself to her full height, muttered something back, grabbed her punch glass and stomped across the room to where Seth stood.

"Did that baronet cause you offence? I could set Chloe on him?"

Matilda smirked. "He suggested that women could never write a book that would still be read in one hundred years – that we lack depth."

"I'll definitely set Chloe on him."

She shook her head. "I did not wish to be a smart-boots, but I reminded him of the book we will reading next month by Mrs Behn from 1688." Her rosy lips twitched. "And do not worry, he came on the coat-tails of a cousin and is not a regular attendee."

Seth wished to seize her hand and bring it to his lips, nip her palm and tell her how very clever she was, but the hostess tinged a glass with a spoon to gain the guests' attention, so he made do with a wink.

"Now," declared Mrs Ashby from the centre of the elegant drawing room, "may we commence discussing this week's choice, which is the Shakespeare sonnet, number thirty-three."

Therein followed a lively debate, but Seth kept his thoughts to himself amongst this canny lot who talked of vicarious experience, metaphysics and artistic alchemy.

They cheerfully chattered upon phrasing, pentameter and alluring alliteration, and he was quite certain that each one of their observations was correct, but for himself, the sonnet's appeal was simply the exquisite use of imagery and the aching sense of loss it conveyed.

"The young could do with reading more words of this calibre," stated the baronet, "and less of that romantic novel drivel which proliferates nowadays."

"And you've read these novels, have you?" asked their hostess, with a curved eyebrow and narrowed eye. "In order to form your opinion?"

"Merely curious as to their popularity amongst the… middle classes. I happened to glance through that work apropos of...prejudice and pride or somesuch, and found it to be the creation of a no doubt flighty unseasoned person – replete with undeveloped characters, trite emotion and magniloquent wordage."

Arsewit, thought Seth.

Frowning, he noted Miss Griffin likewise scrunch her brow, mutter to herself, then lift her head.

"I'm afraid I completely disagree, Sir Henry. I adored *Pride and Prejudice* and thought it portrayed true emotion and timeless struggle, especially for those of my own gender." Her chin tilted. "Perhaps you could do with reading more of that author's work, to appreciate the truth of a woman's plight in this day and age – reliant upon family or the apparition of a husband, threatened with ruin should she wish for more."

Mrs Ashby lightly applauded.

"You must be keeping the wrong company, Miss Griffin." The baronet sniffed with a glance in Seth's direction. "The boorish type that believes we can be more than we should be. That all women and even the working man can enjoy words, when most of them can barely read a song sheet."

Seth could remain silent no longer. "If one finds pleasure in reading a song sheet, then why naysay them? It should not matter what words bring you joy – be they Shakespeare, pig breeding, biblical or romance – but the fact they *do* bring joy to the beholder. On occasion, words are the sole pleasure to be found within this oft chaotic world."

"I daresay that is the common man's view," the baronet twittered. "But you mentioned the Bard, and after all, we are a *literary* salon. Perhaps you would care to share your favourite sonnet? Or are you merely acquainted with song sheets?"

. . .

MATILDA GLOWERED.

What an odious, intolerant sneaksby, but by the hostess's scowl, Matilda knew he'd never be invited back.

It angered her so – that the baronet sought to belittle a man such as Seth Hawkins, a knowledgeable and courageous gentleman who had built his life from naught rather than inherited it, fought hand to hand for a place in this world; she thought to tell the baronet so, straightened her shoulders and–

A broad palm slid to her waist and she glanced up at Seth, who bestowed upon her that tender lopsided smile before placing his claret glass to the table.

He gave the assembled company a short bow before striding to the centre of their circle, and with merely a pause and that Herculean stance, his magnificence stole everyone's breath.

The striped waistcoat of mustard and black with a honeycomb design and brass buttons accorded him sophistication, but the scarred eyebrow and calloused hands reminded all that this was no ordinary gentleman.

She recalled Mr Finlay's words – how Seth never did anything he did not wish to, how he hid a will of iron beneath that amenable poise.

Now she witnessed it.

The room stilled, recognising a master showman of the ring.

"This afternoon you discussed a sonnet of loss and pain, but these lines will remind us of another emotion. One which eases life's burdens and should forever be written of and cherished."

And so he began...

"'Love's not Time's fool, though rosy lips and
cheeks
Within his bending sickle's compass come;
Love alters not with his brief hours and weeks,
But bears it out even to the edge of doom.
If this be error and upon me proved,
I never writ, nor no man ever loved.'"

Mrs Ashby sighed with a hand to heart, the slender hawk-nosed poet fell to the chaise in rapture and the baronet grouched.

"And on that beautiful note," called their hostess, "I declare our salon concluded. We are to be at Mrs Tenby's next month. Mr Keats?" She patted the young poet as he recuperated upon the green chaise. "I'll make you up a food bag, dear."

Seth strode back to Matilda's side, a wicked tilt to his lips.

But she waggled a reproving finger. "I recall at my interview how you declared you'd little time for literature? You, Mr Seth Hawkins, have honeyed lying lips."

"I used to badger the charity school teacher for spare books, and later, I swept the floors of a circulating library in return for borrowing them, but I only ever had snatched moments to read. And even now, I rarely get more than an hour. So 'tis true, I have little time for literature, but..." He leaned close. "I never said I didn't enjoy it."

"Semantics," she whispered as their hostess approached.

Mrs Ashby held out her hands to them. "Well, Mr Hawkins, please accept my thanks for such a moving sonnet." She slanted a brow. "And next month, will we be seeing you...both?"

"In all probability, Mrs Ashby. And my thanks also," Seth replied whilst a heat crawled to Matilda's cheeks.

The hostess smiled, bidding them farewell, and the guests all made their rounds in the drawing room, gentlemen shaking hands, ladies bussing one another's cheeks in the French style. Matilda listened as Seth chatted with ease to both lawyer and countess – indeed his innate composure caused others to seek his company.

They all drifted to the hallway, where a butler and maid stood readied with their outdoor attire, assisting with flapping greatcoats and the many-buttoned pelisses.

Seth straightened Matilda's bonnet ribbons and she handed him his ebony cane.

The butler held open the door with the grave solemnity of an undertaker, and no wonder, as Matilda scrunched her nose from the top step.

For a fine drizzle greeted them, not that this year had brought much else. Leaden grey clouds pulled mocking faces overhead and she clutched Seth's arm tight, the four steps slick with moisture. In the street, hawkers still yelled their wares but now from beneath makeshift cloth-covered stands, while the monotonous clatter of hammers from the building with no roof continued in earnest, the labourers bawling and whistling loud.

Seth tipped his hat low and tugged his collar high as they descended to the pavement, and the groom brought their carriage to a halt across the road.

"A daisy fer the pretty lady, Sir?"

They turned to a woebegone flower girl, her straw bonnet sagging in tandem with her fulsome bucket of unsold daisies.

"I believe," said Seth with a wink, "that this lady deserves more than one." And he turned to rummage for coin.

Matilda smiled, thoughts shifting with the gusting wet wind.

Within their hostess's drawing room, as Seth had reached that sonnet's end, such a feeling of contentment had swathed Matilda. She had felt…part of him, had basked in his subtle confidence and magnificent bearing.

For all his lowly fighting background, he was a *true* gentleman.

A gentleman who had commanded all those present with his recitation, and yet…yet his sparkling gaze had never strayed from her as he'd delivered Shakespeare's timeless words of life and love.

That gaze had seeped into her very bones, her heart pounding with that same life, could not mista–

"Miss Griffin! No!"

She glanced in the direction of the loud yell, but the clang of hammers and thunder of hooves disorientated her, and she spun to… Wild eyes of an immense chestnut horse. Frothed lather spraying and muscular breast rippling so close. The rider swung sideways, thrust out a fist and she screame–

Sheer bulk barrelled into her, tumbling her to the cobbles, the scream still upon her lips.

Shoulders stung as she lay, striving for air, a hefty weight pinning her and she fought to open her gritted eyes.

Through misted, crooked glasses, she found Seth lying atop, his lids closed then lifting with a hiss of breath, a broad palm cushioning the back of her head, their legs enmeshed.

"W-what happened?"

He slumped for a moment. "I heard Kian's shout. Saw a rider gallop from the side street heading straight for you, all so fast. You were daydreaming."

"I never daydream," she countered, hauling breath to her lungs. "I couldn't hear anything… The hammers…"

"Hell, Matilda, you could have–" A trembling hand caressed her cheek. "I–"

Boots and hems surrounded them, the salon guests gasping their concern. Outstretched hands aided Seth to his feet, the abrupt lack of his warmth shivering Matilda's bones. Then she too was hauled from the grimy cobbles by their wool-clad fingers and leather-gloved palms, the guests now tutting of reckless horsemanship and how the cloaked fellow had not even bothered to stop.

Mr Keats placed a steadying hand to her elbow, staring intently into her eyes as a shudder took her, violent and swift.

"Have you pain, Miss Griffin? Can you see me clearly?"

"I-I can see you, Mr Keats. It's my back that hurts."

"Hmm. Can you describe the pain?"

Placing a palm to her forehead, she endeavoured to concentrate but an odd light-headedness had taken hold, wilting her limbs and muddling her thoughts. "It's a…a dulled pain."

Mr Keats nodded but stayed his hand as she brushed her muddied skirts with fingers that refused to cease their tremor.

The street had quietened, hammering ceased as the labourers all squinted over at the commotion, hawkers shaking their heads.

Retrieving Seth's muddied hat and cane, the baronet then wiped them with a handkerchief whilst the countess gathered the strewn daisies.

Matilda noted Seth's lips were tight, his habitually straight shoulders hunched as he thanked the baronet for the return of his possessions and fervently assured them all that he was unhurt.

Drizzle had coated each one of them in sparkles of

silver, hair tipped with sudden age, and a bitter cold suffused Matilda – icy fingers clawing their way to her soul.

Her bedraggled reticule appeared before her. "Matilda dear," whispered Mrs Ashby. "You must both come in from the rain. For some tea. You can change into dry clothes."

That curious weakness amplified, a sensation that her sodden skirts were towing her down, all too weighty, and she could barely summon the resolve to reply.

But a firm palm clasped her waist and she glanced up, took strength from Seth's touch and patient hazel eyes. For all their hostess's goodwill and kindness, Matilda just wished to be alone with Seth. To go home.

"Thank you, Mrs Ashby, for your kindness. Thank you everyone, but...but I believe we should return home. We are fine. Merely shaken, I think."

"Well, if you are sure, Matilda. But if there is anything at all you need, do send word."

The good people all reiterated Mrs Ashby's offer before drifting away to their various coaches, shaking their heads, demeanours subdued, and Seth opened his own carriage door for Matilda to ascend.

Acutely aware of his wince as he pitched heavily into the seat, she sat beside him, skirts soggy.

The door slammed shut and grave blue eyes appeared at the open window, lips parted in a pant. "I'll take the reins. How are yer, lass?"

"I can't seem to stop my hands trembling, Mr Finlay, but I'm unhurt, thank you." She fumbled with her bonnet ribbons and discarded the damp item to the opposite seat. "That was your shout I heard, was it not?"

"Aye. But it was Seth that got yer out the way of those hooves. Seth? Yer all good?"

A tight nod was his sole answer, which she presumed meant 'adequate' in man speak.

Mr Finlay disappeared from view, and after a brief rock of the carriage as he ascended to the coachman's seat, the horses snorted and the carriage lurched into motion.

She leaned into Seth and his fingers caught her shoulder, drew her closer. He must have felt her uncontrollable quiver as he touched a palm to her hair and stroked, loosening her chignon.

"Seth?" she said softly, glancing up. "That horseman tried to grab me, didn't he?"

The wheels jolted over cobbles and he grunted but cocked his head in that way Matilda had become so fond of. "Yes, Matilda, and at that speed, on that horse, he'd be miles away by now."

"But you saved me." She cupped his jaw. "Didn't you?" And with a light caress, she released him to bury her head once more within that striped waistcoat, to seek his warmth.

Lips murmured in her hair. Had she heard a whisper of… *Always*.

"But surely my cousin would not resort to this?" she mumbled into the silk. "My marriage can't be that important."

Seth's hand halted its motion to slide around and tip her chin. His lips firmed.

"That is what we must discover, Matilda."

CHAPTER NINETEEN

"Be respectful and obedient to your governess."

PRIVATE EDUCATION: A PRACTICAL PLAN FOR THE STUDIES OF YOUNG LADIES. ELIZABETH APPLETON. 1815.

"Find out all you can, Kian."

"Right yer are," the Scotsman declared, retrieving his greatcoat from the library sofa and swishing it about his shoulders. "I reckon me and her betrothed'll have a wee chat." And he flapped his metal-laden apparel.

"You're all mouth," Seth stated, rotating his shoulder and stretching his arms.

"And yer all beaten. Get to the basement. I'll see yer on the morrow."

Seth tipped his brandy glass in Kian's direction as his friend departed with a doff of hat, and then he took himself to linger by the oval window and watch the last of the daylight hours bleed into night. The drizzle of this afternoon had lessened, leaving turbid fog that slunk across the lawns of Green Park with menace.

Thank blazes Kian had been there today, as what would he have done if…

He slugged the brandy, savoured the burn and tossed the thought to hell – *if* was a word invented by the devil to drive you to Bedlam. He'd learned that with time.

In the dusk-black pane, his wearied reflection grimaced: shadowed eyes, furrowed brow and tight jaw. Punches to the gut and clobbers to the chops he was accustomed to, but a bloody iron hoof stung like a hive of bees. The basement beckoned, so he set down his glass and–

With a crash, the door burst open, thumping against its stop as a mahogany tea trolley trundled into the room.

But this was unlike any tea trolley his housekeeper brought him.

For instead of the usual Hawkins fine bone-china tea service with potted cream and buttered crumpets, there lay every last item of curative paraphernalia from the Academy's medical mishap cupboard, along with the entire assemblage of Betty's tonics, ointments, powders and potions – items that he'd not seen for years…many years. And were most probably noxious by now.

The tea trolley's middle tier held three voluminous books beside an array of bandages, tourniquet lengths, linen strips and flannels while the lower tier was laden with sharp pins, gouging instruments, bone nippers, probing scissors and blades of every conceivable width.

More fearsome than the contents of a tooth-puller's back room.

Its huffing peddler appeared – Matilda wearing that buttercup gown which could melt his gizzards to pottage, barefoot with hair loose and a little damp. She halted, pushed up her glasses and glared.

"Don't move," she commanded before twisting to dart from the library.

He remained motionless.

And was that a...bone saw?

Upon their return from the literary event, a pallid Matilda had been ushered to her bedchamber by his housekeeper for a hot bath and a few tipples of *Betty's Special Tonic*, which Seth knew consisted of her husband's stash of illegal whisky and...well, that was it, actually, although certain herbs had always been alluded to.

It could send a farm ox to the land of nod, yet it appeared Matilda was made of sterner stuff.

In fact, a quarter-full glass of it nestled in the corner of the trolley.

Not a moment later, a bundle of white towels arrived with Matilda somewhere beneath. She flopped them to the round reading table.

"I am here to tend your wound. Take off your shirt." And she tapped a foot, her bare pink toes negating the sternness somewhat.

"I don't–"

"Do not tell me it's nothing. I know that hoof caught you, Seth Hawkins, so sit down."

She put hands to hips. He shivered... "I am perfectly well–"

"Bruising can lead to sepsis, dropsy or the flux if not seen to. So sit." Her voice softened. "And let me tend to you."

Seth gingerly lowered himself to the indigo sofa. What he would have given to have Nurse Griffin in his corner as bottleman at a prizefight.

. . .

MATILDA APPROACHED HER PATIENT, brandishing a bandage as though she knew what to do with it.

But whilst bathing and sipping Betty's restorative to banish the trembles, she'd swotted up on *Marine Practice of Physik and Surgery, Including the Nature and Treatment of Gunshot Wounds*, by Dr J Ranby, Esquire; Surgeon General to the British Army. Third Edition 1781.

So how hard could it be?

And in any case, Betty had given lots of practical instruction should the written theory prove erroneous.

His waistcoat had been shed earlier, and she perused his remaining attire, ready to assist. "Do you require me to cut your shirt off with a sharp blade?"

"Er, no," he said rather breathlessly. "I don't believe that will be necessary."

Even so, he winced as she edged the material up his spine and then along that injured shoulder. She'd noted every clench of his jaw as the coach had jolted them, despite his manly assurance that all was well – a fearsome fib, if ever she'd heard one.

Tugging the shirt over his head proved more problematic as the laces caught on his chin and she was forced to yank, nigh removing his ears. Who'd have known it would be so arduous to unclothe a man? Surely it would have been easier to cut the material, as Dr J Ranby, Esq. had directed?

In order to accurately diagnose from her medical tome, she crossed to the trolley, had another quick nip of *Betty's Special Tonic* to fortify herself, and then trundled it nearer the sofa, the implements rattling.

She sat behind Seth to scrutinise the affected area, hefty book in hand.

A fierce scarlet brand in a wide U shape marred his shoulder, the area swollen. "Hmm." She flipped past Fevers and Vomiting. "I think..." She paused at Gangrene and softly prodded the skin: somewhat hot and puffy. "I do believe... I believe it to be an *ecchymosis* of the *musculus trapezius*, perhaps even the *rhomboideus major*."

"And that would be?"

"An abominable bruise to the shoulder. Shame it's not a gunshot wound as I know all about those. But we'd best clean it, just in case." Dr J Ranby had been rather cavalier as regards cleanliness, but Betty had advocated that a good slosh of brandy never went amiss, so Matilda would tend her hero with all due diligence.

Seth's eyes flickered in the low lamplight, and she smiled reassuringly before investigating the hodge-podge of bottles on the trolley.

"Has it broken the skin?" he rasped.

"No..." She turned back to examine once more; without doubt it would turn black and blue in the next few days and ache for a month, but it would be remiss of her not to consider all possibilities, so just in case, she glanced to the Splints and Fractures chapter, twisting her head at Diagram 5b. "Can you rotate your shoulder without fierce pain?"

"I've dislocated it before," he asserted, but nonetheless rotated it as requested. "And that hurts in a different way, but do carry on, Nurse Matilda," he said with a wink, "for I cherish your gentle touch."

She blushed, batted a hand to his waist and flicked past Intermittent Fevers, Jaundice and The Itch. Although... "Does it itch?"

"Er, no."

So gathering a strip of linen, she splashed around plenty of brandy and then smoothed the cloth over the red swelling.

He flinched and a groan emerged from her patient, so she softly prodded once more to judge whether any fluid had built up beneath the skin. "If it's that painful, perhaps it requires lancing." And she spun to the tea trolley, knocking over a tin of… "What's this?" she asked, holding up a peculiar cotton-like item.

"Ligature thread made of cat gut, I believe."

Ugh.

Seth threw a wary glance at the silver instruments. "I'm quite sure lancing is not yet necessary."

"Hmm…" She pursed her lips. "In that case, I prescribe arnica ointment, as although Dr J Ranby may know his gunshot wounds, I shall defer to Betty in this instance."

"Foul stuff, that," remarked Seth with a wipe of forehead. "It's the jar that smells of mothballs and gin."

She uncapped and recapped the many glass vessels, sniffing until a pernicious mix of camphor and alcohol nigh seared the hair from her nostrils, so she placed the jar to her lap and swiped a finger over the waxy substance. Too firm and cold for Seth's injured skin, hence she dug out a dollop and warmed it between her palms.

The bruise would be uncomfortable to sleep upon and no doubt other aches would assail him on the morrow. She exhaled heavily. "This is all my fault."

He swivelled, eyes gleaming. "No, Matilda. A swine of a man with no care for you did this. Can you imagine if you had stayed at his house and then refused to marry Sidlow? What he might have done to compel you?" Seth turned back. "It will heal and I've had worse. The cut above my eye hurt like the deuce when it was stitched. I swear Mother used an embroidery needle."

"How did you come by it?" She peered to her lap and gathered more ointment, the more the better as far as she was concerned.

"When I was a boy. Someone clobbered me."

Frowning, she glanced up, his broad back and shoulders confronting her like Hadrian's Wall – unconquerable and defiant. She recalled mention of his childhood, a brutal place where fists ruled. "Was...was your father violent?"

His face slanted to profile, scarred eyebrow raised. "Shall I tell you of my father?"

"Well, if you do not mind." She tentatively smiled. "I would like to know more of your past, Seth."

He rubbed a hand upon his chin, the rasp of stubble so very loud in the silence of the evening. Even the clock hands had paused at a half after the hour, it's owner too distracted to have wound it.

"The Rookery's a tough place, Matilda, where a boy can have all compassion trampled out of him before he reaches manhood." He lifted his chin. "But I grew up with a father who made sure that never happened, who although had the body of a brute, had the soul of a saint. One who loathed violence, any kind of violence against man, woman or beast."

"A gentle man, then?"

"Yes, and the very epitome of the word gentleman." He stretched his legs. "Honest and dependable. If a child went missing in our street, he'd be the first one out hunting and the last to come home. He'd toil till midnight and beyond if our bellies were empty, and I recall him shovelling manure, just to afford daisies for Mother's birthday." With a twist of torso, Seth grinned. "Many a lad down our street had a father too handy with his fists. But not mine. Built like a brick privy but with hands that could cradle a new-born kitten."

She smiled to herself. Like father, like son.

"So how did you receive the scar?" And she commenced smoothing the warmed ointment onto the outer edges of his wound.

"I told you Father was a coal heaver?"

"Yes, I remember."

He rolled his shoulders, so Matilda slicked upwards and onto the swollen hoof mark, keeping her touch tender.

"Hell, that's good," he murmured, head tipping low. "'Tis a hard job, paying fifteen shillings a week, if you're lucky, with the rest paid in ale as his employer was an innkeeper. I started helping when I was thirteen."

Chloe's age.

So young for Seth to lift such hefty sacks of cumbersome coal.

"But I found... You cannot imagine, Matilda," he said, "how it feels when the man you love and adore, a father to be proud of, is beaten by another. By a fiend not worthy to lick his worn boots."

With waxy palm aloft, she frowned. "Beaten? How awful. But why would someone beat him?"

"Father had dropped a coal sack, not surprising after a shift of ten hours, and it had split at the seams. So the innkeeper clobbered him – not a quick clip, mind, but brutal punches about the face and chest. He didn't put up a fight, even though he could've laid the fiend low with a fist. It just wasn't in him."

Matilda scowled. "Your poor father. And what a bullying huff-cap." Seth's back rippled and she kneaded outwards, attempting to keep all fury from her touch.

"Mother and I had seen bruises on him before, but he'd always scoffed it was the hundredweight coal sacks or that he'd fallen." Seth breathed deep. "I raged, asked him why he didn't fight back or find other work, but he said employment was scarce as hen's teeth, and what was better? A few bruises? Or no food on the table? All of us on the streets or in the workhouse?" He twisted, her fingers falling. "How would you have felt, Matilda, if you'd been me as a lad?"

Her eyes slitted, lips flattened. "Angry. I feel angry now."

Seth nodded, gaze fixed to hers. "Then one day, it was my turn for a beating, and the innkeeper clobbered me about the head – fierce and painful. But I fought back..." He snorted. "I knew nothing, not even how to punch, and he smacked me so hard I crashed into a shelf of bottles, and glass embedded itself in my eyebrow. I could've been blinded."

Fury gushed through Matilda, that such a vicious tyrant would not only abuse Seth's hard-working father but also a mere boy, and she jerkily reached out to stroke his eyebrow. "Yet your family was reliant upon the wage."

His lips thinned as he cast a nod. "Yet I also knew it would never stop. For the first time, I could see my own life stretching ahead of me, violent and short, of watching my father beaten down like a dog till one day the punch would hit him wrong and he'd never rise."

She scrunched her fingers in the brandy-soaked linen, tearing the material in her wrath. "So you turned that anger to resolve and began prizefighting?"

"Exactly so. I had my mother's pluck combined with my father's build, and it's not unusual in the coal trade. Same with butchers, bargemen and heavers – they all have a go, but most only use their brawn. I knew if I had any chance, I needed more. So I began sneaking into fights at Five Courts, where they do demonstrations and benefits for retired fighters. I'd watch the champions – their technique and stance."

"And you started winning?"

Seth smirked. "Losing, more like... but learning each time my arse hit the floor, then finally winning. Only for coppers in the early years as I was so young. Hell, Father couldn't bear to watch, but Mother would cheer me on. Her language, you'd not believe it..." He chuckled, deep and strong, and

Matilda marvelled at his steely determination. Driven to fight by circumstance and yet, like his father, never violent in nature.

"Were your parents alive when you gained the championship? They would have been so proud." She attempted to place the cap back on the jar but her fingers fumbled and he took it from her with a broad grin.

"What makes you think they've cocked their toes?"

"Well…" She frowned, twisted her hands and shuffled her bare feet. "Neither you nor Chloe has ever mentioned them."

"Fair enough. But that's probably because they are in Rome, last we heard. On a Grand Tour of the Continent. Like the young nobs do."

Matilda goggled and slid her glasses back up her nose.

"My wife may have lost patience with me, but my parents never did." He shook his head. "They battled on, watched me, supported me, my father still working for that bloody fiend." His gaze firmed. "But eventually I got us all out. Not just me and Chloe, but all of us. My parents have a little place in Richmond now." He brushed her cheek. "But like you, they always wanted to travel. So once Napoleon had been seen to last year, off they went." He kissed her lips, light and tender.

"Well, I never," Matilda murmured, his tale leaving her strangely serene but oddly befuddled.

"I suppose," he said with a tilt to his head, "that happy endings do exist. Hardship can turn to comfort. Despair to hope. I only wish all stories could end thus… Your parents. Kian's wife."

"I wish that too, Seth. But it cheers me so to hear of happy endings for others. It reminds me that life can also be wonderful." Matilda tipped her head back. "Next you'll be telling me that the vicious innkeeper repented his ways and is now a vicar."

"Nah, he drank himself to death."

Her bare toes burrowed into the rug and she smiled. A drowsy lassitude encased Matilda, a rush of satisfaction that Seth's life was now a contented one, that happy endings existed. She brushed his cheek, fingers tingling with the rough stubble, emotions a blur but all containing this man before her. "I hope you won't think me brazen but... I admire you so much, Seth Hawkins."

SETH'S SHOULDER no longer ached; it was his whole being that ached for this woman. "And I so admire you, Matilda Griffin." He'd thought never to allow another woman so close to his heart. Thought to spend his life devoted to his Academy, books and daughter.

Yet with her boldness, cleverness, golden spectacles and sherry eyes, Matilda had burst into his life, a yellow spring blossom flowering before him, casting her scent and luring him in.

She bit that ripe lip and he softly halted her with a brief kiss. "Thank you, Matilda. Never have I been granted such tender care." Nor had a woman cared to read medical tomes or gather ligature thread for him, or ask of his childhood, and listen.

Tomorrow they must talk of Astwood, and mayhap of feelings for each other, but for now, her glasses had slid down her nose one more, eyes not wide but slumberous.

"Would you..." Her black lashes lifted. "Would you mind holding me? Just for a moment. You see, I..."

She'd no need to continue, for he knew.

Knew that after today, she needed comfort. As did he.

Knew she craved the reassurance of a tight embrace. As did he.

Knew she did not wish to be alone. As neither did he.

He thumped a sizeable cushion and placed it at the head of the sofa, reclined, careful not to undo all her good work on his shoulder, and held out his arms. "Come, Matilda."

A slow smile and she keeled into his embrace, tucking her legs and skirt up onto the sofa. He buried one hand in her hair, felt the slip of silk through his fingers, and brought the other tight about her waist.

Her head fitted so perfectly beneath his chin, the scent of fresh flowers overwhelming his senses. The evening held a stillness of promise, and he laid his head back, content, lips rested and brow smooth.

At some hour soon, she would have to retire to her chambers, but for now, he would relish this closeness.

"I'm so sleepy, Seth," she mumbled into his chest.

"Then sleep, sweet Matilda, 'the honey-heavy dew of slumber'."

Her lips curved against his skin as she smiled, her body lax and pliant, moulding to his nude torso. A hand that had been stroking his forearm fell still and her breathing deepened.

Softly, he kissed her hair, as *Betty's Special Tonic,* which could fell the strongest of fellows within a moment, finally claimed the bravest, kindest, most caring woman he'd ever known.

CHAPTER TWENTY

"Nature or truth is our guide."

Private Education: A Practical Plan for the Studies of Young Ladies.

Elizabeth Appleton. 1815.

The distant bells of St James's Church woke Matilda to a moonlit chamber and she blearily counted the chimes to ten.

Heavy blankets smothered her to the chin, dress twisted about her legs and a blur of yellow flickered quietly in the corner, so Matilda scrabbled for her spectacles, finding them folded upon the bedside cabinet. Never was she that neat, habitually flinging them off with abandon, so Seth must have carried her up the stairs, placed her upon the bed, removed her glasses, folded them and perchance stroked her hair – how she wished she'd been awake.

Betty's Special Tonic, she surmised, held some effective herbs within its sweet whisky.

As she sat up and stretched, her lower back twinged,

reminding her of Astwood and all that had transpired this afternoon. Sighing, she rose to pad for the tapers upon the mantelpiece, lighting the lantern from the fire and casting light where there'd been gloom.

A china pitcher rested upon the dresser but it was empty, so gathering it up, she ambled for the door. The range would still be lit and mayhap Betty would be around for tea and a natter.

The Academy closed its doors at sunset most days and the house wore a strange silence by night, the din of male shouts and grunts leaving an eerie trace within the walls.

Candles were not stinted upon within the Hawkins' household so the corridor remained well lit by its many sconces, otherwise, and with no one else about, she'd suppose herself in the middle of an outlandish tale, all the other inhabitants falling foul of a mad ghoul.

Signs of life could be heard from the kitchen, the clatter of plates and patter of feet.

"Evening, Betts." And she swung the door open.

Behind the table, stacking crockery, Betty gawked. "My *Special Tonic* ain't as strong as I thought." She tutted. "Yer should've slept till Christmastide, girlie. Might have to up the whisky."

"I believe the St James's bells woke me, but my back rather aches now." Matilda shuffled on her bare feet. "I can only imagine how poor Mr Hawkins' shoulder feels. He did take a hoof for me, you know, Betty, and has an awful swelling."

Betty grinned and waved a plate. "Did yer have to lance it?"

"Would you believe, he wasn't all that keen."

"That's men for yer."

Matilda nodded, rolled her eyes and huffed. "Anyhow, I

wondered if I might have some hot water? To soak some linen in it for my back."

The housekeeper tapped her chin in thought. "I could fetch yer some of my special camomile ointment. Whiffs a bit, but if it don't whiff, it ain't doing yer no good."

"Er..."

"Or perhaps," continued Betty with an odd glance, "yer should pop to the basement. That'll soothe yer aches and pains."

Matilda frowned. "I was told it was out of bounds."

"Academy's closed and I don't think yer forbidden any longer, girlie. Here, take this in case it's locked." And she opened a little cupboard on the kitchen wall to extract a large brass key. "It'll still be warm."

"What will?"

"The basement. Now don't dally. Yer ain't got all night, and yer'll sleep like a tot after some time down there."

And Matilda was shooed from the kitchen by a flapping apron and waggling fingers, as though she was the kitchen cat being put out for the night.

Left in the hall with an empty pitcher but with herself full of intrigue, she thought to follow Betty's advice, and so pottered along the hallway, discarding the pitcher on a side table.

The black-painted door leading to the basement had a heavy brass handle that turned with ease, no key required. In Matilda's limited experience, such places below ground were unpleasant, having no windows and little light. Or air. But considering the amount of time Seth spent down here, might it be a...personal gymnasium?

Lined with four sconces, the stairs were at least lit, but a herby fragrance wafted, light glowing from beneath a further door at the bottom.

Tentatively, she trailed down and halted, her nostrils twitching at…rosemary?

She twisted the handle, pushed open the door and gasped.

A medium-sized room presented itself, painted in sky blue and deep burgundy, shadowed but lit by lanterns upon ornate brackets on all four sides. Patterned carvings decorated the walls, giving an opulent feel, and the ceiling was rendered with gods and nymphs reclining upon fluffy clouds.

But that wasn't the sole reason she'd gasped, for central to it all was a circular blue pool, some eight foot in diameter, sunk into the floor with petite marble steps and surrounded by sea-green tiles decorated with frolicking mermaids.

Not a ripple to the water, it appeared inviting and limpid.

What a delightful secret treasure.

Her eyes flickered up.

In one corner was an open arched structure, like a room within a room, a wall with stucco plasterwork and decorative cornices separating it from another door. Towels lay upon a shelf, a simple burgundy daybed set against the rear, a table next to it with an open book and empty glass.

What chiefly drew her attention, however, was the muscular man who lay slumbering upon that burgundy daybed.

In solely loose cotton sailor's slops.

He dozed upon an arm, exposing his chest to her gaze, and drawn like a moth to a flame, she drifted along the poolside.

Mother had always said men appeared like innocent little boys when asleep but the same could not be said for Seth Hawkins.

Darkness beneath his eyes and that scar upon his brow gave a menacing air, fists twitching as his chest heaved.

He rolled onto his injured shoulder, grunted, and now disturbed it was an honour to watch him wake – unhurried and languid, arms stretching, torso expanding, eyes opening...

"Matilda?" He startled and jolted upright but made no effort to cover himself with the banyan on the hook.

Truly, what a delectable view.

Although a befogged one as her glasses had steamed up.

"Betty suggested I come to the basement."

"Did she now," Seth murmured.

"Hmm." She wiped her glasses on her skirts. "I mentioned my aches, you see. From the cobbles."

Instantly he rose to his feet, placed broad palms to her shoulders. "No damage, I hope?"

"No, just sore." His slops rode low on his waist, damp and almost see-through. She didn't quite know where to look.

Very well. She did know where to look, but an unbeknown shyness had descended.

"What a beautiful place, Seth. I had no notion."

"No, I thought to show you all this tonight, but, well, you fell asleep." He released her shoulders...leisurely. "This area is for my personal use, but..." And he prowled to the other door, opened it for her to peek through.

Speechless.

Another sunken pool, but much larger and oval shaped – some sixteen foot by ten. Hooks lined one wall of the room with benches below, a row of sinks opposite. Pitchers and towels were laid neatly upon shelves, and some type of rain-like bathing contraption that she'd seen advertised in *The Times* occupied the far end.

It reminded her of the bathhouses of ancient times and solely lacked men in togas chomping grapes.

"This larger room is equipped for the members. Wimpole

Estate first gave me the idea as it has a similar basement, and of course, I had books on the Roman baths. I not only wanted an academy of excellence but also somewhere gentlemen could relax." He rolled his neck this way and that. "I couldn't resist having my own private pool, however – my one indulgence."

"It's a marvel. No wonder you have dukes squabbling in a queue."

He grinned, shut the door to the members' area and scratched a hand across the hair on his chest. Matilda flapped a collar.

Heat coiled around her.

"Well..." She cleared her throat. "Perhaps you could show me how this pool will ease my aches. Can I bathe in my chemise?"

The request was shameless, wicked and sinful but Matilda no longer cared. This was Seth, the man who had carried her to her bedchamber, who'd saved her from kidnap and who filled her every thought.

His throat bobbed, head tilted, skin gleaming with moisture. "Matilda, I warn you, if you strip to your chemise, I *will* kiss you."

"And I shall want you to," she whispered, knowing it to be the truth.

His jaw firmed. "And if we kiss on this occasion, Matilda, I will not cease."

"And I shall not want you to."

His breath hitched, rumbled. "And if I do not cease, then fair warning, I will never let you go."

"And I shall not want you to," she whispered once more, conscious of what she was saying, that she wished for a lifetime of adventures with this man.

. . .

A KICK of pure blinding lust struck Seth, harder than any hoof, halting his breath and scorching his skin. The humid air shimmered with anticipation and want, each knowing the other's heart but perhaps afraid to reveal such sentiment in words.

He swallowed to ease the knot of tension.

"The pools are heated by a parallel series of hot pipes from the latest Walker coal-fired boiler."

Clay-brained addle-pate! Why the hell had he said that? He ought to have whispered words of devotion and passion…

"It's wondrous, Seth." And she spun, commenced unfastening the buttons at her throat, which put paid to any more words from him whatsoever. "And I can smell herbs. From the pool?"

"Yes," he more or less grunted.

Ribbons were loosened and he assisted in pushing the cotton dress from her shoulders.

Palming her hair to the side, he kissed her arched throat as a last warning of what would ensue.

A breathless sigh assured him; nails lightly dug at his bared waist, tormenting him.

He sought the calm mien he invoked for a prize bout – the Seth who never lost his control – but that man had never been confronted with Matilda Griffin in solely silk paraphernalia and fragile chemise.

Creamy skin abounded, her coal-black hair the perfect frame.

Petticoats dropped to coat the floor, no stockings to bother with, but the short stays about her midriff still restricted.

"May I?" he growled, elegant diction beyond his capability.

She smiled her acquiescence and he tugged laces, then wrenched, kissed the skin above her chemise – smooth and with the scent of meadows.

The corset fell away, in harmony with his breath.

Crisp white linen hinted at curves, shadows beneath implying treasure beyond his most feral imagination.

And oh, how he had imagined. Night after anguished night.

Five steep steps led into the round pool and he grasped her hand, aware his own attire hid little of his aching need – but Matilda, with a light blush, kept her eyes raised.

The water still retained its warmth, yet it did nothing to ease Seth's strangled breath and thrumming pulse.

As Matilda drifted down the steps, her chemise floated up in the water and she laughed, patting it down. "How wonderful," she whispered, swirling fingers and gathering palmfuls to sluice her arms.

Seth considered asking how the temperature felt, but his vocal cords refused to comply as the water lapped at her breasts, teasing his gaze till nigh blinded yet refusing to blink.

"Yes, indeed," he barely managed.

"And deep enough to luxuriate in but not to drown, for I can't swim, you see."

She abruptly ducked beneath the water and then surfaced with a spluttering chuckle, glasses skew-whiff, black hair streaming and chemise transparent – a bedraggled bespectacled mermaid, and he could withhold no longer, lost to her lure, so seized her nape and kissed her.

Damnation, he could feel every curve, every lush part of her mould to him.

Though broad, he wasn't a tall man and she fitted so very perfectly, responded as if she'd been waiting forever.

Since these bathhouses had been added, Seth would sit here most nights, alone. To now have Matilda in his arms – his brave and bold Matilda – fulfilled every midnight dream of the last weeks.

He kissed her wet throat, groaned as her fingers slicked up his arm.

Driving her backwards through the water till her spine met the circular wall, he threaded his fingers through her hair and kissed her till she took what little breath remained.

Her fingers tentatively roamed his back, slipped shyly to his lower spine, then boldly explored his backside, the wet cotton a sensual addition.

"Callipygian," she murmured. "That's the word. Do you know, I've admired your callipygian figure since the interview."

He laughed – his delicious Matilda and her elaborate wordage – but he aimed to induce a gasp as he slid a hand over her breast, cupped the weight, thumb abrading the tip until he received a gratifying moan for his impudence.

Further his hand teased, to her waist and hip. So perfect, and he yanked her near to grind his aching groin against her softness whilst their lips met in carnal need.

Clasping her derrière, he lifted her beneath the water, and their hips clashed just so. Her legs parted, chemise rising in the water, and... Hell, it would only take a ripping away of cotton and he would be deep inside her, burning and tight.

Grinding once more, he felt the heat of her, and she cried out, her legs tangling around his thighs in the water, fingers gripping the hair at his nape.

Damnation, he must...

Seth hauled back, rasped. "To the bed, Matilda."

. . .

Seth Hawkins tousled her wits, scattered her senses and then, to Matilda's dismay, untangled her legs from about his waist.

Stepping away with a growl, he climbed two of the pool steps and held out a rough palm.

Matilda hesitated, not through shyness but sheer gogglement.

Now that her glasses had taken a soaking to clear the fog, she could see better and…

Water sluiced Seth's powerful torso, rivulets over muscle she wished to trace with her lips and fingers. The sailor attire now rode so low she could see his hips, so different to her own – slender and indented, a line of hair arrowing lower.

Matilda's gaze skittered from the sight of his potent want, because if she inspected too closely she was sure her maidenly upbringing might cause her to swoon in shock. She'd felt that blatant arousal though, thrusting against her in the water, seeking entry, immense, blunt and demanding.

Breathing deep and with a tentative step, she rose, held Seth's gaze as the water level dropped beneath her chemise-clad breasts, stomach and then hips.

Seth's jaw clenched, a quiver to his held-out hand granting her confidence.

"Do you still ache?" he all but rasped.

"Yes. But in an entirely different manner."

Their hands gripped, sparked, and he drew her to the arched construction, where he grabbed a towel from the shelf and dried her hair with measured, firm strokes. That one was tossed to the floor and a new towel now whispered over her shoulders, then the translucent chemise. And finally, on one knee, he dried her lower legs with delicate exquisiteness.

Matilda wished to do likewise to Seth – be slow and investigative – but it appeared his patience was limited, as he whipped a towel over his own body with undue haste and hurled it aside, drawing her toward the daybed.

He reeled her close for a ruthless kiss, but her glasses slid, knocking his cheek, so she flung them off without a care as to where they landed. "I can see no further than four feet, but my near sight is adequate."

"Then I shall stay unbearably close." He cupped her cheeks within broad hands. "I will be so gentle. I do not wish to cause you any discomfort."

"The procreational mechanics of mammals cannot be so bad otherwise the human species would have gone extinct," she said in all seriousness.

Besides which, Matilda wasn't entirely sure she wished for gentleness – maybe later, but for now she yearned for a Seth untamed and wildly groaning with passion.

So with absolutely no idea what she was doing – except for the knowledge that he appeared to enjoy her touch – she traced a finger upon his chin, newly shaven and smooth, tracked a chord in his neck, outlined his magnificent *pectoralis major,* flexed her fingers through the slight hair, sketched the muscles at his stomach, and dipped to the indentations of his hip; then internal curiosity having won out, she allowed her hand to stray over his cotton-clad manhood, tentatively brushing.

Seth groaned; she grinned.

"Bad governess," he growled, tumbling her backwards to the daybed, lips and hands all over her, peeling off straps and coating her bared skin with bites and kisses.

The untamed Seth she'd desired yanked her chemise down, revealing her breasts, and although his expression was fierce, his lips were yet tender, nipping and laving.

One candle flickered and guttered, the remainder casting shadows that leaped upon the walls, and she stroked his vigorous back and nape as he drew her up and stripped the chemise from her body, kissing his way to her toes.

Shyness ought to have overtaken her, but like all the adventures of these past weeks, she would relish each moment with all her body, soul and heart.

Seth reared, his mighty chest heaving, eyes roaming, and never had she felt such emotion, such thundering need for another.

Thought to tell him so...but insistent lips returned to hers, hands now driving her thighs apart. She allowed it, trusted Seth completely, gasped as his fingers caressed and dipped in a rhythmic stroke that coincided with rough kisses upon her throat and breast.

It snaked within, the pleasure, a never-ending tightness and tension as she twisted within his embrace and pushed against his palm.

"Seth," she gasped.

"My beautiful, exquisite Matilda," he whispered, and with those words – ones no one else had ever applied to her – that tightness released and the rosemary-scented room ceased to be as her eyelids closed, rapture flooding to every tip of limb, submerging her beneath warmth and light.

With a rip of cotton, a heady, muscled weight was upon her, powerful hips and thighs parting her legs further before a thrust against her core, raw and rude and resolute.

A stretched pain robbed her breath and she lifted her gaze, witnessed Seth with jaw tense yet eyes tender, and aching need shook her once more as she arched into him, heard a harsh groan.

"My Matilda," he bit out, low and agonised. And he

dragged back, only to plunge anew, a guttural grunt locked in his throat.

The tightness caused a sharp inhale but the rapture of before still simmered, and as he rocked, gentle and short, that hurtling bliss returned – faster and tauter.

"More," she gasped, aware he held back from whatever he wished to do, aware his strained arms and clenched teeth hid a sharp longing. So she caressed his back, scratched those magnificent buttocks.

His hips jerked, and a growling Seth began to pound. A broad hand claimed her thigh, hitching it aloft as she cried out, and he plunged deeper.

Seizing her hands within his, he pressed them to the cushions to prevent any more daring assaults. Lips scalded her breast and so, like this, restrained in his arms with his persistent heavy thrusts driving so deep, the pressure surged anew, thrashing her body with fervour and torrid bliss.

His raw groan likewise echoed from the tiled walls, fingers clasping, flexing against hers as Seth raised his chest and wrenched his head back. Her eyes fell to where their bodies blended – so as one as he roared his pleasure, hips brutally lunging.

Their panted breaths mingled as his head slumped, ragged kisses exchanged as his forehead dropped to meet hers. Seth's hips still bucked, but now diminishing to lackadaisical thrusts, each inciting a gasp, a nuzzle to her breast producing a languid smile.

Rolling her head to the side, her imperfect vision transformed the room to a distorted landscape of mere colour – sky blue and earthly burgundy – so she twisted back to focus upon Seth, the sole defined treasure.

He grinned that lopsided smile and causally flipped them both over as though she weighed naught, still joined so intimately that she felt a blush rise from her toes to her forehead as she lay atop.

On many occasions she'd dreamed of those rugged knuckles and now they kneaded her backside, those wonderful rough-skinned fingers splaying and tightening, then rising to her waist and spine – calloused pads clutching.

And all the while, she too explored – lips grazing his chest, nails teasing his hips, toes brushing his calves.

A mounting heat, which had nothing to do with the humid surroundings, swirled afresh, their bodies rocking in accord.

"I believe," she whispered, pushing up to her forearms to gaze into sultry hazel eyes, "that no adventure could better that."

Seth gripped her nape and surged his hips, unabashed and voracious as she gasped anew.

"Our adventures," he rasped, "are never to end."

CHAPTER TWENTY-ONE

"Of marriage and domestic comforts you should banish every idea. A governess cannot expect offers from men of birth and fortune."

Private Education: A Practical Plan for the Studies of Young Ladies. Elizabeth Appleton. 1815.

Matilda scrunched her nose.

'Love is full of anxious fears.'

Not in the least reassuring, and she discarded the poems of Ovid to flick through the pages of the next tome gathered to her side upon the library sofa.

'Love is the wisdom of the fool and the folly of the wise.'

Pah, what did Samuel Johnson know?

Matilda had decided to while away the evening consulting the great names of literature in order to discover whether her feelings for Seth coincided with their stanzas and prose on love. Yet not one of them had endorsed her hypothesis, for it seemed each held a differing view – love could be fierce or gentle, jealous or trusting, selfish or altruistic, protective or unbound.

She eyed a leather-cased book of Plato. Now there was a man who surely knew himself and everything else, so she settled into the sofa cushions to begin somewhere in the middle.

'Love is a grave mental disease.'

Oh, good grief, and she abandoned it to the stack upon the floor before reclining to twiddle her thumbs as night descended.

All day she'd waited for Seth to return from who knows where...and still she waited.

Matilda tugged out his note, wedged as a bookmark amongst the pages of Shakespeare – *'The course of true love never did run smooth.'*

Hah.

And she re-read Seth's words.

Dearest Matilda,
Kian has some information. I shall be out for the morning.
Yours, Seth

Functional but not altogether informative. Incorrect as he'd not returned. But she appreciated the 'Dearest'. And the 'Yours'.

Indeed, at eight this morning, Matilda had greeted the day with vivid elation, full of promise and hope, but that note amid the breakfast toast had rather dampened her spirits, reminding her of Astwood's shadow.

The daylight hours had been spent well enough in lessons with Chloe, but by six of the evening, they'd congregated in the kitchen where Betts and herself had glugged the master's claret and they'd all dined upon his beef pie.

She reached for the last unread book by her side, to caress the leather spine of the keepsake that Seth had gifted her and–

Memories flickered. Of words... Words from this book that her father would recite before casting a soft glance upon Mother.

> *'Why did I love her? ...Because it was her; because it was me.'*

And that was why no love was the same, for it was something intangible, deep in one's own self that connected with another.

She wanted for nothing more than to witness Seth smile, to revel in that sonorous voice, to caress his Herculean body.

To be the recipient of his kindness, loyalty, devotion and protection.

To give him everything of herself. To care for him.

Why did she love him? ...Because he was Seth; because she was Matilda.

She hugged the book close and knew her heart.

But how did one divulge such an emotion?

Not once had she confessed to a real person that she loved them, and Miss Appleton's half-baked governess tome failed to instruct on how one could convey more tender sentiments to one's employer.

Did one blurt it out? Expose it by degree? Or steer a path of conversation to it?

The clock chimed a quarter after nine and she rose, placing her beloved book on the sofa. She'd left the curtains open, savouring the sight of Green Park as night had claimed it, and now she ambled over for a closer inspection.

A London drizzle had commenced again, a warning that summer was in no way ready to lay its warmth upon them and–

The creak of a gate took her attention, followed by the low rumble of voices, and she squished her nose to the window, could make out two figures stalking up the garden path, both with greatcoats and easy lopes.

Seth and Mr Finlay.

She dallied, shifting from foot to foot. Should she descend and greet them? Or stay here? Or just go to bed?

The bold and brave lady that Seth had called her would dash downstairs and find out what was happening... So that's exactly what she chose to do, extinguishing the lantern and grabbing the candlestick.

From the stairs, she could hear their murmurs and the banging of cupboards from the kitchen – they wouldn't find any leftover beef pie for supper.

"Whatever is in those vaults is worth a tidy amount," came a Scottish burr, "if a man is willing to kidnap for it."

"Any clues at all?" Seth replied, and Matilda paused outside the door.

"None. And Miss Griffin's birthday won't solve it as the vault's contents still go to her husband should she be forced to marry by more sinister means."

"Damnation!" And a thump, as though a fist struck a table. "But we can't risk it."

"Risk what?" asked Matilda wandering in.

Both men leaped to their feet, Mr Finlay with a bow and Seth... His gaze appeared to devour her appearance yet his lips were arrow straight, brow furrowed.

Their damp cloaks lay haphazard upon the chairs – hopeless men – and she ambled over to hang them on the hooks by the warm range.

Mr Finlay cleared his throat. "Well, lass, we've been digging around a bit. On yer cousin."

"Oh, I see. Well, please sit. I'll make some tea, shall I?" Both men crumpled their noses as they reclaimed their seats and Matilda sniggered, lifting the kettle to the iron surface. "With a tot of whisky, of course."

"I always said yer were a fine lass, Miss Griffin. And I know Seth agrees. Eh, Seth?"

But *Seth* remained silent. Merely stared with eyes she could not fathom – not alight with rapture as of last night but gravely dark. With hair damp from the rain and wearing his 'ale-house' togs, he looked every inch the malevolent prizefighter and Matilda silently quivered, locked within his gaze.

"Ahem," said Mr Finlay.

She blinked and twisted. "Sorry, you were saying?"

"I wasna, but... Astwood has turf debts up to his red eyeballs and a cut-throat lender on his tail, did yer realise any o' this?"

Matilda slung more firewood in the range and stoked it as Betty had shown her. "I had my suspicions as I came across quite a few vowels in his study desk when... reconnoitring. But as heir, he inherited all my parents' money, and he has access to my dowry – supposedly for my yearly needs."

"Och, that's all gone, lass."

Her head bowed. She'd thought that might be the truth of the matter but was astonished anyone could spend such an amount in so little time.

"It appears, however," rasped Seth, "that personal effects remain secure in the bank vaults, deeded to yourself and to be passed directly through the Griffin line to your children. Not to be touched until you are...married."

Mr Finlay dallied with a kitchen knife. "Sidlow parted with that knowledge..." His blue eyes were now of a January lake. "Once they'd got yer married, they planned to sell these effects and split the proceeds. I dunno what it is about them nobles and spending."

"No appreciation of what they have, I suppose," she ventured, removing the boiling kettle to steep the tea.

Seth rose, and for the first time that day she felt his nearness and then his touch, a hand upon her shoulder. "So, Matilda, do you have any clue what is in those vaults?"

"Well... I suppose it might be... I'd not realised they were still there but..." She screwed her eyes shut. "Father kept a selection of old books, you see, in a vault. If I remember correctly, the 1477 edition of *The Canterbury Tales,* a manuscript comprising Da Vinci's own writings, and, er, I believe various copies of Shakespeare's Folios, amongst some other bits and bobs. Illuminated manuscripts, Saxton's maps and so forth. Oh, and some old jewel of Anne Boleyn's."

"Folio..." Seth's eyes widened. "Shakespeare's First Folio, you mean?"

"Well, yes. Father acquired one of those. In calfskin. But I presumed all his chattels had been sold at some point."

"Never mind the bloody Folio," interrupted Mr Finlay. "What about the jewel?"

"Well, I don't know too much. It was given to an ancestor who was a lady-in-waiting. It's been passed down the female line. I thought never to marry, you see, and I'd never sell it, of course, hence it would be inherited by my thrice-removed half-cousin's daughter. Phyllis is her name. Her father is the Duke of Aberdare. I told you about him at the interview."

Seth breathed deep. "Matilda, all this must still be in those vaults then and will be yours on your birthday, and if you marry, would, of course, become the property of your husband. These have much value."

"Do you think? But they're items to be treasured for future generations, not to be bartered for gambling debts." She scowled and paced the kitchen floor. "Are you saying that Cousin Astwood attempted to kidnap me in order to leg shackle me to a mutton-mongering buck fitch, just so he can sell my books? What an utter...shagbag!"

"It would appear so, lass. Astwood has sold all that's not entailed or nailed down, but 'tisn't enough. He owes money to a villain not to be messed with, one who's becoming a mite impatient. It's his life we're talking about."

She crossed her arms and muttered.

"Kian believes Astwood will try and take you again as he's running out of time."

The Scotsman leaned back in his chair, causing the spindles to creak. "My idea is to draw him out. Easier and quicker to catch the smetchet in the act rather than guarding yer all hours. Then we can fetch the magistrate."

"He wants to use you as bait," Seth grouched, seating himself once more with crossed feet and folded arms.

"Well, 'tis either that or I...get rid of him, but I thought yer might not approve."

"Hmm..." Matilda tapped a lip. "But no, I don't believe we'd best do that, Mr Finlay." She rummaged for three mugs. "So instead you want to use me as a worm on a hook. Good idea. As you said, you cannot guard me all hours."

"Exactly so," he agreed. "And we'll take good care of yer. But tell us, lass, how smart is this cousin, d'yer reckon?"

With a certain weariness abruptly taking its toll, Matilda sat. "He's not stupid, by any means, but arrogance causes him to blunder."

"Most likely he's got someone keeping an eye on us," rumbled Seth.

Mr Finlay poured the tea with expert aplomb. "I reckon if we attend a few events about Town, or lurk in some theatre gaffs, he won't be able to resist another attempt to grab yer. There's a Gaelic saying... 'Desperation drives on cowards', and I reckon yer cousin to be both."

Seth's gaze remained sombre. "But are you sure, Matilda?"

"Yes, quite sure. And besides what choice do I have?"

"Well," muttered Mr Finlay with a smirk, "if yer married a certain someone at Gretna post-haste, that'd end it."

With a bashful smile, Matilda peeped to Seth, to exchange a clandestine wink or wait for him to tell his mischievous friend to mind his own business, but...

Silence.

Those hazel eyes weighty and troubled, a hostile scowl upon his lips.

Matilda's smile wilted.

Confusion and doubt, that treacherous doubt, filled the void where elation had earlier dwelled.

"I..." She placed her own mug down. "I don't believe I will join you for tea after all. I'll–"

Abruptly Seth rose and forestalled her departure with a

firm hand to her wrist. "Matilda, meet me in the library. I shall be but a moment." He stared deeply. "Please."

At the soft plea, she nodded and twisted away. "Good night, Mr Finlay."

"Good night, lass."

Matilda seized the candlestick and without looking back wandered from the kitchen, legs and thoughts sluggish with weariness and befuddlement as she ascended the stairs. Why had Seth kept so very silent and solemn at the prospect of marriage to her?

Perhaps he did not wish for another wife having been previously forsaken, but surely he never would have made such passionate love to her if that were the case.

She relit the library lantern from the candlestick, the silence solitary, and meandered to the circular reading table in the centre. An exquisite book with illustrations lay open, of the *Ancient Mariner* and his many trials. She flipped the pages one by one, eyes blind.

At the light tread of footstep upon the stairs, she did not turn. Neither at the footfall within the library as it approached her. Not even as a warm breath whispered over her nape. Or as a soft kiss was bestowed upon it. A calloused hand brushed her smooth arm, slid down her wrist till it covered her hand upon Coleridge's legacy.

"Some words," Seth uttered softly, "were left unspoken last night. Words that caught in my throat because I knew not the right moment or the right way. But in all the hours of daylight, I have called myself every type of fool for not uttering them."

"Seth..." His body caged hers. She was unable to twist, to see his eyes, solely his hand interlacing, the warmth of his body against her back.

"And once more I shall steal another's lines because I am a

simple man, Matilda, and so many others express it better than I." Lips kissed her ear and she shivered. "'Doubt thou the stars are fire, Doubt that the sun doth move, Doubt truth to be a liar, But never doubt I love.'" His arm encircled her waist. "Never doubt I love *you,* Matilda. With all that I am – humble prizefighter and a man at your feet."

A tear streaked her cheek – such a soggy goosecap she was – and leaning back into his chest, she twisted her head to gaze up at him. "I had a hundred verbose ways to tell you my feelings, Seth Hawkins. Yet now I find only three words matter." His hazel eyes glinted, that band of gold searing with flame. "I love you."

WITH A SOUL ALIGHT and spirit ablaze, Seth beamed at his beloved.

At dawn, he'd beamed also, awakening with body sated and mind at rest. Yet a day spent gathering information by fair means and foul had beaten at that serenity, his lips refusing to cooperate in the kitchen through unease at the plan and his ire at Astwood.

And Kian was perfectly correct in that taking Matilda to Gretna Green would solve many a problem. No need for her guardian's permission or the lengthy calling of banns.

Yet...

Today he'd realised how much had been taken from Matilda already – her beautiful home, her parents' legacy and her future as a daughter of the *Ton.*

He would take no more.

So he drew away and as she twisted in his arms, he cupped her delicate but bold jaw in his palms and gazed into the depths of her sherry eyes.

"When I ask for your hand in marriage," he said hoarsely,

"and it is a *when,* not an if – I want you to be utterly free to answer. Not because of threats or escape or lack of money, but because of love, and nothing else. I was troubled by Kian's suggestion because I do not want you to ever feel forced or compelled to marry me. Otherwise I would be no better than Astwood or Sidlow – granting you no choice. I stayed silent because if you agreed to such a proposal, it would mean a clandestine and arduous elopement to Scotland. All as though it were *us* who were ashamed of our love."

"Seth–" He placed a finger to her lips.

"I stayed silent because I want to listen as the banns are read loud to all and sundry, feel the anticipation and emotion. I stayed silent because I want to say and hear those solemn words of devotion and respect which will bind us together for eternity before my daughter, family, friends and God. Not in front of a wearied Scottish blacksmith who solely wants the coin."

Ebony eyelashes fluttered, fingers clasped.

"I stayed silent because I want to watch you dance at our wedding breakfast with Betty, Kian and all those who adore you. To see you drink champagne with Mrs Ashby and your literary group. To wear any bloody colour you choose. To not be looking over your shoulder." He breathed deep. "I stayed silent because I love you so very much and you deserve better, nay you deserve *everything,* Matilda Griffin."

He waited.

The rasp of their breath, the patter of rain, the scent of book and flower...*'this bloody tyrant, time.'*

Then she tugged him close and kissed him, firm and rough, which he hoped might signal her forgiveness for his silence in the kitchen.

Lips teased his earlobe. "Never have I met a man more

considerate or selfless than you," she whispered before drawing away with eyes that glittered bright with love in the lantern light. "But know this... I shall indeed drink champagne at my wedding and wear whatever I wish...but I shall dance with none but my new husband." She cupped his jaw. "I love you with all my heart. And so together, *we* shall wait, Seth Hawkins."

CHAPTER TWENTY-TWO

"Tis only for the guilty to tremble."

PRIVATE EDUCATION: A PRACTICAL PLAN FOR THE STUDIES OF YOUNG LADIES. ELIZABETH APPLETON. 1815.

"My lords, ladies and gentlemen, may I present for your delectation and pleasure, The Knights of Yore!"

Wild applause rolled as four muscular horses galloped into the sawdust-covered arena below, their riders dressed in medieval tunics of scarlet and black, unicorns and swirled dragons decorating their chests.

Leaning her elbows on the velvet-cushioned balustrade of their box, Matilda's breath caught at the sight, each rider hidden by a lavish mask – king, jester, lion and ghoul.

Pounding drums from the orchestra accompanied the thunder of hooves in the amphitheatre as the great beasts galloped in an endless circle, fast and reckless, faces a deceiving blur.

Matilda drew back from the edge and placed a palm to

her chest in a vain attempt to slow her racing heart. But a savage yell erupted from the masked king as shortened jousting lances appeared from beneath their cloaks and Matilda tipped forward once more, not wanting to miss a single moment.

Never had she visited Astley's Amphitheatre before – had thought it would entail preposterous circus tricks and tumbling fools – yet tonight, lithesome female acrobats in sensuous silks had defied gravity upon pole and rope, and black-clad sorcerers had appeared in puffs of smoke as though arising from hell.

A magical haze layered this fantastical circus world – trickery, the sleight of hand, the scent of leather, horse and exotic perfume.

Matilda briefly closed her eyes to allay the assault on her senses.

Over the past days, there'd been no sight nor sound of her cousin, despite an agreeable walk in Hyde Park and a visit to Dulwich Picture Gallery, so this glamorous venue had been suggested by Mr Finlay for its popularity and…ease of guarding the exits.

Was her cousin here within this melee – watching and waiting?

The amphitheatre was crammed from pit to rafter. Hidden in the lower shadowed seats, couples furtively kissed or raucously argued, penniless bucks waved spotted handkerchiefs and impish children scampered amongst the benches.

Their own small party was situated within a private box first tier up and not far from the ring, a clear exit via the curtain behind them to the hall and stairs. Two further tiers of boxes wove around the theatre, the ladies' frocks and gentlemen's waistcoats a riot of colour. From above boomed frequent unruly cheers, an occasional scarf, ostrich feather or glove drifting past their box as items tumbled over the precipitous edge.

Illuminating the entire spectacle was a vast chandelier suspended from the domed ceiling, enough candlelight to see the acts but not to diminish their mystique, costumes glinting, faces shadowed. Green and gold decorated the ornate boxes and Corinthian columns rose tall, fluted in gilt and white. Beyond the orchestra rose a further stage with fastened crimson curtains, denying, for the time being, the audience its attractions.

Matilda clenched her fists in her skirts as the king and jester now galloped in differing directions, circling, lances held straight and true – no fear in these lean men whose bodies lifted and fell with their beasts as though one. Centaurs come to life.

A thud and roar as they clashed, the jester tumbling sideways from his saddle, one foot caught in the stirrup, fingers carving into the sawdust as his horse continued its gallop. In fright, Matilda leaped to her feet along with half the audience, the hooves pounding so close to his skin.

But the jester abruptly swung himself upright and into the saddle, laughing loud at his cunning deception.

"Are you enjoying it, Matilda?"

She gulped, flopped into her chair and turned to a chortling Seth seated beside her, an enthralled Chloe to his left.

Seth's demeanour appeared jovial, yet she sensed an implacable alertness beneath that jacket of black and waistcoat of silver – primed and forceful.

"I'm not sure enjoyment is the right word. For it's..." Side by side, the ghoul and lion now circled the ring, their horses' eyes flaring, midnight manes flying, the brisk beat of drum and hoof spearing her soul and heart with its rhythm. "It's dangerous and exciting and…irresistible."

With a flash of scarlet and kick of boot from stirrup, the lion man now stood balanced upon his saddle, arms aloft and black cloak whipping, until he deftly leaped from his steed to fall astride the ghoul's mount.

Accompanied by rapturous cheers, the two men mock wrestled, their horses galloping without guidance, before the ghoul rose and somersaulted from its back, landing to the sawdust upon one knee.

An unearthly apparition indeed.

The crowd stood as one to applaud as all the knights came forth and bowed, faces still veiled behind those sumptuous masks – they might have been Romany or royalty, wicked or worthy, and Matilda drew breath at the tantalising, seductive thought.

And although in truth this was all to flush out Astwood, a menacing shadow that refused to come to the light, she could not help but feel invigorated by yet another new adventure – so much to experience with Seth at her side.

Clowns with vivid coloured outfits now burst into the ring, faces painted pure white, lips overly rouged to an upward tilt and their hair caught in peculiar red bunches upon their heads.

Two of them began to juggle…with knives, their lethal edges catching the candlelight in flashes of gold.

Then, with apparent hilarity, they commenced flinging them at one another – on each occasion, catching the knives by the hilt. Matilda placed a hand to her eyes, dared not look, dared not look away, so peeked through open fingers, pulse numbing as one cork-brained fool turned his back to capture the knife blind.

Further clowns prowled the ring, one with an ugly scowl, shaking his fists at the roaring crowd.

He wasn't very funny.

As the angry clown passed their box, he leered at Matilda and stuck his tongue out, teeth yellow.

"Seth..." she whispered, not taking her eyes from the bizarre fellow. "The clown... I think... He could be hired by Astwood."

A hand reached out for hers, patted in mollification, and then Seth leaned close. "That's one of Kian's men. Keeping an eye on you."

Grief.

No wonder he wasn't very funny.

And how on earth did Mr Finlay arrange these matters?

Not that the crowd cared, hooting and whistling before the clowns scampered from view at the whistle of their ringmaster.

The red-tailcoated gentleman strode the sawdust in Hessian boots, whip in hand – to echo the days when his father, Mr Astley, would command the amphitheatre in his military finery.

"Retake your seats, if you please," he bellowed over the hubbub. "For now, my lords, ladies and gentlemen, may we humbly present further sights of astonishment from our act..." He bowed with a sweep of starched cuff. "Broken Heartstrings."

Behind the orchestra, two men dressed in black pushed the scarlet stage curtain aside to reveal an Italian ruin painted on an enormous backcloth, lit either side by lofty candelabras, wax dripping.

The amphitheatre quietened. Matilda fidgeted. Seth scrutinised the pit below. Chloe goggled.

From upon high, a dainty pair of slippered feet appeared

from behind the pelmet of the stage curtain. Slender ankles drifted down from the heavens to gasps of amazement, followed by a patched, ragged skirt and black bodice. Lastly, a face lowered into view – eyes fastened closed, smothered in a heavy kohl, white-painted skin with ebony tresses and red pursed lips.

A forlorn Columbine.

Strains of a violin ballad rose and Matilda drew a sharp breath. For as the woman's toes touched the stage boards, she saw that attached to Columbine's ankles and wrists were stout ropes. They stretched up high, beyond the enraptured audience's view, and as the music played, a rope yanked so that her arm curled skyward. Another rope jerked, her leg swung out and she was twisted into an *Arabesque*. A mortal marionette compelled to dance upon a stage.

The gentlemen cheered and whistled as her skirts rode high, but Matilda's lips refused to curve upwards for it was odd and peculiar and she didn't care for it at all. If anything, it reminded her of a woman's plight, strings pulled to another's command.

A tall and slight figure sauntered into the ring below them with a costume of coloured diamonds and a mask of black. This Harlequin lover held a bow and arrow, and as poor Columbine was tugged back and forth upon the stage, he nocked an arrow and aimed at the sorrowful marionette.

Matilda closed her eyes, but a firm hand took hold of hers, a deep whisper in her ear.

"Watch."

She unsealed one eye.

The bow pulled back. Columbine's lips parted. Violins reached a crescendo. The arrow took flight over the orchestra and to the stage where it sliced high through the rope binding her ankle.

A smattering of astonished applause broke out, but the tension ratcheted as Harlequin nocked another arrow.

He readied. Aimed. Arched. The crowd edged forward. Breath caugh–

Matilda screeched as their box curtain was wrenched aside, a black figure loomed, and Seth spun with fists drawn.

"Only me," whispered Mr Finlay, winking as he pulled up a chair. "Been in the rafters."

Seth shook his head with a glare and retook his seat; Mr Finlay nonchalantly settled with a hand just inside that deadly greatcoat of his; Chloe grinned; and Matilda considered whether circuses were good for one's nerves as Harlequin released his arrow.

She gazed to poor Columbine, left bound by the two remaining ropes.

Another arrow was nocked, the bow raised, aimed, and she gasped as the silver tip flew skyward...

Columbine flopped like a broken doll, hanging from the one rope left tied about her right wrist.

After a smug bow, Harlequin's fingers reached to the quiver upon his back, only for them to return empty, and he mimed his utter despair to the crowd's utter delight.

Columbine, he silently mouthed to the dangling girl.

My Columbine...

All of a sudden, her free hand twitched.

Harlequin mouthed her name once more and she angled a leg.

Yet again the lover pleaded and her spine stiffened, neck rising like an automaton.

Then her eyes abruptly opened wide.

She appeared as though woken from a profound sleep and the audience hushed as she first stared this way and that, then to the beseeching Harlequin and finally beheld the knot at her wrist.

With a flash of ragged skirts, she snatched hard on the rope.

A yell, and a bundle of white silk tumbled from the heavens to astonished gasps, the rope swinging free before it too dropped to the stage – her fallen puppet master Poirot in his clown costume lay motionless upon the boards, lips painted a failed black.

Everyone surged to their feet in applause as Columbine pirouetted in freedom upon the stage, Harlequin bowed in triumph and the curtains were dragged closed.

Matilda crumpled into her seat, utterly exhausted, but this Mr Astley Jr. certainly made good on the entrance fee as now the clowns tumbled back into the ring, and she gulped, hand to heart, as they bent their bodies back and forth like saplings in the wind.

The audience clapped their somewhat perilous somersaults while another clown strode to the centre with a wooden barrel containing many lit torches.

Awe and chatter resounded as the ringmaster's disembodied voice appeared to bellow from somewhere in the rafters. "My friends, we now give you, The Horsemen of Hellfire."

The clowns dove to the centre of the arena as three swarthy men dressed in midnight black galloped into the ring upon sable steeds with leather mantels. Each horseman seized three flaming torches and whilst riding in fleet circles, they hurled them aloft, juggling the golden blazes.

Matilda rose to cheer, Seth whistled, Chloe waved and even Mr Finlay looked a little bit impressed.

Faster and tighter they cantered in giddying loops, hooves thundering, drums hammering a spirited beat, and the crowd roared their approval as one horseman caught a torch betwixt his teeth.

The clowns danced and cavorted in the centre of the ring, faces fiendish in the firelight, and all around the amphitheatre, gentlemen hung over balustrades to better view the spinning blurs of flashing inferno, ladies fluttering their fans against the smoke, heat and reek of oil.

A horseman wildly shrieked as he rode by, his many torches circling to unfeasible heights, and with a flick of arm and twisted grin, one was thrown directly at their box.

SETH ROARED, yanking Matilda to his chest, the blazing torch plunging aside.

He exhaled with sharp breath but the spiting flame had caught the front corner drape and fire curled up the green silk like ivy. Kian seized a handful and wrenched, dragging the entire rail to the floor.

Shielding both Matilda and his daughter, Seth tugged them to the rear of the box, Matilda stumbling.

"Kian!" Chloe cried, fingers stretching forth.

And glancing back, he beheld his friend stamping on the drapes, almost out, but that bloody greatcoat of his was aflame at the hem and Kian abruptly twisted, batting with a gloved hand.

"Go help him!" screamed Matilda and his daughter wriggled from his grip. He darted over, endeavoured to tear the coat from Kian's shoulders, but buttons snared and it wouldn't budge.

"Leave me, damn it. Get the women out," Kian hissed, but the fire had snaked to his shoulder capes, so with no time, Seth twisted him, curled his heel around the back of his friend's ankle and swept him from his feet.

Following him down, he rolled him upon the boards, beating at the eager flames, burned wool singing his palms.

The blaze spluttered, smoked, snuffed, and Seth breathed deep. "You good?"

Wild cheers and Seth's head shot up, saw the culprit pinned to the sawdust of the arena by Kian's clown, the audience applauding, the fire doused, all believing it part of the bloody show.

And he twisted to–

"Matilda! Chloe!" he yelled to the empty box.

A rush of air as Kian hurtled past him for the curtain.

MATILDA'S SCREAM was severed as the arm encircling her throat from behind wrenched tight.

Through eyes that watered, she saw Mr Finlay wrestled to the hall floor by broad-shouldered men hammering him with blows, while another gripped Chloe, fingers twisted in her hair.

Seth tore towards her, and Matilda fought for breath, to warn, but all she could do was lock eyes – too late as the awaiting villain spun him, knuckles crashing into his jaw.

Raking the arm which grasped her, she strove to wrest it from her neck, fright overwhelming all else as the callous grip began to drag her backwards, her throat aflame, lungs empty.

Matilda's heart roared its pulse in her ears as she was hauled to the deserted staircase, slippers finding no purchase on the rugs, Seth and Mr Finlay a blur of shadow and fists as her glasses knocked sideways.

Stubble pressed to her cheek, harsh breath in her ear.

"You bloody harridan. I'm your guardian and you'll do as you're told."

Guardian?

And Matilda stilled...

As far back as she could remember, she'd considered herself a calm, level-headed sort of person, not prone to histrionics, bad humour or bouts of petulance. Her confidant, Evelyn, referred to her as rational, and even Seth appeared to think her quite sensible.

Yet at this moment and at that voice, an ember of unbeknownst temper lit within her.

It flared and flourished.

This *guardian* had squandered her beloved parents' money, her dowry, threatened Seth, his daughter and their splendid academy, shaken her harshly, bruised her wrists, stolen her future and sought to marry her off to a diseased libertine with fetid tongue.

A savage rage now flamed and spat, overwhelming all fear, all sound, all else.

And so, with the last remnants of her breath and all her gathered might, she pitched her head back to bestow a reverse nobbler to his ivories.

The grip loosened, allowing her a lungful, so fisting her right mitt, she shifted her hip to one side and burst a box of fives in Astwood's ballocks.

Yowls of pain disturbed her ear, the arm dropping, and she spun on a yellow-slippered heel.

He bent to clutch his ballocks and she spied her chance, so without remorse, peppered his lugholes with thumb-curled fists.

No time to dally and she pitched a chopper to his chin, chipped him low, and then, for good measure, bashed a rattler to his potato trap.

Her guardian fell upon his arse on the crimson rug and Matilda raised her right foot to stomp on his talliwa–

"Mercy!" he cried.

Matilda took no notice and walloped down.

Lamentably, in her enthusiasm, the slipper merely grazed his thigh but 'twas good enoug–

"Miss Griffin!" With skirts hoisted and blond mop flopping, Chloe hurtled towards her. "That was magnificent," she cried breathlessly. "I saw it all."

Matilda pushed her bent spectacles up her nose and breathed deep. "Do you think so?" She bit her lip. "I'd not thought I had the wherewithal but... All at once, I found myself so intensely irritated with the man."

"You were perfect."

Matilda blushed and glanced up.

The villain who'd trapped her young charge lay inert, legs akimbo, while a phoenix-like Mr Finlay was poking a sound nobbler to the breadbasket of another. Her beloved Seth was milling a rather burly brute with a stout sneezer to the conk followed by a rib tickler to the...ribs.

"Do you think we should assist them?"

"Nah, they'll be fine," declared Chloe. "Here, I gathered some curtain ties for your cousin." And they commenced on Astwood's ankles, snaking it none too gently till he resembled a mast in port.

A lost straggler from one of the other boxes lurched towards them, blinked and paused, parted his lips, closed them, and then peered to his gin bottle. Matilda merely glared and shooed a hand before stuffing a handkerchief in Astwood's mouth as a precaution.

The agreeable Mr Finlay bust a whiffler to his opponent's whisker bed, toppling him like a felled oak, and Seth's assailant, mayhap realising his chances were now slim, turned tail to scarper down the stairs.

She and Chloe dashed to surround the two men, and

Matilda tumbled into Seth's embrace. His cravat had loosened in the fray and a swelling marred his clean jaw, but he felt so very warm and safe.

Strong arms swamped her and she grinned, tilting her chin in pride. "I whiffled him good and proper, Seth."

"Did you see it, Pa?" Chloe gushed. "Miss Griffin gave him a plumper to the nutmegs. It was amazing. I've never been so proud."

Matilda felt rather proud. And exhausted and jubilant and she desperately wished to return home. To float in the bathhouse pool and let this evening seep away, let freedom saturate.

Seth kissed her knuckles. "Those doubts, my Matilda, are traitors no more. You can do anything."

"Well done, lass," Mr Finlay likewise declared with a grin, dusting off his attire. "Remind me not to meet yer in a dark alleyway." He bundled the remnants of his charred coat under one arm. "Now then, what would yer like to do with yer cousin? I could fetch the magistrate or... I wonder..." He tapped a finger to his chin. "Perhaps we could give the smetchet a choice. If I recall, the Prince has a ship leaving for China in a couple of days. D'yer think he'd be any good at swabbing decks? By the time he gets back from there, all should be settled, aye?"

In the crimson shadowed hall of Astley's Amphitheatre, with the scent of burned cloth, exotic perfume and magic in the air, Matilda grinned within Seth's arms. "That sounds perfect, Mr Finlay."

CHAPTER TWENTY-THREE

"You are so very giddy that you will not give yourself time to think before you speak."

Private Education: A Practical Plan for the Studies of Young Ladies. Elizabeth Appleton. 1815.

Meet me in the basement.
S.

In Gothic novels, such a message read beneath the ghostly radiance of the moon would send a shiver of dread down the heroine's spine, but Matilda's *medulla spinalis* tingled solely with elation.

Before indulgence of that elation could take place, however, she hastened from her bedchamber and into the hall, dropped her linen towel to the side table and made for the door opposite.

A light knock and she entered. "Chloe?"

"Hmm. I'm still awake. I'm writing a book."

Gosh.

Sitting propped up in bed beside a lantern, Chloe scribbled away with pencil in hand while strewn over the coverlet were sheets of paper smothered in diagrams and arrows.

Matilda squinted from the doorway. "And what is the subject matter, dearest?"

"Well, it's entitled *How to Defend Oneself Against Villainous Relatives: Volume One.*"

Miss Appleton did advise that themed compositions were a necessary part of a lady's blossoming education, so Matilda nodded in approval. "That will be an undoubted success." She smiled and wandered in, adoring her young charge's bedchamber, caught at that moment between girl and woman, yet nonetheless all Chloe – books and boxing gloves, ragged dolls and…illustrations of half-naked pugilists.

Perching on the bed, she lightly patted Chloe's hand. "I just wished to thank you for today. I never could have fought off my cousin without your fine instruction. Initially I was so frightened, but I could hear your words in my head – that it's the element of surprise that makes it possible."

A blush lit Chloe's cheek – the first she'd ever seen. "I'm so glad it worked."

"And I would like to learn more techniques, Chloe. If you will?"

"Of course," she gushed. "I should love to. And…and if you like, we could work on overcoming that fright. Pa says it's all about finding the calm within yourself…which I've never found. But then I'm only thirteen. Fourteen in November." She bit her lip, green eyes bright. "And yes."

"Yes?"

The jumble of papers was shoved aside. "When we got back, Pa asked if I'd be agreeable with the two of you marrying, and I said yes. Just in case you thought I might not. In truth, I can't wait."

"Oh..." A fervid heat crept into Matilda cheeks and she fiddled with the blue coverlet. "Well, I haven't actually been... We may need more time... I wouldn't like to presume..."

Chloe rolled her eyes and tucked her knees up. "You make Pa happy. He's spent so long working, to look after me and build our academy. And you're not exactly a wicked stepmother."

"Even if I make you quill tea caddies?"

Sniggering, Chloe flung her arms around Matilda's neck, all gangly limbs and messy blond plait, lavender wafting.

Tears smarted, and although affection still felt peculiar to Matilda, now it was a comfortable sort of peculiar – one she relished – and she returned the hug, keen and tender.

This loving girl would become a glorious woman, with or without a lady's accomplishments, and she drew away to bestow a soft kiss to her young charge's forehead. "Good night, Chloe. Do not stay up too late writing."

"Good night, Miss Griffin. I won't, and I'm so glad you chose to come here as my governess."

"Me also, Chloe." And after a last squeeze, Matilda rose to cross the room, shutting the door softly behind her and letting her spine rest back upon it for a moment.

Had she chosen to come here?

Once, Matilda had thought fate to be cruel but mayhap its nature was fluid, its guise shifting like the Saharan sands. For if fate had indeed guided her to this household, then it could also be miraculous and benevolent.

The lantern flickered. The basement beckoned.

So she grabbed the linen towel from the table and in an exceedingly unladylike manner darted along the hallway, vaulted down the stairs, sprinted for the black-painted door, tugged it open and...

SETH HEARD THE GASP, knew Matilda had discovered the apple blossom and ivy which littered the basement stairs.

Roses would have been preferred but the spring had been so bitter, the gardens failing to produce even a single bud, so he and Chloe had swiftly gathered what they could in the pitch dark.

Footsteps scampered down the steps, the door was thrust wide and then another gasp...

Never would he label himself a romantic man, but when he put his mind to a task, he tended to carry it out to the best of his ability, and in the past days, aside from keeping Matilda safe, he'd planned for this moment.

Small boats of candles floated in the pool, with rosemary scattered in the water; Pears soap had been melted and added to the beeswax to scent the room; a new lady's silk bathrobe – not in yellow – hung on the peg; and in the corner, he'd managed to procure a bronze statue of her beloved Bird of Paradise with outstretched wings, an upright tail and haughty expression.

"Oh, Seth, it's beauteous."

As was his enchanting Matilda in a gown of saffron, barefooted and with her midnight hair loose and free. Maybe he himself should have togged up in a silk jacket and frilled shirt but he wished her to look upon him and accept him for who he was – a man in mere cotton slops but with a heart full of love.

"Betty says if we get wax in the pool, she'll resign."

That wasn't quite the romantic line he'd wished to begin

with, but Matilda smirked and commenced unbuttoning her dress, so it couldn't have been all that bad.

Of course he was well aware, as he aided in slipping the garment from her shoulders, that she might refuse his proposal, sell the books and jewel on her birthday and travel to the Molucca Islands with some fellow who knew the difference between the Gold-breasted Bird of Paradise and the Red-breasted Bird of Paradise – besides the obvious.

But he also knew that Matilda Griffin possessed not a fickle bone within her delectable body, and that when she said she loved a man, she meant it wholeheartedly and forever.

For some, that might taint the anticipation of this night, but instead it made him a creature of lust, want and ragged need – to possess the exquisite Matilda with a signature and God's blessing.

At last, his bold lady stood before him in merely chemise, the candlelight glinting off her spectacles. After the menace of their day, they ought to have felt exhausted, but he observed that same heightened aliveness in her sherry eyes that shimmered within him – that of a contest fought…and won.

Of now awaiting their prize.

"I had no idea," he declared, aiding her across the sea-green tiles and then the steps to the warm waters, "that employing a governess would also grant me my heart's desire."

"'Love sought is good, but given unsought is better,'" Matilda murmured with an impish tilt to her lips.

"That's my line."

"From another discarded theatre print, Mr Hawkins? What corkers you told when we first met." She flapped down her floating chemise in the water. "Indeed, you sought to hide your impressive light under that muscled bushel of yours, did you not? When in truth, you had an extensive library and a penchant for Shakespeare."

His lips twitched in silent culpability and he bobbed a floating candle across the pool, water now lapping their chests, the scent of meadow heady in the rising steam. A candle flickered, casting the bronze Bird of Paradise to a soaring shadow of momentous proportions upon the wall.

"All this is so splendid," Matilda whispered, eyes drifting over the *scène à faire* before they came to rest upon him. "Treasures surround me."

No longer could he contain himself. "I love you, my Matilda."

Her eyes turned serious but with lips soft. "I love you also, Seth, truly and deeply." She seized his hand and touched her gentle cheek to his rough knuckles. "I love your bravery and determination to succeed, to escape and better your life." She leaned forward and brushed his lips with her own like a caress of moth's wings. "I love your ingenuity in building this wonderful Academy. I love the warm home that you have created for your talented daughter. I love your appreciation of literature and deep knowledge. I love your sincere heart and kind soul that treats all men equal."

Pure emotion clogged his throat and clattered his chest, so while he searched for words, he drew Matilda near and toyed with a black lock, dipping it in the water before stroking it over her neck. "You claim I have bravery and determination, Matilda, but you have more so."

"Me? No. I'm just an over-wordy nitterwit."

Seth shook his head and smiled. "Bravery comes in many guises, my love. You were presented with a path not of your choosing, threatened by a man who should have protected you. But rather than submitting to a life of misery, you sought your own future, using your wits and intellect. And in a boxing academy of all places."

"I was a dab worried initially," she confessed.

"And yet you remained strong, defying conventions and the dictates of your guardian. And...before I go on, you must... You must realise that you will continue to defy the *beau monde* if you freely admit to your love for an ex-prizefighter who was born in St Giles Rookery and whose daughter adores boxing."

"Seth? You–"

"I may be welcomed at salons and the occasional soiree or ball by an Academy member, but I am looked upon as a curiosity, never to fit within their world." He dropped his hands from her shoulders and rubbed his nape. "You must understand what you will lose should you decide to be with me."

Seth had no wish to point out his disadvantages, yet Matilda had to know the consequences, had to realise the limits of his life. He was no aristocrat who could provide the trappings of society. Some would even argue with the term 'gentleman'.

Slender fingers teased his chest, slid upwards. "Society with its balls and soirees do not make me happy, Seth," she whispered. "*You* do. Every hour, every moment that we are together. We will build our own beautiful world, with Chloe and..." She cast a shy glance. "Perhaps further siblings for her. But for now, I wish to experience all the adventures of a life with you, Seth." She pressed close, wet chemise abrading. "I've read of love in books, never thought to feel it for myself, but now I never want to be without it...never want to be without you. My *true* gentleman."

Her words stole his breath and he cupped her cheeks, tilting his head.

"So then, Matilda, I will now be plain and simple, without use of another's prose or poetry." He kissed her rough and wanting. "Please take me from torment and marry me? I shall be true and loving. I shall protect you and let you fly. I shall listen and be yours forever."

Her eyes gleamed a moist amber, fingers gripping him tight.

"With no other reason than I love you so much and wish to spend my entire life with you, I will marry you, Mr Seth Hawkins."

Lost for words, he let his kiss declare his joy.

That joy seeped like water into every joint, muscle and bone, the scent of meadows enveloping him.

In riches and in poverty, Seth had watched men and women seek their dreams, toiling all the years with the hope that maybe, just maybe, life would reward them.

Drawing back, he gazed to Matilda and knew fortune had looked kindly upon him. Gifted him a bride of beauty and intelligence, who'd sparked a cinder of a long-forgotten dream within him and fulfilled it this very night.

"Then let us embark on all life's unending adventures..." Seth cupped her cheek. "Together and as one, my love."

EPILOGUE

"Adieu. Be good, be lovely on earth."

Private Education: A Practical Plan for the Studies of Young Ladies.

Elizabeth Appleton. 1815.

"Monsieur Hawkins, we are ready, *oui*?"

With a wink to the swarthy Frenchman, Seth twisted to remove the silk blindfold from his beloved's eyes.

Matilda blinked in the bright sunshine of Vauxhall Gardens, gifting him a loving glance before her attention was caught by the scene in front of her, palms rising to her cheeks, teeth gripping that ripe lower lip.

"Oh, how exciting!" she cried, spectacles glittering. "I've always wished to view a balloon ascent." And Matilda flung her arms around his neck, kissing him to raucous applause from the small crowd that surrounded them.

He clasped her tight and reciprocated wholeheartedly.

For now, they were man and wife.

Bound together that very morning in St James's Church

before family and friends – Kian as best man, Chloe skipping along as bridesmaid and Betty giving Matilda away, her bilberry eyes moist with the honour.

He shifted his lips to her ear. "We are not just here to view the ascent of this balloon, Matilda, for I have arranged a little something as my wedding gift." The chatter of their guests faded as they clutched one another, lips brushing. "In a few years, I hope we can visit the Molucca Islands, to see those Birds of Paradise you so adore." He hushed her protest. "But for now, I want you to feel the freedom of the treetops, the breeze within your hair and the land down far below."

"You mean... Are we to ascend *in* the balloon? Oh, Seth..."

His wife drew back, a red flush to her cheeks, ebony hair tumbling in fat curls with gold ribbons. A wedding dress the colour of honey gilded her, along with a pelisse of flaxen, as she'd admitted that through their rather unconventional courtship, she had in fact grown to adore yellow's varied hues – revealing a truth that some things were not truly disliked, merely tainted by circumstance until viewed in a different light.

"We are to rise just above the treetops."

"It's... How?"

A single tear trailed and her glasses steamed. He removed them, cleaned them on his cuff, kissed the tear away and replaced them.

"I have my ways." In fact, he'd asked a member of the Academy – a scientifically minded earl who'd been on balloon jaunts before – and with a cod of blunt, the entire affair had been arranged. To be truthful, he wasn't entirely sure he possessed a head for heights, but all would be worth it to see Matilda's joy.

Champagne corks abruptly flew to boisterous cheers, the

champions and their wives handing out glasses, Tonks filling them to the brim. A scarlet-clad Prince lurked under a tree and the scowling young fighter, Liam, loitered by Chloe.

The balloon lurched a touch in the light breeze as if impatient, so with congratulatory thumps on his back from Bill Richmond and John Jackson, and somewhat gentler rose petals floating down upon his bride from Mrs Ashby and Mr Keats, they clasped hands and–

All at once, Matilda twisted, fingers slipping away, but Seth merely grinned and followed as she darted towards the couple standing quietly to the side and threw herself into their open arms.

His father withstood the assault with a laugh, and Mother, whom he'd never seen shed a tear, surreptitiously wiped her eyes.

A letter had been sent to their last known whereabouts and Seth had prayed it would reach them, but not having any idea of when or if they might be able to return, himself, Matilda and Chloe had decided to call the banns and…hope.

In fact they'd been in Paris, the last city of their Grand Tour, when Father had declared he'd a funny feeling in his gizzards, a need to return home at once, so disregarding Ma's suggestion that it might be the exotic food, they'd travelled by carriage and sea, arriving in the nick of time to see their son wed. Once more proving that happy endings were forever possible.

With a wink, Father patted Matilda's shoulder and she turned to clasp Seth's outstretched hand, smile as bright as her dress.

They raced toward their gallant Gallic pilot who bowed and commenced chucking sandbags over the side.

The oval basket was strewn with yellow silk swags to match the striped balloon and a small set of steps was available to ascend, but Seth swept his bride into his arms and with the beaming Frenchman holding the many ropes apart, he settled her within.

Clambering in himself, he clasped her so tight, not entirely sure it was from joy as the ropes pulled and scraped.

"*Mes amis*, we go to the sky, oui?"

At Seth's nod, more sandbags were freed, and gradually, with hardly perceptible movement, the basket creaked and lifted from the grass. A lengthy tether began to uncoil from the ground for a few broad-shouldered fellows to later haul them back down to earth.

"It feels so insubstantial," his bride whispered, tentatively prodding the wicker with her slipper. "Yet strong at the same time."

Seth concurred with the former, wasn't sure about the latter, but Matilda's wide smile and even wider eyes eased his concern.

A cheer rang out as they hovered twenty feet or so off the ground and waved at the onlookers that huddled below – fighters and nobles all watching in awe. His daughter bounced upon her toes, gesturing madly, Kian waggled his feather-clad hat, and Betty's eyes were as wide as her husband's agape mouth.

"I thought it would be bumpy for some reason," declared Matilda, "but it's gentle, like floating on a cloud. Oh, Seth, I can imagine how a bird must feel – so serene and free." She peered up above to the sealed balloon. "I've read of all this, but to see it and feel it? 'Tis miraculous."

Further they rose to the sky, the air cooling a little, the Frenchman testing wind speed with some type of cogged metal device. The grassy field grew smaller; they could view the thick branches of Vauxhall's elms over yonder, then higher, till they overtook the verdant leaf canopy – seventy feet or so from the ground.

"Enough, *oui?*" the Frenchman enquired, black eyes flashing with verve.

Matilda laughed and shook her head; Seth swallowed and nodded, but the pilot allowed the balloon to drift another foot or twenty before, with a contented inhale, he turned to fiddle with some knots.

They tentatively peered down below at the cluster of faces, beaver hats and beribboned bonnets – Matilda pointed and waved at her friend Evelyn, the lady's red hair a beacon within the crowd. Next to her loomed her husband, a member of Seth's Academy, but there was no way on earth – or sky – that he was letting go of the basket to acknowledge him – duke or no duke.

A gust abruptly caught them, the balloon seeking further freedom from its earth-bound tether, ropes groaning like an old ship to be broken up.

Seth gulped.

"Have no worry, *Monsieur et Madame.*" The Frenchman shrugged.

Matilda giggled. "Seth, it's a wonder – like flying."

He clasped one arm around her waist from behind, that chill breeze rippling against their faces, the sky a never-ending blue. A bird flitted past with a startled blink of beady eye and Seth laughed loud, nerves easing.

"You are the wonder, my love." And he kissed her hair, earlobe and nape, heard her soft sigh and savoured this moment.

The balloon dipped a little, London unfurling behind the lattice of ropes, its ancient river below them – the lifeblood of the city – wending its way across the land, and the medieval Palace that declared its age with squat defiance.

But Seth merely watched his beloved wife, bold and brave and relishing every adventure.

MATILDA HEAVED in great lungfuls of the cold, pure air, felt dizzy from the expanse of blue and awed by the many ropes that twisted about them before they smothered the striped balloon like a tremendous fisherman's net.

It made one feel minuscule yet immense, audacious yet fainthearted.

In the distance, London's rooftops melded into verdant fields and scattered villages, the perspective from far above on such a clear day making the bustling city appear so insignificant as compared to nature's abundance beyond.

Yet so many lives unfolded within this metropolis, fortunes lost and found, folk working and at leisure, families grieving and rejoicing.

A warm whisper of breath touched her ear. "Do you ever wonder," he murmured, lips teasing the tendrils, "how we managed to find this love in such a large and busy world?" His arms tightened. "The lady and the pugilist – I mean, we never should've even crossed paths, and yet now, holding you in my embrace, I cannot imagine a life without you."

Matilda rested her head on his shoulder and smiled at the colourful balloon, surrounded as it was by the blue boundless sky, before she turned her back on London to plait her fingers at her husband's nape, to watch the breeze ruffling his hair, that lopsided smile and those twinkling hazel eyes saturating her with joy. And she knew that this enthralling adventure would be one of many that married life would hold for her.

"Mayhap an unseen hand guides us." She smoothed a glove across his honey-coloured waistcoat, the one she and

Chloe had chosen together, felt his heart race and muscles tauten. "But had I known such a love as ours existed, I would have searched forever to find you, Seth."

Lips met in eternal devotion as the balloon ropes softly creaked in the breeze, and recollections of her dear father drifted to the fore…

> *'Why did I love her? ...Because it was her; because it was me.'*

Why had love chosen them?
…Because he was Seth; because she was Matilda.

The End

THANK YOU

Thank you for reading *A Governess Should Never... Tempt A Prizefighter.* I truly hope you enjoyed Seth and Matilda's tale.

Read on for a Glossary of Pugilism (!)

EMILY'S GLOSSARY OF REGENCY PUGILISM

If, like Matilda, some words left you a little flummoxed, here is a glossary of some Regency boxing / general cant. Not all of these were used in Seth and Matilda's tale, but I hope it helps!

Enjoy!
Love Emily xxx

- Bantling – youngster
- Belfry – head
- Bowsing ken – ale house
- Breadbasket – stomach
- Buffer – prizefighter
- Burst a box of fives – punch a fist of five fingers at...
- Burster – knockout punch
- Cannister – head
- Chipper – a jab
- Chopper – a punch
- Claret – blood

- Clicker to the gob – a punch to the mouth
- Clobber to the chops – a punch to the mouth
- Cock robin – weak opponent
- Cod of blunt – a good sum of money
- Conk – nose
- Coppers – pennies
- Culp to the lughole – a punch to the ear
- Dew beaters – feet
- Dub – punch (usually to the head)
- Famble – a punch ('dandle' is made-up, so means what you wish!)
- Grub-up – dinner
- Ivories – teeth
- Mill – to punch / throw
- Mill a plumper to 'is kissin' trap, yer calf's 'ead – throw a punch to his mouth, you idiot!
- Milling cove – prizefighter
- Milling-set-to – a prizefight
- Mitt to the sneezer – fist to the nose
- Mitten / mitt – hand
- Mufflers – a blow to the mouth
- Mug – face
- Muzzlers – punch to the mouth
- Nitterwit – a made-up word but perhaps self-explanatory!
- Nobbler – punch to the head
- Noddle – head
- Noggin – head
- Nous – sense
- Ogler in the gaslights – punch to the eyes
- Pepper – hit fast and hard
- Pitch a chopper – aim a punch
- Plump to the brisket – wallop to the chest

- Plumper to the nutmegs – punch to a male's nether appendages!
- Poke a sound nobbler – wallop a good punch to the head
- Poke to the brisket – punch in the chest
- Rattler to the rails – punch to the teeth
- Raw buffer – young, inexperienced fighter
- Reverse nobbler to the ivories – backwards headbutt to the teeth
- Rib tickler – punch to the...ribs
- Settler – knockout punch
- Smeller – nose
- Sneezer – punch to the nose
- Snorter to the snout – punch to the nose
- Teaser – a punch in order to provoke
- Top-loft – head
- Tripe shop – stomach
- Trotters – feet
- Whiffle – a punch
- Whisker bed – chin

ALSO BY EMILY WINDSOR

GAMES OF GENTLEMEN SERIES

The Duke of Diamonds - Out Now

Casper Brook, the eighth Duke of Rothwell, has forever spurned frivolous pleasures, his restless emotions remaining buried beneath duty and command.
Yet when a titian-haired minx perches upon his ducal desk and claims to know the whereabouts of his one burning obsession, a game of wits and passion erupts...

RULES OF THE ROGUE SERIES

An Earl in Wolf's Clothing (Book 1)

From the hallowed halls of London's Almack's to the unkempt taverns of Drury Lane, from whispered words in glittering theatres to seductive encounters at Vauxhall Gardens – an earl must pursue his love.

A determined lady. An even more determined gentleman.
Let the pursuit begin…

Merry Christmas, my Viscount (Book 2)

Seduce a rogue? By Christmas Eve? What a troubling resolution for the most proper widow Mrs Lily Mereworth to be left with… How? And more importantly, who? Ghost stories on a windy night, swordplay down the Great Portrait Gallery, a lady and a spymaster with no thought to love… Merry Christmas.

Let Sleeping Dukes Lie (Book 3)

"Strait-laced. Ruthless. Arrogant." – The Duke of Rakecombe has forever spurned love…and with good reason.
"Forthright. Impudent. Capricious saucebox." – The fiery Miss Aideen Quinlan refuses to be spurned, unable to erase the memory of the duke's vehement kiss…
An unlikely couple, an unquenchable passion.
Resistance is futile.

Marquess to a Flame (Book 4)

The Marquess of Winterbourne has long been guided by his *Rules of the Rogue*, but as spy for the Crown, his next mission will break every single one. Sent to the wilds of Cornwall to beguile secrets from a lady, the last thing this rogue expects is to unearth his own buried heart.

CAPTIVATING DEBUTANTES SERIES

Captivated by the Viscount

ALSO BY EMILY WINDSOR

My Captive Earl

Her Noble Captive

ABOUT THE AUTHOR

Emily grew up in the north of England on a diet of historical romance and classical mythology.

Unfortunately, you couldn't study Georgian slang or the Regency London Season, so she did the next best thing and gained a degree in Classics and History instead. This 'led' to an eight-year stint in engineering.

Having left city life, she now lives in a dilapidated farmhouse in the country where her days are spent writing, fixing the leaky roof, battling the endless vegetation and finding pictures of well-tied cravats.

Happy Reading,
Love,
Emily
x

facebook.com/AuthorEmilyWindsor
pinterest.com/EmilyWindsorBks
instagram.com/emilywindsorwritesregency
bookbub.com/authors/emily-windsor
goodreads.com/EmilyWindsor
amazon.com/author/emilywindsor

Printed in France by Amazon
Brétigny-sur-Orge, FR

24256290R00162